PENGUIN BOOKS

BOGMAIL

Born in Donegal, Ireland, and educated at Galway
University, Patrick McGinley now works in London in publishing.

BOGMAIL

PATRICK McGINLEY

PENGUIN BOOKS

Penguin Books Ltd, Harmondsworth,
Middlesex, England
Penguin Books, 625 Madison Avenue,
New York, New York 10022, U.S.A.
Penguin Books Australia Ltd, Ringwood,
Victoria, Australia
Penguin Books Canada Limited, 2801 John Street,
Markham, Ontario, Canada L3R 1B4
Penguin Books (N.Z.) Ltd, 182–190 Wairau Road,
Auckland 10, New Zealand

First published in Great Britain by
Martin Brian & O'Keeffe Limited 1978
First published in the United States of America by
Ticknor & Fields 1981
Published in Penguin Books 1982
Reprinted 1982

LIBRARY OF CONGRESS CATALOGING IN PUBLICATION DATA
McGinley, Patrick, 1937–
Bogmail.
I. Title.
PR6063.A21787B6   1982   823'.914   82-375
ISBN 0 14 00.6195 9   AACR2

Printed in the United States of America by
George Banta Company, Inc., Harrisonburg, Virginia
Set in Caslon

ACKNOWLEDGMENTS
The quotation on page 163 comes from J. B. S. Haldane's "Cancer's a
Funny Thing," and the extract on page 169 is from P. M. Young's *The
Tragic Muse: Robert Schumann* (Dennis Dobson, 1961).

For my father, who gave me the germ of the story

ONE

Roarty was making an omelette with the mushrooms Eamonn Eales had collected in Davy Long's park that morning. They were good mushrooms, medium sized and delicately succulent, just right for a special omelette, an omelette surprise. He had chosen the best mushrooms for his own omelette; the one he was making for Eales was special because it contained not only mushrooms from Davy Long's park but also a handful of obnoxious, black-gilled toadstools which he himself had picked on the dunghill behind the byre. He was hoping that four of them would be enough to poison the bastard; he dared not put in any more in case he should suspect. Eales was a fastidious feeder who never touched bacon rind or pork crackling or the thin veins of white fat that made the best gammon so tasty. He never ate the frizzled fat of grilled lamb chops or sirloin steak, nor the crisp, earthy jackets of baked potatoes. Normally he would not have blamed him for avoiding the latter because the jackets of some potatoes were rough with scabs and excrescences. But Roarty's potatoes were different, grown lovingly in the sandy soil by the estuary and smooth to the touch as sea-scoured beach pebbles. The man who was not moved to eat the jackets of such potatoes was nothing if not untrustworthy. He was blind to the beauties of life and the true delights of a wholesome table. He was probably a man who harboured evil thoughts against his neighbour, a man from whom wise men one and all would lock up their daughters, at least those of them who still retained their maidenheads. The outcome was inescapable: Eales must be destroyed.

The toadstools were a brilliant idea, better than the ragwort which was his first thought and which would have had serious shortcomings as a poison, if poison it was. McGing had been talking in the bar about what he called its toxic properties only last week, and if traces of the weed were found in Eales's alimentary canal during the inevitable autopsy, McGing might put two and two together. 'How did the ragwort get into the stomach of the deceased?' he would ask aloud with unselfconscious pomposity. 'After all Eales was not a cow.' It was not the type of thing that got into a man's stomach by accident whereas a toadstool might. Eales had picked the mushrooms himself, and it was all too possible that in his haste he had picked a few wrong ones. Roarty would sorrowfully admit to having made the omelette but, since a motive for murder could not be attributed to him, he would go free. It would be a perfect murder, executed cleanly with a minimum of fuss and exertion, better than the spilling of blood which was for stupid men who could not control their passions.

Eales, in the sickly yellow waistcoat which he wore on weekdays, was perched on a high stool behind the bar, reading the racing results to Old Crubog. He was a young man of twenty, tall, swarthy and narrow faced, with an uncommon self-possession that showed in his unconcealed assumption that other people lived only for his amusement.

8

Old Crubog, the sole customer, was listening intently, head tilted and an untouched pint of stout before him.

'Your tea is ready,' Roarty called from the kitchen doorway.

Eales folded the newspaper, placed it on the counter before Crubog, and dived hungrily past Roarty.

'The paper's wasted on me, I'm afraid. I've left me specs behind,' said Crubog, taking an experimental sip from his glass and smacking two puckered lips that collapsed over his loose false teeth. 'The first this afternoon,' he said, his watery eyes brightening with eager pleasure.

Roarty leaned over the counter and listened to him praising times past as he wondered in a remote chamber of the mind when Eales would snuff it. Would he go out like a light after he'd eaten? Or would he struggle manfully through the evening and quietly slip away in his sleep that night? To be rid of him so easily, so perfectly, seemed too good to be true.

With his hand on the stout pump, he looked out of the west window at the sharp evening sunlight on the sea, a plain of winking water with not even a flash of foam round Rannyweal, the submerged reef that reached from the south shore almost half-way across the bay. It had been a glorious summer, the best anyone, except Old Crubog, could remember. Not a drop of rain had fallen since Easter, and it was now the first week of August. The corn was only half its usual height, and the potatoes, though floury, were meagre in both size and numbers. The farmers had been grumbling since June and the parish priest, who was a farmer himself, had taken to praying for rain on Sundays. Only the tourists, turfcutters and fishermen were happy. It was a good summer for publicans too, however.

Never had he seen men so thirsty in the evenings; never had he sold so much ale and stout. There was always someone in the pub from morning to night, always someone with a thirst that needed slaking. Noticing that the stout shelf was almost bare, he brought in two crates from the storeroom and placed the bottles in three neat rows in readiness for the evening swill. Then he poured himself a large Irish whiskey and water and said to Crubog: 'It's a rare day when you don't see it breaking white over Rannyweal'.

'They were good mushrooms, those,' said Eales, returning from the kitchen. 'I've never enjoyed better.'

'I thought some of them tasted a bit strong,' said Roarty.

'Imagination,' said Eales. 'Mine were perfect.'

'Where did you pick them?' asked Crubog.

'In Davy Long's park,' said Eales.

'It's the foremost place for mushrooms in the three parishes,' said Crubog authoritatively. 'You'd never find a bad mushroom in Davy Long's park, every one as juicy as a Jaffa orange.'

He left Eales and Crubog to talk and wandered out behind the house, the sight of the withered conifer banishing all thought of Eales from his mind. He filled two buckets of water from the outside tap and poured them on the roots of the dying tree. The cracked earth absorbed the water as if it were a thimbleful, and he carried six more bucketfuls, dogged and determined but with a black sense of hopelessness in his heart. He had planted the tree seventeen years ago, on the day after Cecily was born and his wife had died. During its first winter, a storm from the west uprooted it one night but he put it standing again, this time with a supporting stake, and it grew with Cecily, tall, dark green and tapering with branches that drooped with a heaviness of needles. He came to associate the growing tree with the changes in Cecily, the subtle change in the shape of her nose when she was six, the darkening of her flaxen hair at nine, the lengthening of her spindly schoolgirl's legs, and finally the bulging of her breasts. She was a sweet-natured girl, not unlike her mother in looks and yet so different, but now when he thought of her he could not help feel a twinge of foreboding. He had been right to send her to London—he could do nothing else—but he could not bear the thought of her so vulnerable and so far away. Since the tree had begun to wither he had been unable to think of her without holding his breath.

He grasped a branch above his head and the brittle needles turned to dust in his hand. The branches had begun to curl up and the dark green had given way to a lighter green with a yellow tinge, yet he refused to believe that the tree would die. All the other trees in the garden were thriving, probably because of their deeper roots. If only he'd realised that the conifer was sensitive to drought. If only he'd noticed the lightening of the colour in time.

With the corner of his eye he saw one of Eales's cats spring from the flowerbed onto the low bird table. He bounded across the garden and caught the miserable creature by the neck but he was too late—the sparrow in its mouth was already dead. Eales was evil, and he rued the day he had so innocently made him his barman. He had sauntered into the bar one evening last summer with a knapsack on his back and a black cat under each arm, one Scherzo and the other Trio.

'A pint of porter,' he said, 'and a job if you've got one.'

He should have known that a man who goes about with

two black cats was not a man to tangle with, but he needed a barman and none of the locals wanted the job.

'What brings you to me?' he asked Eales.

'I enquired in the pub at the other end of the village and they told me you might have work for me. I've worked in a bar before.'

He was a good barman, quick to pull pints and give change on busy evenings, industrious even when there was little to be done, and popular with the regulars. But there was something unnatural about him, not simply because he was a cunning Kerryman in remote Donegal but because he was secretive, sharp-tongued, overconfident and lacked intimate friends; and though he went out with every girl who would look at him, he behaved as if he would not even consider the possibility that one of them could become his wife.

He had an unnatural sense of humour too. On his day off he would put a plate of breadcrumbs on the bird table and sit by the kitchen window waiting for Scherzo or Trio to pounce. He had deliberately placed the low bird table near the flowerbeds so that they might provide cover for the cats. And whenever one of them caught a bird, he would slap his bony thigh, laugh uproariously, and say something like 'Good old Trio, the second today'.

One evening at the end of May, Roarty had watched him shaking the sycamore tree until a little nestling fell from one of the upper branches. The poor bird, paralysed by fright, could make only the most feeble attempt to fly. The two parents in the nearby ash tree were scolding furiously, and Eales went off, laughing like a maniac, to find Scherzo and Trio. Roarty was so horrified that he got out the ladder and put the fledgling back in the nest. And when Eales saw the white and yellow stain on his shirt sleeve, he laughed like a madman and said:

'That's the thanks you get for rescuing a scaldy, bird shit on your sleeve.'

Eales was evil beyond reasonable doubt. Eales must be destroyed.

Throughout the evening he kept a watchful eye on him but there was not a sign of him weakening. Never had he seemed so alert, pulling pints as if it were a funeral day and joking and arguing with Old Crubog, Rory Rua, the Englishman Potter, Cor Mogaill Maloney and Gimp Gillespie. It was a good evening for business. The bar was packed, the farmers arguing about the storm clouds that were piling up in the east, making the air heavy with humidity. Some shook their heads and said that they'd expect rain when they saw it but Crubog with all the authority of his eighty years said that he had never seen a sky that had the makings of a bigger rain storm.

TWO

The following morning Crubog was the first customer, complaining of the rain storm that never came.

'Did you see what happened?' he asked. 'The clouds travelled right across the sky from the east to the west. That rain fell over the sea where it was least wanted.'

Roarty pulled a pint of stout for him and took a crimped pound note from his trembling hand. After he had given him sixty-two pence in change, he poured out a large whiskey and placed it on the counter beside the pint.

'What's on your mind?' asked Crubog.

'Nothing that can't wait,' said Roarty with a distant look at Rannyweal and the blueness of the bay.

'Whenever you put up a drink on the house I know there's mischief on your mind. *Do shláinte, a chailleach!*'

'*Sláinte na bhfear agus go ndoiridh tú bean roimh oiche.*'

Crubog raised the glass and poured the neat whiskey down his throat. The action was certainly one of pouring rather than drinking, Roarty thought. He had watched his Adam's apple, and it hadn't moved.

'There's nothing like whiskey first thing in the morning for clearing out the old tubes. If only a man could afford it...'

'You could if you had a mind to,' Roarty smiled.

'How?' asked Crubog, flattening the single tuft of hair that sprang from the top of his otherwise bald head. It was like a tuft of couch-grass, and he had split it in two and combed one strand down over each ear. He was an uncommon sight, small, thin and sun-tanned, and cunning as an old dog fox.

'I've told you before. All you've got to do is sell your land.'

'And how much are you offering today?' Crubog asked slyly, showing a hint of interest yet treating the conversation as a familiar joke.

'The same as last week: four thousand. It's a fair price; it would keep you in whiskey while there's breath in you.'

'That's a point of view, as Sir Valentine Matlock used to say. But it's a sore temptation.'

'Then what's stopping you?'

'Love of the land. It was my father's and his father's before him. If I sell, it will be to a farmer. What would the likes of you be doing with it?'

'I see it as an investment. I don't think money should lie fallow in the bank.'

'You'd just buy to sell when it suited you.'

'I have no plans. I might build on it or I might stock it as the whim took me.'

'If you want to buy it, you must first tell me what you'd do with it. That would be part of the bargain.'

Crubog was impossible. Roarty had been prodding him for the past four years but he still had not got even a promise to sell. It did not make sense. Crubog was poor. He lived on his pension, and his land lay under the crows when it could be earning him a modest income. It wasn't good land. The farm was only six acres, most of it rocky, but he also had what he called 'a large mountain acreage' and that was what interested Roarty. It was rumoured that the Tourist Board was going to build a scenic road across the hill right through Crubog's land, and Roarty could foresee the day when the roadside would be lined with week-end cottages and tourist chalets. If he owned Crubog's mountain acreage when the road came to pass, he would stand a good chance of making a killing.

'Well, I must collect my pension,' said Crubog, finishing his pint. 'Don't worry, I'll be back to leave some of it with you before dinnertime.'

Roarty poured himself another whiskey and looked at the sea. The bar was empty. It was always quiet until eleven, and the demon Eales had gone to Garron for the day. He took his glass upstairs to Eales's bedroom. The window was open but there was a smell in the room, not an unpleasant smell but still a smell, a smell perhaps of used lotions and talcum powders. The room, however, was tidier than his own, the low dressing table covered with an assortment of bottles and hair brushes. What vanity! What misplaced conceit! He certainly looked after his mangy carcass. Always washing his hair and having baths, yet his feet smelt like a midden. The mushrooms had failed; he was up at six, chirpy as a lark, calling Scherzo and Trio before the dawn chorus had quite finished. What next? Foxglove? McGing had said that you could make digitalis from the leaves provided you gathered them at the right time. But what was the right time? He felt restricted by ignorance; not even *Britannica* had the answer. He would have to think of something; next Saturday wasn't far away. Perhaps another omelette with a bigger surprise.

He moved to the bed and lifted the pink counterpane, then the flowered pillow. Underneath, rolled in puce pyjamas, was a glossy sex magazine, wherever he'd got it, full of colour pictures of naked women in the most inviting poses, women offering their bare arses, women exhibiting their fuzzy fannies, women with closed eyes swooning as they crushed their enormous breasts between their hands. His head swam with unspeakable possibilities. He looked at the letters page. Troilism. Fellatio. Cunnilingus. It was all there, all the aberration of the civilised world. Eales must be destroyed.

Guiltily he put away the magazine and in relief picked up a coupon advertisement from the bedside table which had been filled in by Eales. Incredulously he read aloud:

> Increase your partner's pleasure—and your own—at a stroke! Send for our new heart-shaped pillow today, place it under your partner's bottom, and 'feel' the difference. Choice of foam rubber or hot-water filled. Ergonomically designed. Guaranteed success. Order before September 3rd and receive free rubber lust finger by return of post, a must for the truly modern lover.

Wondering about the meaning of 'ergonomically', he went into his own bedroom and took an old edition of *The Concise Oxford* from the shelf but the only word that resembled the word he wanted was 'erg', a unit of work or energy. He would ask Potter. He was an engineer and he would know. Absentmindedly he opened the fifth volume of the 1911 edition of *Britannica* and took out a single-page letter. He had bought the encyclopedia for ten shillings at a jumble sale in Sligo one Saturday afternoon over twenty years ago. It was the bargain of a lifetime, the only literary work apart from the dictionary and a biography of Schumann which he possessed. And the fact that many of the articles were long since out of date only increased the esotericism of his pleasure.

He read the letter, wondering at the strangeness of the impulse that made him wish to re-experience the pain and uncertainty that now filled his chest.

> Dear Eamonn,
> Only three more weeks, only twenty-one days and nights. How I long to escape from behind these walls, to see you again, to see you every day. I often think of the evening under the Minister's Bridge and the strange thing you did to me. I've been trying to find out if the other girls know about it, but when I hint they look blank. As our English teacher says, I hold there is no sin but ignorance. It's lights out in a minute. I must end. A hundred kisses and one last one from your loving Cecily.

That was before the Christmas holidays, and he hadn't discovered the letter until after Easter. God only knows what strange things he had done to her since. But mercifully he was still in time to protect her from the unspeakable refinement of the lust finger.

THREE

It was Saturday evening, the pub was crowded, and Roarty was at his most landlordly. After pouring himself the sixth double since dinnertime he had gone with no perceptible outward change through what he called the well-being barrier. It was always like that. The first double had no effect and neither had the second; the third thawed him; the fourth warmed him; and the fifth lit a taper in his mind that shone on the surrounding dark, colouring it like a winter moon bursting through low cloud. The self-destructive edge vanished from his thoughts, words flowed as bright as spring water, and laughter came easily and without overt reason. Between the fifth and the twelfth double he lived on a plateau of unconsidered pleasure which he tried to prolong until after closing time. The twelfth double was followed by a period of deterioration during which the commonest words seemed like tongue-twisters, and thoughts came slowly like the last drops from a squeezed lemon. That was regrettable, and it was a stage which he usually avoided. He liked to arrange matters so that he was on his twelfth double at closing time. Then, after he and Eales had washed up, he would scorn the optic and pour himself what Potter called 'a domestic double' straight from the bottle. This he would take to his bedroom and sip as he read his 'office' for the day, an outmoded article on some aspect of science from the scholar's *Britannica*.

Pulling a pint of stout for a long-haired tourist, Roarty listened with enjoyment to the catechetical conversation between Crubog, Cor Mogaill, Rory Rua, Gimp Gillespie and the Englishman Potter who, though new to the glen, was learning fast.

'Why do seagulls no longer follow the plough?' asked Crubog.

'Because of the lack of earthworms in the sod,' said Rory Rua who had heard this conversation before.

'And why are earthworms as scarce as sovereigns?' Crubog demanded to know.

'Because of the artificial manure.' Cor Mogaill sniggered.

'When we used to put nothing on the land but wrack and cow dung,' said Crubog, 'the sod was alive with earthworms, big fat red ones, wriggling like elvers as the spade or the coulter sliced them. And the air would be thick with a *gliobach* of gulls on a spring day, there would be so many of them. But now you could plough from June to January without even attracting the notice of a robin. The fertiliser has killed the goodness in the soil so that not even an earthworm can live in it. How can you grow good oats in dead earth? Answer me that, Cor Mogaill.'

'What we need is humus,' said Gimp Gillespie, the local journalist. 'Science has upset the natural cycle. Render to the earth the things that are the earth's and to the laboratory the manufactures of science.'

'Hear, hear,' said Potter.

'How many tons of earth does your average earthworm turn over in a year?' Crubog asked darkly. 'Answer me that, Cor Mogaill. And you can consult your personal library if you like.'

Cor Mogaill, a youth of no more than twenty, regarded himself as the village intellectual. He never came to the pub without his knapsack in which he kept his bicycle pump, certain back copies of *The Irish Times* and *A History of Ireland* by Eleanor Hull. He would then spend the evening trying to start an argument that would provide him with an opportunity of consulting what he called his personal library. Now he looked menacingly at Crubog but the knapsack remained on his back.

'What do you know about the physiology of earthworms?' he asked Crubog.

'I've had it on good authority, the best there is. Forty tons, not an ounce less. Now a Bachelor of Agricultural Science could put out the spool of his arse without achieving that.'

'Who told you?' Cor Mogaill demanded.

'Sir Valentine Matlock told my father, and my father told me.'

'With his dying breath,' suggested Cor Mogaill sarcastically.

'They were two good men, may God be good to them, and now they're doing more to improve the quality of the soil than you've ever done, Cor Mogaill. There are some men who wouldn't even make good humus,' Crubog laughed on his way to the outside lavatory.

It was an evening of energetic conversation. Crubog was at his most entertaining, full of trenchant anecdotes and antique lore, and Cor Mogaill and Gimp Gillespie drew him out with unobtrusive skill to the evident delight of the Englishman Potter who presided over the conversation with the intellectual discrimination which he saw as befitting a man of scientific background. Their talk took colour from the obscurity of the topics and the need of the speakers to make up for their relative ignorance by embroidering their thoughts with humorous whimsy. First, they considered whether a doe hare drops all her litter in one form or if she places each leveret in a separate nest for safety sake. When they had failed to find an answer, they turned to the trapping of mountain foxes. Here Rory Rua proved the most knowledgeable or at least the most confident in his opinion. He impressed everyone by saying that he would bet his shirt that a dead cat, preferably in an advanced state of decomposition, was the best bait because a fox could wind it even on a windless night. But Crubog was not to be bested. He demanded to know how curlews, when they are feeding inland, can tell that the tide has begun to ebb and that it is time to make for the shore. And he posed the question with such an air of dark omniscience that Potter said that it was as well they did not have an ornithologist in the company, that his specialist knowledge would kill all conversation.

Now and again they tried to draw Roarty into their circle but he told them that their talk was too abstruse for a mere publican. He felt remote from those on the other side of the bar, the distance between himself and them increasing with each double. Besides he could not banish last night's dream from his thoughts.

He was a boy of twelve chasing his ten-year-old sister Maureen in a field full of daisies when suddenly she stopped and said:

'Bring me that butterfly.'

'Why?' he asked, sensing that his will was not free.

'Because I want to pull its wings apart,' she laughed.

It seemed such a natural desire that he ran after the

butterfly at once, dizzy with its rise and fall in the sunlight and the whiteness of its wings like the whiteness of the daisies in the grass.

Suddenly he stopped on the shore of a lake. The butterfly had escaped him, fluttered over the unruffled surface of the water and rested on a solitary lough lily in the centre.

'You can walk on the water—if you don't look down at your feet,' his sister explained from behind.

Reluctantly he dipped his toe, and the water retreated before him. He stepped off the bank, the water still retreating, exposing the soft, peaty mud that cooled the soles of his feet and oozed between his toes. The earth swallowed the water with a sucking and a gurgling until the entire bottom of the lake was bare and the water lily, lacking the support of its natural element, lay besmirched and bedraggled on the black mud. He examined the stem and how it grew out of the darkness of the mud, and finally the round hole in the delicate heart of the flower. He held it tenderly between his fingers, and an ugly green caterpillar poked its head through the hole and crawled over the leaf with odious contractions.

'You've pursued evil to its lair,' Maureen called from the shore.

'And I've found it at the heart of beauty,' he replied.

The tenderness he experienced as he held the lily between his fingers and his horror at the ravishment of the flower merged in dark vexation, and he lost count of the number of drinks in a round.

'Roarty will have the answer,' said Crubog. 'After all he's the second best snipe shot in the county.'

'What's that?' Roarty asked, measuring a double Scotch for Potter.

'How does the snipe beat his tattoo in the spring?' Crubog asked.

'Tattoo?'

'How does he drum?' Potter rephrased.

'With his outer tail feathers,' Roarty replied. 'He holds them out stiffly at right angles as he swoops.'

'Wrong,' said Eales. 'Every one of you is wrong.'

'Enlighten us,' said Roarty, reddening beneath his beard.

'With his syrinx, of course,' said Eales.

'Fair play to you, Eamonn,' said Cor Mogaill.

'With his syringe?' asked Crubog, who was rather deaf.

'Syrinx,' Eales shouted. 'That's how most birds make sounds.'

'But the snipe's drumming is a different kettle of fish,' said Roarty.

'I'll bet a double whiskey I'm right,' said Eales.

'And I'll bet a bottle,' said Roarty, who did not take kindly to being challenged by his barman.

'I'll keep the bets,' laughed Crubog.

'Can you prove you're right?' asked Eales.

'Not this minute. I'll look it up after closing.'

It was half-past eleven by the clock, and they would expect twenty minutes to drink up. He put two towels over the dispensers and went out the back for a breath of cool air. He was disappointed, however. It was a humid night with a faintly touching land breeze that died away every now and then, leaving him becalmed by the back door with a constriction in his throat that made breathing difficult. The eastern sky was a mass of inky cloud, a low roof that pressed on the tops of the hills and obliterated the moon and stars. These rain clouds had come up since dinnertime, and it surprised him that no one in the pub had mentioned them. He listened to the hum of conversation from the bar, and thought that a pub at that hour of the evening was the most unreal place on earth.

'Where is your proof?' asked Eales self-confidently when they had washed up and the last customer had gone.

'In my encyclopedia. I'll go fetch it.'

He went up to his bedroom and scanned the article on 'Snipe', too distraught to take much pleasure in being right.

The house was quiet now; the last few stragglers had taken the country roads home. Sadness and impossible longing choked him as he remembered summer evenings with Cecily on holiday sitting at the piano in her room, the whole house flowing with liquid music. 'On Wings of Song', 'Für Elise', 'Jesu Joy of Man's Desiring': all the old favourites. The purity of those evenings brought a tear to his eye. The purity of those evenings gone for ever.

After he had found the letter to Eales in the waste-paper basket, he wrote to Maureen asking her to invite Cecily to London for the summer. It was not what he wanted but he did not have a choice. If she came home, it would be to the lust finger; and if he sacked Eales without good reason, Cecily would never forgive him. Even if he did sack him, he felt certain that he would not leave the glen. He would find another job in the neighbourhood so that he could continue to defile Cecily. And now all Roarty's precautions had come to nought because Eales was planning to go to London in a week's time. He didn't say whom he was going to see; he didn't have to. Roarty's hands shook with rage and frustration. Eales was evil. Eales must be destroyed.

He found himself half-way down the stairs, clutching the twenty-fifth volume of *Britannica* in his right hand, the fingers opening and closing involuntarily on the spine.

Eales was behind the bar, bent over a barrel, examining a length of plastic tube.

'Have you found it?' he asked without looking up.

Roarty raised the book in both hands and brought it down with all his might on the back of Eales's head. The breath went out of him with a reedy murmur and his face struck the edge of the barrel. He put both hands on the barrel in an attempt to get up. The barrel moved. Roarty raised the book again but Eales sank on his haunches and fell back on the floor without as much as a whimper.

Roarty shuddered in horror. His act had been involuntary, and being involuntary was unwise. What if someone had been passing and Eales had called out in his agony? But he had been lucky. He had not cracked the skull. There was no blood, and that was a good thing because blood told irrefutable tales. But perhaps Eales was just stunned. He put the evening paper under his head, got a hand mirror from the kitchen and put it to his mouth and nose but there was no condensation that he could see. Difficult though it was to credit, he must have died instantaneously from the severity of the shock. The mirror test, he had heard McGing say, was not foolproof. The surest indication of death was the temperature of the rectum falling to 70°F or below; but, though he had a thermometer in the bedroom, there was a limit to what he was prepared to do in the interest of science. Anyhow, the body was still warm. It might take an hour or more for the temperature of the rectum to fall to that extent. As an afterthought, he felt Eales's pulse but there was no perceptible stir in the blood stream. He noticed that the upper lip had blood on it where it had come against the rim of the barrel, and he got a plastic bag and put it over the head and tied a piece of string round the neck.

He took the stairs two steps at a time and reached the toilet not a moment too soon. His bowel movement was the most violent he had experienced since his mother gave him an overdose of Glauber salts at the age of eleven. Homicide, he was interested to discover, was as good as a physic.

He was sweating profusely, a cold, clammy sweat that drenched his shirt under the arms and made tickling rivulets down his forehead and into his eyebrows. He came downstairs again, weak at the knees and very thirsty. He reached for the Bushmills but as he unscrewed the top of the bottle he remembered the immensity of the next problem—how on earth to get rid of the body—and he put the bottle back on the shelf and filled a tumbler of water from the tap. Though he felt uncomfortably sober, he could not risk taking another drink. If he was to make this a perfect murder, if he was to survive undetected, he would have to act with foresight and intelligence; but when he tried to think of the next step, he found that coherent thought was beyond him. His mind was a sieve; no thought would remain long enough in focus to connect logically with another. To encourage concentration he went into the kitchen and sat at the deal table with an open note-book in front of him. Thought came slowly, and when it did he wrote down seven words:

Fire

Water $\left\{ \begin{array}{l} \text{sea} \\ \text{lough} \end{array} \right.$

Earth $\left\{ \begin{array}{l} \text{garden} \\ \text{bog} \end{array} \right.$

Burning was impracticable; he had only a range, and roasting flesh and bone would raise an unearthly smell. That left him with immersion and burial, and of these he favoured the first because it involved less work. He could drive west to the sea cliffs and heave the body over the brink into the water. Or he could tie a weight to the body, row out into the bay and cast it overboard. But when he began to imagine the details of the actions, he realised that there were snags. He was reluctant to take out his boat in the dark because he did not know the positions of submerged rocks well enough to be entirely confident. There were houses along the shore and it was just possible that he might meet someone. Besides, the body might be washed ashore. There would be an autopsy, the forensic pathologist would discover that there was no salt water in the lungs and that therefore death was not the result of drowning. There would be an investigation into the cause of death, and questions, searching questions, would have to be answered. Of course he could dump the body in one of the mountain loughs but, as they were a long distance from the road, he would have to carry an eleven-stone burden for well over a mile. Not an inviting prospect on a dark night and over rough ground. That left him with the third possibility: disposal by burial. The easiest course would be to bury him in the garden but if there was an investigation it would be the first place the police would look. He would have to choose a less obvious grave, the bog for example. He would drive out the Garron road for two miles, take the right hand bog road, and bury the body in the centre of the moor, away from the areas where turf was now being cut. The bog road was a lonely spot, there was not a house within three miles, and the likelihood of being seen was remote. The only danger was the possibility of meeting another car on the main road, returning perhaps from a dance in Garron. He hastily looked in the *Dispatch* but there were no advertisements for dances in any of the local towns. Nevertheless, you never knew what late-night straggler you might meet on a country road, and his car was known to everyone in the glen. He would need an excuse, and what conceivable excuse could he have for driving towards Garron at two o'clock on Sunday morning? A sudden gripe, a severe stomach pain, that made an urgent visit to Dr McGarrigle unavoidable. If he were seen, he could say that the pain had abated when he was half-way there and that he had come home without seeing the doctor. It was not the best of excuses but it would have to do.

He went to the back door to look at the night sky. The clouds in the east seemed blacker and closer, and the air was still and heavy, hanging like an invisible net over his head, laden with the scent of snuff-dry hay. Though it was nearly one o'clock, there was light in several of the cottages on the south mountain; he would have to wait at least until two before venturing out. He sighed sorely under the weight of the night air and the unbearable burden of his thoughts.

Ploddingly he went upstairs and opened a volume of *Britannica*. He lay on his side on the bed, sipped an orange juice and looked up the article on 'Murder' only to be directed with simple brevity to 'Homicide'. It was a disappointing article, probably written by some verbose solicitor or criminologist rather than a scholar with first-hand experience. It occurred to him that some newspaper editor might welcome the type of account he himself could now write—a story that would tell of the murderer's grim sense of inevitability as he looks on the sprawled body of his victim. From youth he has been conditioned by novels, stories, plays and films that imply at the very least that crime does not pay, that it is the criminal himself who pays; and he cannot help but wonder if he will be one of the rare exceptions. He looks at the cooling body which in death is a more formidable opponent than it ever was in life, aided by all the arcane resources of forensic science. After months perhaps of obsession with his victim, he is truly alone, facing the instinctive revulsion of every decent citizen, the impersonal tenacity of the police and the relentless treadmill of the courts; and all he has to ensure his survival is his cunning and intelligence. Roarty could not help wondering if he were intelligent enough.

There might be so many possibilities which he had not considered, so many things he may have overlooked, when on this night of all nights he needed to anticipate every contingency. He had not thought of the moon, for example. It was only two days before the full, and if the sky should clear he would have to bury Eales in ghostly but too revealing light. Obviously he would have to be careful, dig with one eye on the night sky. Another indication of his incapable abstraction was the way he had looked up the *Donegal Dispatch* when even the most rudimentary presence of mind would have told him that there was never a dance in Garron on Saturday.

He had written down seven options, and now the intimation of an eighth tantalised him beyond endurance, his freedom of action constrained by his inability to extend through imagination his gamut of choice. The man who is most free is the man who is most aware of possibilities, and in the past he had prided himself on being such a man. But now the effective possibilities in his life had shrunk from seven to one, and that one not particularly attractive. For a moment the eighth possibility illumined the internal dark; he would smash the front window, break open the till, hide the money, and pretend that Eales had been struck down by a burglar. It had the advantage that he could stay put, go to bed and get up in the morning at the usual time, and after a black coffee and a hot toddy 'discover' Eales and ring the police. However, that would lead to questions, and murder was better concealed than advertised. His eighth possibility had disintegrated like gossamer, leaving him tantalisingly with just the one. But having thought of the eighth, he was now harassed by the possibility that there might be a ninth. He went downstairs and stared stonily at his note of seven choices but, try as he might, they refused to multiply. He had always regarded himself as intelligent, at least a deal cleverer than most of those he met, and now when intelligence most mattered he was faltering. Many people, he thought, were reasonably intelligent; they had the kind of brightness that is related primarily to memory, that relies on noting how things are done and on an unthinking ability to imitate accurately. The truly intelligent were a race apart, as distinct from the rest of humanity as a salmon in season from a kelt. Their incisiveness went straight to the core of every crux and their capacity for dispassionate reasoning carried them far beyond the bourne of past experience. They possessed the logic of a computer with the intuition and mental agility of a man. This ability could be described in one word—analysis. And that was his present failure: an inability to analyse a situation.

He put a match to the incriminating note of options and ground the ashes into powder with the poker. He changed into an old pair of trousers which he used for painting, a dark shirt which would not show conspicuously in moonlight, and a pair of wellingtons that would keep out the bog water. He went upstairs again, took Eales's hold-all from the wardrobe and stuffed into it the glossy sex magazine, the puce pyjamas, Eales's toothbrush, toothpaste, razor and shaving lather, a spare shirt and three bottles of deodorant. This latter, he thought a brilliant stroke because Eales would not have gone to the door without his deodorant. Not quite analysis that, he decided, but rather good nevertheless. Premature self-congratulation was to be avoided though. The time for hubris, if there was one, was tomorrow morning or perhaps even in three years when Eales would be as remote in time as a fossilised pterodactyl. He would not fossilise, however. Bogs were noted for their powers of preservation. In five hundred years some slow-thinking turfcutter would unearth him with his slane, a time capsule preserved by tannin, the date of the magazine in the hold-all providing a perplexing *terminus a quo* for the rural constabulary.

When he came downstairs again, it was two by the clock, time to make a move now that the glen was abed. He quietly opened the back door of the garage, lifting it slightly so that it did not drag on the concrete floor, and put the hold-all and Eales in the boot of his car. The body had hardly cooled. Rigor mortis had not yet set in though the skin had begun to lose its elasticity. It was difficult to believe that this limp deadweight, this inedible carcase, this uneconomic commodity, had been the man who had threatened the peace and sweetness of his mind for the last four months. Somehow it did not seem possible, and he half-expected him to open one eye and recite once more his favourite piece of verse:

> If ever I marry a wife,
>   I'll marry a landlord's daughter,
> For then I may sit in the bar
>   And drink cold brandy and water.

With a sudden chill of the spine he remembered that the battery of his car was almost flat. If he used the self-starter, the whole village would realise as they turned in their beds whose car was giving trouble. He opened the off-side window and pushed the car into the road, facing it down the hill that ran out of the west end of the village. He would have to start it on the run when he was clear of the houses, double back along the North Circular as they called it, and take the Garron road without re-entering the village. He was about to move off when he remembered that he had forgotten the spade. Brilliant! He went back to the garage and took both a slane and a spade as well as a torch in case he should need it for the car. He put the car in second gear and with his foot on the clutch pedal moved off down the slope. When he was almost half-way down and had begun to gather speed, he let in the clutch. The engine fired at once and he was off with a song of minor achievement in his heart.

The Garron road climbed steeply out of the glen for the first mile. He drove in third with the accelerator to the floor, enjoying the cool rush of the night air coming through the open window. He looked down at the glen on his left; there was not one light along the whole length of the north mountain. Even the ever-vigilant McGing with his arse to his wife was dreaming of suggilation, saponification and a score of other forensic arcana which to his chagrin mattered little in booking men for poteen-making and other rural offences which, he complained, were somewhat beneath his consideration. If only he knew of the opportunity he was missing.

Soon he was driving straight into the black clouds in the east, the heathered hills stretching darkly on either side. Once he had to change down to second because of two foolhardy wethers in the centre of the road, and then suddenly after a sharp bend he had reached the flat plateau of bogland that separated the twin parishes of Glenkeel and Glenroe. He took the narrow bog road, little better than a dirt track, the rushes along the selvage brushing the wings and doors. The swinging rays of headlamps came over the crest of the hill to his left. He stopped and switched off his own lights, and waited for the car to pass down the main road into the glen. He had got off the Garron road just in time.

He parked the car at the end of the road where the tractors usually turned and switched off the lights and the engine, the blackness of the night rushing up simultaneously to his very eyeballs. The night was uncannily quiet, the sky low and opaque and the air heavy with humidity. He listened with strained ears but not a bird, animal or insect stirred. The whole bog was asleep. He alone was abroad.

He took the body from the boot, slung it over one shoulder so that the arms dangled at his back, gripped the legs and hold-all in his right hand, and the spade and slane in the other. Standing on the verge of the road, he groped with the spade for the narrow drain which he knew to run alongside. Then he stepped gingerly over it and set off across the bog, treading slowly in the thick dark in case he should trip on a stump of bog fir or fall into a hole or drain. It was so dark that he could not see the turf stacks until he was right beside them, but soon he was on the open bog which stretched flat and unbroken for two miles. He would bury Eales in the centre, in an out-of-the-way spot untrodden by human foot except perhaps that of a sheep farmer in search of a straying ewe or wether. He jumped involuntarily as a flushed snipe rose with a loud 'scape'. It was a hard summer on the poor buggers. They favoured damp or marshy ground but even the bogs were now quite dry.

When he had walked for fifteen minutes, he tested the ground with his boot and put down the body with a sense of well-deserved relief. After urinating at some length he began to pare the top sod from a patch six feet by three, just wide enough to allow comfort in the digging. The entangled roots of the mountain grass were so tough that he had to put all his strength behind each drive of the spade, and soon the sweat was making runnels down his forehead and into his beard but he worked like a man possessed until he had dug two spits and could turn to the slane which he preferred to the spade. In spite of four months of dry weather, there was a surprising amount of water in the lower layers of the bog, and before long his trousers and shirt were filthy from rubbing against the sides of the grave. When his shoulder was level with the brink, he stopped digging. He put Eales lying on his back on the bottom, clutching the hold-all over his chest, the plastic bag still over his head. He filled the grave quickly with the spade and made sure that he had cleared all the turf before putting the top sods back in place. When he had finished, he tamped the sods with his boot and stood for a moment in the centre, savouring the spring of the ground. In next to no time, he thought, Eales would be shooting up the most picturesque of bog cotton.

What he now wanted most was to get home without mishap and pour himself a quadruple whiskey. An over-whelming tiredness had begun to creep up his legs and arms, but he walked back doggedly to the car, the slane and spade on his right shoulder. As he neared the road, a ragged splotch of ghostly light appeared in the southern sky. The moon momentarily showed a veiled face before vanishing behind an enormous swag of cloud, but in that moment something caught his eye, a movement perhaps at the end of a turf stack. His grip on the spade tightened and he stole across to the stack and leaned against the end, listening for the faintest stir in the dark. He must have imagined it. There was no one there. Who could there be? Not at this hour of the night—except perhaps someone planning to steal a neighbour's turf. But that was unlikely, and with an effort he put the disquieting thought from his mind. When he reached the car, he took off his wellingtons, trousers and shirt, stowed them in the boot and put on clean clothes and shoes.

It was almost four o'clock when he got home. As he closed the garage door a great raindrop stung the back of his neck. He took no notice, however, but went straight to the bar and poured himself half a tumbler of whiskey. There were several things he should do. He should wash the floor where Eales had fallen, have a bath, and burn the trousers and shirt he had worn because in the event of an investigation he would find it difficult to explain how they had become so turf-caked. But he decided to put off until tomorrow what he need not do that night. He would get up in time for eleven o'clock Mass and open the pub as usual at twelve. Then in the holy hours between two and four, when all good Catholics were at lunch, he would attend to what was necessary.

He wanted above all to sleep and forget, but his mind was still too active, racing madly, dwelling on minutiae, now that the action of the night was over. He put Schumann's cello concerto on the gramophone and lay over the bed clothes, sipping the whiskey and listening to the recurring sadness of the first movement. He needed ambiguous music, sound that would bring glimpses of heaven while hinting at the depth of the darkness in the well of life, and Schumann in this respect was the composer par excellence, particularly the Schumann of the cello concerto. Never was the struggle between light and dark, between conscious and unconscious, keener than in Schumann, and yet it was not expressed as a struggle but as a fusion of opposites, weighing the very air with mystery, leaving it laden with an uneasy sense of other, less imperfect, musical possibilities. Listening to him was like looking into a well after a pebble had disturbed the water: a precise reflection threatened to form but the water continued to tilt and sway, distorting the image, teasing the mind in search of facile symmetry. And yet as you looked, it was possible to gain an indistinct idea of the reflection. Though the image was broken, it was recognisable as something remote yet deeply personal.

With a gratifying awareness of rhythmic abridgement he closed his eyes while his fingers clasped the tumbler on the bedside table. He opened his eyes again, aware of nothing but the searing pain in his rectum, a keenly stinging pain that made salty tears run into his mouth. He realised that he must have slept. The record had finished and he could not remember having heard the end of the last movement. He ground his teeth and pressed hard as if pressing would expel the pain. Was this to be his punishment, a summary visitation, cancer of the rectum followed by total colostomy to prolong a life no longer worth prolonging. God! As a punishment it was more appropriate to buggery than homicide. Bent in two he groped his way to the toilet in the dark and sat hunched on the naked bowl, too absorbed in his pain to remember the wooden seat. What he now desired was an elephantine defecation,

37

to discharge in one blistering avalanche the ache in his arse, but, though he pressed, the pain continued to cut like a twisting knife and nothing came. Was this, not cancer, to be his punishment: a phantom crap to plague and trouble till the end of time? He pressed again, the blood rising to his face until a fart, fierce as a shot from a gun barrel, ripped through his rear, dispelling in a moment all but the memory of pain. What relief! It was as if he had been reprieved at the point of death. The absence of pain was pure pleasure. Tears came to his eyes as he remembered how he had inflicted the ultimate pain on a fellow creature and yet could not himself stand the agony of a recalcitrant fart.

He was about to go to bed when he realised that he was at the centre of a rushing river. A clap of thunder, a cracking, splintering sound, reminded him of his tree, and he went to the open window and pulled back the heavy curtains. They were stiff to saturation and the carpet was wet under his feet. The rain was falling out of the sky, not in drops but in a continuous, splashing stream that came through the window and poured down his face and neck. The night was shaken by horrendous thunder, the sky torn by fleeing light that seemed to have neither pattern nor purpose, neither beginning nor end.

He put on his slippers and went downstairs and out into the garden. It was within half-an-hour of dawn, and he could see before him the dark pyramidal outline of the stricken tree. In a moment he was soaking from head to foot as if someone had emptied a keeler of water on his head. He stood under the conifer as the rain made rivulets down his face and chest, imagining the heavenly water being absorbed by the tinder-dry leaves, into the sapwood, into the very heartwood. The sky was a mass of flame, and he saw the darkness over the bog being rent by blu.. light and the water flooding in streams where there had never been a stream before, expunging footprints, swelling the surface of the sod, burying his secret deeper, making a fathom unfathomable. It all ended as quickly as it had presumably begun. The streaming and splashing became a flurry of droplets and he became aware of the dripping of the tree like the susurration of blood in his ears.

As the storm receded into the north-west he went inside, towelled himself with luxurious care, and went to bed in his pelt. He woke in daylight, refreshed by a sleep without dreams. After a copious breakfast of black pudding, bacon, eggs and tomatoes, he went into the garden again to savour the freshest, most intoxicating smell in the world, the smell of the earth after rain. Under the warmth of the forenoon sun the flowers, grass and leaves, after a long parching, gave off a subtle odour that cleansed his mind of the remaining shades of agitation. It was as if he had never heard of Eales. Suddenly he was strong and full of purpose. It seemed to him that there was nothing he could not do.

FOUR

Potter would have liked a bath before dinner but a bathroom was not among the amenities of the cottage he had rented from Rory Rua. As a makeshift solution he had arranged with Roarty to use his bath once a week; and though Sunday was not his regular bath night, he got out his towel, wrapped it round a bottle of bath oil, and put it in the car at the gable of the house.

He had been in the glen since May and after three months he was at last beginning to feel at home, thanks largely to Roarty and his pub. For the first month he had done his drinking in McGonigle's at the top end of the village, which was much frequented by sheep farmers from the depths of the north mountain who talked mainly about yeld ewes, louping-ill, liver fluke, grass tetany, mastitis and reactor cattle. Night after night he had listened to the sing-song of their conversation, regretting that his knowledge of sheep-shearing and dipping was so scant, and wondering if they might be interested to hear of the problems of lawn-mowing in suburban London. Then one evening he went into Roarty's for a change and he never went back to McGonigle's again. Roarty's was smaller and smokier with an old-fashioned flagged floor and a bar so arranged that the farmers and fishermen who drank in it could all take part in the same conversation. Whoever designed it had probably done so unthinkingly but he had provided a place of converse for the like of which many a sophisticated architect strove in vain.

On that first evening the customers eyed him as he entered but continued their conversation as if they had not seen him. He ordered a large Scotch, and a small hungry-looking youth whom he later came to know as Cor Mogaill looked at him with a smile and said: 'I've often wondered how many centuries it takes a people to evolve your pronunciation of the word "Scotch"'.

'Precisely the length of time it took to evolve your pronunciation of the word,' he replied, not wishing to become embroiled in a discussion on social history which might explode in politics.

'You must be English,' said Cor Mogaill. 'I can recognise the effete tones of southern England even here in rarefied Donegal.'

The other customers had turned their heads and were looking at Cor Mogaill and himself with open amusement.

'Yes, I'm English,' he said. 'I'm pleased you can tell.'

'Put English on *ruamheirg*, then,' said the youth with apparent innocence.

A few of the regulars laughed and waited with open mouths for Potter's reply.

'If you tell me what it is, I might conceivably be able to oblige you,' he said drily.

'It's a trick question,' said a tall, mule-faced man at his elbow whom he later discovered to be Gimp Gillespie. 'A question without a straight answer.'

'It must have an English name,' said Potter with a trace of chauvinism that was not lost on the company.

'It's the red-brown water you find here in the hillside

streams that run over iron ore in the ground. Rusty water, you might say, but the literal meaning of *ruamheirg* is "red rust".'

'I'm sure there's an English name for it,' Potter insisted. 'I just don't know it.'

That was how he first made the acquaintance of Gimp Gillespie, now his boon companion. Gillespie was a journalist who took his vocation seriously; he used Roarty's not merely to dull his too-active senses but to snap up what little news there was in the glen. Gillespie told him that the hungry-looking youth was the village intellectual and that 'Put English on *ruamheirg*' was a local phrase that meant 'Square the circle'.

'So, if I'd known the English word, I'd have become a local hero,' Potter laughed.

'We don't take it quite so seriously,' said Gillespie. 'There are certain key-words which occur again and again in the conversation here and have as a result acquired a certain comic resonance. *Ruamheirg* is one and *cál leannógach* is another. We all laugh whenever we hear them. It keeps us from having to think up new jokes to amuse ourselves in the long winter nights. If you wish to enjoy yourself here, you'd better begin finding words like *ruamheirg* and *cál leannógach* entertaining.'

He looked at Gillespie, at the seriousness of his long, ugly face, and he laughed warmly at his rueful Irish humour.

'Are all your key-words in Irish?' he asked.

'Most are Irish words for which there is no exact English equivalent. I can remember only one in English, and that's "replevy".'

'Replevy? Isn't that a legal term, something to do with the recovery of goods and chattels? But I think it's more commonly called "replevin".'

'Here we use it to mean a loud noise. If you had the misfortune to fart vehemently in company, Cor Mogaill might say: "He discharged a replevy that would wake the dead".'

'I wonder what the Law Society would say to that.'

'I thought I'd mention it to save you possible confusion.'

'It's very kind of you, I'm sure,' said Potter.

From that evening he was one of the locals. Whenever he entered the pub, Roarty would pour him a double Scotch without waiting to be asked, and the regulars would involve him in their disputatious conversations as if he were a countryman born and bred. Their talk was mainly of the country, oddly enough of matters which could well form the subject of the last letter in *The Times*. They would argue for hours about whether wild duck feed with curlews because of the vigilance of the latter. One group would contend that the curlews acted as sentinels for the whole flock while another group would argue that curlews were too restless and noisy to make easy companions for other wild fowl. The essence of these arguments was that no one knew the answers, and for this reason Potter's olympian adjudications were much appreciated by the company.

He looked out of the kitchen window at the rocks and knolls that fell away steeply to the sea. The waves were winking in the evening sun and Rory Rua in a red shirt was lifting lobster pots in the bay. He felt that it would be nice to sit by the west window in Roarty's bar and watch the evening drift into night. After a drink or two he would have a bath, and after another few drinks he would come home to dinner. He left the door on the latch, glad that he could do so in the knowledge that burglary was unknown in the glen. It was a lovely evening after the rain of the previous night, and he drove slowly to the village enjoying the view of the north mountain, a jigsaw of small fields, roads and cottages with here and there a straight plume of smoke rising from a potless chimney.

The bar would be empty at this hour of the evening; the locals never came in until about nine o'clock. Roarty would be alone as Eales always went dancing on Sunday evenings, and if Roarty was alone he would be game for an off-beat conversation. He was a treasury of useless information. He could talk of everything from phlogiston to fish-plates but his favourite topic was drink and all its concomitants, ancient and modern—pins and firkins and hogsheads, faucets, spiles and spigots not to mention the kilderkin, tierce and puncheon. Potter could listen to him for hours theorising about the effect of Irish whiskey on the dark side of the Celtic soul, and as for his knowledge of fishing and shooting, it was unsurpassed.

He parked his car opposite the pub where the road was widest, and bent his head under the low lintel as he entered. Roarty was immersed in the Sunday newspapers and Gimp Gillespie was sitting by the window with a creamy pint of stout before him. He had just washed his hair, and a pendulous lock that stuck out at the back gave him an uncanny resemblance to a tufted duck.

'I didn't expect you at this hour,' said Gillespie.

'I felt like a snifter before dinner, or what I take on Sunday by way of dinner, and I didn't have any Scotch in the house.'

He sat on a stool beside Gillespie and sipped his whisky while he listened pleasurably to his companion praising the forbearance of the Irish bachelor in the face of the sexual rapacity of village widows. Gillespie was a good conversationalist; there was a hint of rumination in every

44

thing he said which gave his lightest remark a substance that reflected the sadness of his ugly face on the verge of spontaneous laughter.

Roarty was sitting behind the bar, holding the newspaper at arm's length as he read. Even in his present hunched position he looked impressive. He was tall, broad-backed, bald and bearded with an air of stillness that reminded Potter of early mornings on the mountain. Was it the stillness of self-possession or self-absorption, he wondered without knowing why. When you met him in the street, the first thing you noticed was the width of his shoulders and his bow-legged walk. But when he was behind the bar, you could only see his top half, and then it was the head that impressed. It was a noble head with a grizzled beard from the depth of which emerged a sand-blasted, straight-stemmed pipe. Beardless, he would have been red faced. As it was, the flush of his cheeks showed above the greyness of his beard, contrasting oddly with the pale skin of his bald head. The thickness of his beard concealed his closely placed ears. You could not see them if you looked him full in the face, and this gave his head its unforgettable outline. Pulling a pint of stout, he would eye the rising froth, his head tilted sideways, the cast of his half-hidden lips betraying serious concern. But when the pint was nicely topped, his eyes would light up momentarily as he placed it before the expectant customer. At such moments one felt that because of some pessimistic streak in his nature he did not expect the pint to be perfect and that he was continually surprised by the successful combination of brewer's technology and his own handiwork. The pint served, he would put out a big hand with well-kept nails and take your money with an absentmindedness that robbed the transaction of anything approaching the cold-blooded self-interest of commerce.

Looking at him now, Potter became aware of the difference between him and the farmers and fishermen who drank in his pub, hardy, bony men who went out unthinkingly in all weathers. They were men who reminded him of bare uplands, grey rocks and forlorn roads in the mountains. Even in the twilight of the pub they wore their peaked caps down over their eyes, and though they could be seen occasionally squinting from beneath them there was an unflinchingness in their gaze as if they believed that looking could change the object looked at. Their lean faces bore spiders' webs of deeply etched lines that branched from eye corners or criss-crossed stubbled chins, expressing for Potter a noble stoicism in the grip of life's adversity. But Roarty did not look like that at all. He was big-boned and fleshy rather than hardy, with the look of a man who has led a comfortable life, who has never experienced sun or wind except from personal choice.

'Where is Eales this evening?' Gillespie asked. 'Dancing in Glenties or maybe Garron?'

Roarty put down his paper with an air of impatience and said: 'I wish I knew. I got up this morning to find him gone, his room empty, the bed not slept in. But wherever he is, he took his hold-all with him.'

'Do you mean to say he's gone?'

'I don't know what else to think.'

'And the bugger owes me a fiver!' said Gillespie.

'That's the younger generation—no sense of responsibility,' said Roarty.

'I should have known better. Never trust a Kerryman, not even if he's been caught young,' said Gillespie, looking mournfully through his wallet.

'He must have left after I went to bed,' Roarty grumbled.

'He must have got a lift,' said Gillespie. 'He would never have walked out over the hill in the middle of the night.'

'I wonder what lift he got at that hour,' said Roarty.

'There's a woman behind this,' said Gillespie. 'I've never known a man so given over to women. He couldn't meet a girl on the road without putting the comether on her. They tell me that he was even after some of the schoolgirls.'

'He's left me in the lurch,' said Roarty. 'If you hear of anyone looking for a job as barman, let me know.'

After another drink Potter went out to get his towel and bath oil from his car. In the street, Cor Mogaill with a knapsack on his back was looking up the exhaust pipe of his Volvo. Potter opened the car door without speaking and Cor Mogaill still kept his eye to the exhaust pipe. He lay in the bath for half-an-hour looking out through the open window at the evening sky turning from screened to solid pink in the west. Between the sky and the window was a mountain ash, and on its topmost branch a blackbird was whistling his heart out, the sparrows and thrushes mute with admiration. There was a magic in the Donegal evenings, in the luminous twilights that were long enough to seem like days in miniature. And he soaped his arms and thought of the long evening ahead, knowing that his dinner would wait till after closing time.

'Ireland is full of wonders,' he said to Gillespie when he returned to the bar. 'When I went outside, I found Cor Mogaill with one eye to the exhaust pipe of my car.'

'Cor Mogaill looks up the exhaust pipes of cars as a journalist might look up a dictionary.'

'Or a woman's skirt?' suggested Potter.

'A sexual fixation, would you say?'

'Undoubtedly,' said Potter. 'How interesting that the

love of cars should manifest itself so extremely in rural Ireland.'

'And in a man who rides a woman's bicycle too!'

'Now, in England that would never happen. I know several suburban men whose lives are their cars. They dream about them, talk about them, copulate in them, and when they drive into the country on Sundays they sit in them eating sandwiches. Yet not one of them would be seen dead looking up the exhaust of another man's car.'

'You English are so sophisticated.'

'Or sexually self-aware. Compared with us Cor Mogaill is an innocent. He could well provide the basis for a brief monograph for one of the trendier London academic publishers, a sociological survey of the phenomenon of car love with special reference to exhaust—or should I say anal—eroticism to capture the general market.'

'Cor Mogaill would provide the basis for more than a study of exhaust eroticism.'

'You say he is the village intellectual but he's closer in my opinion to being the village idiot. I came upon him by the roadside on the hottest day last week enraptured by a bag of fish he'd placed on the wall.'

'On the ditch?'

'On the ditch as you Irish inexplicably call it. There was a hole in the bag surrounded by a cloud of blue bottles. "Guess what's in the bag," he said to me. "Fish, by the smell of it," I said. "Pollack," he said. "Four whoppers that I killed myself at the back of Rannyweal. And do you see the flies trying to lay their eggs?" he asked enthusiastically. "Now an entomologist would take a power of knowledge out of that. Do you think that if we observed them closely we'd make a discovery?" I told him to put the bag on his back and go home quickly and salt his fish or put them in the fridge before they went bad in the sun. If *he* is the village intellectual—'

'Perhaps not,' said Gillespie pensively. 'But he's certainly the village atheist.'

Outside, the sky had darkened except for a lingering streak of pink in the west, and the breezes of late evening coming through the window enclosed them both in a cocoon of comfort. The pub was full without being crowded, and Roarty had half-a-dozen pints of stout lined up on the counter for topping.

'Have a chew of dulse,' said Crubog, who had just joined them. 'If you do, you'll never regret it.'

'What is it?' asked Potter, half-suspiciously.

'Seaweed.'

'Is it good for the virility?'

'And what is the virility?' asked the old man.

'Does it make you more attractive to women?' Potter shouted in his ear.

'No.'

'What is it good for then?'

'Worms.'

'Worms?'

'Intestinal worms. You'll never again pass a worm if you eat a fistful of dulse first thing in the morning and last thing at night.'

'If it's an anthelmintic, I'll try a spot of it,' said Potter.

'A word of advice about that greedy bugger you've rented a cottage from,' said Crubog.

'Rory Rua?'

'The devil was out in the bay at six this evening lifting lobsters in the middle of Sunday.'

'Presumably they were his own,' said Potter.

'That is not my story,' said Crubog, grasping Potter by

the sleeve. 'He's a great one for the sloke, you see, but if he offers you a chew of it, be careful. Don't refuse it because he might put up your rent but don't eat more of it than you can help. Sloke, you see, especially spring sloke —*slóc earraigh* as we say—is as good as a tonic but it makes you fart like thunder.'

'You mean replevy of course,' said Potter.

'The very word,' said Crubog. 'After sloke you must choose your company but after dulse you could dine with the Queen. That's the difference. Here, have another chew.'

'It's certainly got a distinctive taste.'

'Does it go well with Scotch?'

'Not as well as water.'

'Let me tell you something else then. Never come out for a drink in the evening without first swigging back a pint of new milk. The milk lines the walls of the stomach and when you take a drink the cream rises to the top and keeps the spirits from rising to the brain.'

'How much are you charging for all this good advice?'

'I can see you haven't been in this country long, fair play to you. Here the best things are free.'

He felt sure that the old man was angling for a drink and he was in no mood to disappoint a diverting octogenarian.

'Can I buy you a drink?' he asked, placing his empty glass on the counter.

'Not tonight, sir. In six months' time maybe, when you know me better.'

'You've made an impression on Crubog,' said Gillespie when the old man had gone.

'I wonder why.'

'It must be your sporting English manner. For all his

years and wisdom Crubog is an incorrigible snob. He remembers the old days, days of English landlords. His father was Sir Valentine Matlock's head gamekeeper, and he himself was his gillie. Sir Valentine was the local landlord, and ever since Old Crubog dearly loves an Englishman provided he's ·got the right swagger and a hint of rhotacism in his speech.'

'I don't know whether or not I should feel flattered,' said Potter. 'I can see I'll have to handle him with care in future.'

'Are you sufficiently English to wish not to disappoint him?' Gimp Gillespie asked with disarming directness.

'Would it be immodest to say that I'm convinced I shan't?'

'Do you ever miss England?' Gillespie asked.

'I wouldn't be English if I didn't miss England. I miss the little things most: the hush of Kent pubs after opening time on Sunday mornings, the Sunday newspapers with breakfast, the contrast between the urban week and the suburban weekend, and the occasional, peculiarly English experience which lights up life like a lamp, an unsought happening, a kind of epiphany.'

'Be more precise.'

'I once lived in Chelsfield in Kent and I used to travel home every evening on the same train from Charing Cross. One evening there were seven of us sitting in the same compartment, seven bored, slightly complacent men reading evening papers, when a girl got on at Waterloo. She was about eighteen, dressed casually in an open-neck shirt and scruffy jeans, and she sat opposite me looking vacantly out of the window, aware, I suppose, of how quickly the wall of newspapers opposite her had come down. The truth of it was that none of us could take his

51

eyes off her. She was beautiful in that delicate English way you must know, and she was shyly aware of it because she would glance fleetingly at each of us in turn without ever catching a single eye. I could not but marvel at the way she had transformed the drab compartment, not to mention the thoughts of the seven of us who until then had not a worthwhile purpose in common. She had the fairest skin I had ever seen and long, fair hair which looked the more attractive for being somewhat unkempt at the ends. As I looked, I began to wonder where she'd get off. If she rode on to Chelsfield, I might possibly have her all to myself for the last few stops of the journey, but that seemed unlikely because she did not look like a Chelsfield person. I should explain that on this line it is possible in a rough and ready way to judge a man's social class by his stop. Anyone who continues beyond a certain station has some pretensions to being middle class. He may be a milk-man but he has met bank managers. I was convinced that she would just qualify for the middle-class belt but to my surprise she got off at the first stop after London Bridge.'

'And what does this lesson in Bradshaw mean?'

'Let me finish. The girl got off and we were left staring at one another, beagles that had lost the scent. If she had once opened her mouth, she might have shattered the illusion as many women do. But of this I am sure. She would never have said in any circumstances: "That was a clitoral".'

He felt a remote sadness like water in a deep well into which a boy drops a pebble, and he paused as if to listen for the splash.

'Potter, you are stricken by class-consciousness.'

'It's the Englishman's burden,' he laughed.

'And where is all this leading? Where is the epiphany?'

'Being wrong about the girl's station, that's the epiphany. If I were wrong about a girl in Ireland, it would merely reinforce my sense of detachment but being wrong in England enhanced my pleasure in her beauty. It almost restored my faith in our class system. But now, my dear Gillespie, I must pee.'

He did not go to the loo, though. He went outside and into Roarty's garden, bitter tears of loss welling in his eyes. In the dark he leaned against a tree and asked himself why he needed to escape, to be for a moment alone. Was he weeping because of the way he had vulgarised the experience in recounting it, linking it so unnecessarily to a class-consciousness which wasn't his, demonstrating so painfully the difficulty of being oneself? Or was it that in his present loneliness he saw what the girl had represented for him was lost for ever. His loneliness was not of the country nor of the remoteness of this narrow glen. He had felt it increasingly since he was forty and the warmth of his marriage had begun to cool. He had married Margaret for several reasons but mainly because in being herself she had given him a point of rest from which to confront the world. She had given him form and direction as well as something of the unconsidered gladness of boyhood, and she did it unobtrusively, merely by her presence. Together they were not self-analytical; they talked only of the trifles of daily living, clothing them at first in mutual magic, making them into symbols from which they drew strength and encouragement. But as the first decade of their marriage ended, their power to transmute had faded. Margaret had not stood still and neither had he. While she had turned to her Irish past, he gave more and more of himself to his job. Increasingly, they sank into their separate preoccupations, two strangers who had mislaid the flint that lights the annealing fire of life. Margaret talked increasingly of her ailing mother, and when she begged him to take her to Dublin so that she might be near to her he was not taken by surprise. Though he was reluctant to give up his London job, which he liked, he hoped that his wife and he might rediscover each other in new surroundings. Within six months he had landed a job in the Dublin office of an American firm, and after a further four months he had found himself heading a six-man team prospecting for barytes in the Donegal mountains. He had been excited by the prospect of living in the wilderness of the western seaboard but it was an excitement that Margaret did not share. She told him dismissively that anyone who was born outside the Pale in Ireland was only half-civilised, and that Donegal people spoke an unspeakable lingo made up of Scots and Irish which even she could not construe. 'You may be understood,' she warned him, 'but you won't understand.' And so she remained in Dublin with her arthritic mother while he braved the vaunted rigours of the north-west alone.

He came to Ireland determined to experience as much of the genius of the country as he could. As soon as he arrived in Donegal he rented a fisherman's cottage and settled down to a life without Margaret. He was suffering from a severe bout of conjugal withdrawal symptoms. He found it difficult to sleep at night, and he shivered in bed for the first week though the May weather was mild. But he soon began to savour the pleasures of self-sufficiency. After coming home in the evenings he would make himself a bowl of soup, and then as he waited for a simple dinner to cook he would listen to a record and drink a Scotch or two. The bachelor life was not without its benefits, and when the people of the glen began referring to him as a bachelor he did not undeceive them. Now and again, however, his loneliness clouded the day, and then he could only look forward to Roarty's in the evening and a chat with Gimp Gillespie, Cor Mogaill and the rest.

Roarty was sharing a joke with Gillespie when he returned, and there was another large Scotch waiting for him on the counter. He felt slightly tipsy though it was still an hour off closing time, and he knew from experience that the next sixty minutes would slip past before he had a chance to grasp even one of them. Better not to look at the clock; better to seek the comfort of half-truths in the bottom of one's glass.

'Why does all drunken conversation become unintelligible before you're quite drunk?' Gillespie asked.

'All conversation, drunken or sober, tends towards the unintelligible. We are merely deluded by occasional shafts of light.'

'Let's talk about something we understand. Have you had any good rural rides since you've been here?'

'Why do you ask? You know I haven't got a horse.'

'I wasn't thinking of mares,' said Gillespie, pouring a too-high stout with unavailing care. 'I was thinking of women.'

'Only a journalist could make such an execrable pun.'

'You haven't answered my question.'

'The answer is no.'

'But there have been women in your life?'

'Enough to satisfy my curiosity.'

'Now you've said it. Once a man has satisfied his curiosity the rest is routine.'

'I'd like to think about that when I'm sober.'

'I've had only one woman in my time and that was to see what it was like. I went to work on the buildings in

London when I was eighteen, and I blew my first week's wages on a prostitute I met in a pub in Shepherd's Bush. She wasn't a proper prostitute; she was just an old tart that drank free gin in exchange for a tumble. She had a mouthful of rotten teeth but oddly enough it isn't her teeth I remember—it's her reddish hair. It was so stiff with lacquer that it felt like wire in my fingers, and in the bedroom she took off an old pair of stays that hadn't seen the wash since before I was born.'

'When I think of stays, I think of my great-aunt Letty. What was it like with stays?'

'Amn't I telling you that she took them off before we began?'

'And with all those handicaps how did you manage to raise it?'

'The virility of youth and an oblivion I owed to a dozen Guinness. I achieved my object, however; satisfied my curiosity. Before, I never knew what to say when other men talked of sex. Now, after one night, I was an authority, and better still I was cured of women.'

'Because you were put off?'

'It cured me of women but not of *a woman*. I've been in love with the same woman since I was fourteen and in thirty years I've never had as much as a kiss off her.'

'Surely no woman is worth such devotion.'

'A man can't help it if a woman lights a candle inside him. This woman has kept me warm through colder winters than you've known in London.'

Gillespie was looking into his glass as if reading his past in the physiognomy of the creamy top. His long face seemed to grow longer, his lower lip drooped, and for one disconcerting moment Potter thought that he would weep. His heart went out to him for the ugliness of his face, the ungainliness of his stride and the true simplicity of his conversation. Gillespie looked up and smiled sorrowfully.

'Without her I'd be a sapless stick,' he said.

'Does she live locally?'

'I see her from a distance at least once a week, at eleven o'clock Mass on Sundays. You're a different case, however. You're still foot loose, still capable of fancying a touch of the old *orificium urethrae*.'

'A bit of the other, as we say in England.'

'If you were to have an affair here, what kind would you wish for?'

'Something light-hearted and amusing, something to engage the mind more than the heart.'

'You mean you want conversation as well as copulation.'

'In a nutshell. I'm nearly forty-five, you see, at an age when the demands of the intellect begin to loom larger than those of the flesh.'

'Are you serious?'

'As serious as I can be after three-quarters of a bottle of Scotch.'

'Don't say another word. I'll have you fixed up before the night is out or I'm no Milesian.'

Potter scrutinised Gillespie's face to see if he were being serious but Gillespie was drawing on a burnt-down cigarette, one eye closed against the smoke and his right arm flung drunkenly between the bottles on the counter. Potter could not help laughing but he stopped when it occurred to him that the best Irish humour is entirely without malice.

'There are three possibilities,' said Gillespie. 'There's Monica Manus but she's a man-eater. There's Biddy Mhor but I'm told her natural juices are dry, and who wants to be bothered with axle grease? And there's Maggie Hession.'

'Who is Maggie Hession?'

'She's the local nurse and a snappy conversationalist. You did say you wanted conversation.'

'Among other things. But what's her age?' asked Potter, beginning to appreciate the humour of his situation.

'She's barely thirty-five, ripe for the plucking. When she was a girl of sixteen, she dropped her knickers for a kilted Scotsman who was here on holiday, and whatever he did to her she pulled them up again and she hasn't taken them off for any man since. There isn't a sinner of my age in the glen who hasn't put the comether on her but all she'd ever say is: "Come back when you're wiser".'

'Perhaps she's still waiting for her Scotsman.'

'I think he hurt her.'

'Her feelings?'

'Not her feelings. He was a bull of a man, you see, and she's only a sliver. Some say he was equipped with a veritable caber.'

'But that doesn't mean a thing!'

'You're a strange engineer. It's a question of volumes, man. You can't put a quart into a pint pot.'

'Now I know why you're still a bachelor.'

'Finish your drink. We'll corner her before bedtime.'

'But it's nearly eleven.'

'No glen person goes to bed before twelve.'

They both got up to go, laughing at the way they jostled each other on the way out. It was a lovely night with cool airs and what sounded like recitatives coming up from the sea. They lingered for a moment in the street, listening to the wild rumble of conversation inside and Roarty shouting 'Time', hoarse with exertion.

'Roarty is a landlord in a thousand,' said Potter. 'In a sense he is wasted here.'

'You know he's a spoilt priest.'

'That explains his learning but not his unusual physical presence.'

'He looks like a leader of men, the kind of chap who in another age would have made successful expeditions to the Antarctic.'

'He is too uneasy in his mind to be a natural leader. He saw the glory of the golden city and turned his back on it.'

'He asked me this morning the meaning of "ergonomically designed".'

'I wonder why he wanted to know that. What on earth did you tell him?'

'Designed for efficiency, to minimise human effort.'

'He must be going to install a newfangled stout dispenser,' said Gillespie.

At the crossroads outside the village they turned left and climbed the hill with the fenceless road, the moonlit mountains to the north and south gleaming with dots of light. The night was blissfully quiet except for the deep breathing of cattle in wayside byres and the occasionally piercing cry of a curlew from the shore. They walked in silence, Potter wondering what on earth he was doing on such an errand but too drunkenly amused to turn back. He felt truly happy, replete with the peace of the country and the seemingly inviolable sense of detachment that came with Scotch.

Half-way up the hill Gillespie stopped by a blackthorn bush and farted with venomous vigour. Potter, pretending not to hear, faced the ditch and waited for his water to come. Holding his insentient penis between his forefinger and thumb, he looked up at the southern sky

59

dappled with light cloud, a mackerel sky with patches of empty blue. At the centre of this field of cloud was a full moon with its rim so bright that it seemed impossible for such brilliance to be mere reflection. The clouds were so fluffy and light that you could not see them pass over its face. They looked as if they were behind the moon with the bottomless blue of the night sky behind them both. He watched the moon ride high and fast until it sailed straight into a sea of pure blue in which it seemed to lie becalmed, suddenly bereft of its yellowy halo.

'It takes rain to settle the wind,' said Gillespie as his water splashed rudely against a rock, but Potter, buttoning with deep concentration, did not answer.

'Maggie Hession lives in the groin of the hill. You can see her light from here,' said Gillespie.

'I've had second thoughts. I'm not going in.'

'I've got a plan. You pretend you've sprained your ankle and that you've come to have it bandaged.'

'But I haven't sprained my ankle!'

'How is she to know?'

'She's a nurse, isn't she?'

'You're thinking like a clapped-out bachelor. What you need is another Scotch.'

'I don't need another Scotch. I feel as if I'd had a skinful.'

'A word of advice then. Surrender to the genius of the country.'

'Brilliant, my dear Gillespie. Lead the way.'

When they reached the laneway that led to the house, they could see the light from the kitchen window cutting cater across the lawn into the untrimmed fuchsia hedge at the end. They stood in the shadow of the gable making some final adjustments to their clothes and expressions, suppressing laughter like two schoolboys.

'This has got to look good,' said Gillespie. 'Hop on my back and I'll carry you in.'

'What if you should let me fall? You're not exactly sober.'

'Then she'll have to bandage both of us.'

He stood with his back to Potter and, bending forward, gripped him at the knees while Potter placed a hand on each of Gillespie's shoulders.

'Hup!' said Gillespie, hoisting Potter onto his back.

'We'll be had up for attempted buggery if we're not careful,' Potter laughed.

'But we'll plead that it was all in the service of hetero-sexuality.'

With a sway and a stagger Gillespie turned the corner of the house into the light from the open door, keeping close to the wall in case he should have need of support.

'*Dia sa teach*. That means "God in the house", you heathen Sassenach.'

'Come in, will you, and rest your burden on the settle.' said a young woman who was knitting by the fire.

'My burden is nothing less than an English gentleman. Nora Hession, Kenneth Potter.'

She reached up and took Potter's hand, smiling with small teeth at his discomfort. She was better looking than he had expected, and younger too, but the lines of laughter and possibly sadness about her mouth and eyes gave her face a touch of quiet inwardness that told him she might be a girl who did not take life easy. The main impression she left on him was one of extreme fragility. Physically she was skin and bone, her neck and shoulders, arms and hips making straight lines where a connoisseur of feminine beauty would have demanded curves. A rare water bird, he thought, that lights once in a wonder on some secluded mountain tarn.

61

'Nora is the nurse's sister, you see, the one who is going to bandage you.'

'I see,' said Potter, realising his mistake.

'What ails you?' she asked Potter.

'My ankle,' he said lamely, not wishing to invite interrogation before he had concocted a plausible story.

'We were coming up Gara's brae when he slipped on the verge and turned out on his foot. Where's Maggie?' asked Gillespie.

'She's down in Paddy Og's—his wife's in labour.'

Potter stretched his leg on the settle and gingerly felt his ankle with his fingertips.

'Take off your shoe and sock and I'll bathe it for you.' said Nora Hession.

'I'll take him down to see Maggie,' said Gillespie, showing a restlessness which surprised Potter.

'It's a rough lane down to Paddy Og's, and it's dark under the trees. If you slipped, we'd have two patients on our hands. No, stay as you are, and I'll see what I can do.'

She poured hot water from the kettle into an aluminium basin and placed it on the floor beside the settle. He put his foot in the basin and she knelt beside him with a sponge. She wasn't pretty but she was arresting. Her black hair, sallow complexion, high cheekbones and hollow cheeks formed a picture of light and shadow which reminded him of a figure from El Greco. Then she smiled, and he almost felt the light of her smile on his face, a rare burst of sunshine on a January day turning all that was mutable to silver rather than gold. She was wearing light blue jeans and an open-collared shirt of darker blue which crinkled rather than swelled where her breasts were. And her squarely pared but unpolished toe-nails peeping through her sandals made him catch his breath as if he

62

had seen something that was not meant for his eyes. He thought of his too-obviously pretty wife, realising that here was a kind of girl he had never seen before, a girl who did not live for men but who might almost unthinkingly lead a lost man out of a labyrinth. He cleared his throat and said:

'You're the first girl I've seen here in jeans.'

'It's my day off. I don't wear them usually because Canon Loftus doesn't approve.'

'What has he got to do with you?'

'I'm his housekeeper.'

'Have you sold your soul to him?'

'He's only a parish priest, not the devil,' she laughed, looking up into his face with wide, black eyes.

'I don't think it's sprained,' he said. 'The pain is going already.'

'That's good.'

She carefully towelled his foot and went outside to empty the basin into the runnel. As she crossed the floor he noticed that her feet were not white but brown as if she'd been standing all day in bog water, a thought he found curiously affecting.

'We'll go now,' said Gillespie. 'We'll go down to Paddy Og's to see Maggie.'

'Enough is enough,' said Potter firmly.

When Nora returned, she offered to make them tea but Gillespie said that it was bedtime, that they really must go.

The sky had changed while they were inside. A great continent of cloud had risen in the east, propelled by a wind from the land. It was expanding in all directions, thinning at the edges, passing over the face of the moon which became a pale plate, all its brilliance gone. The cloud continued to expand until its black heart swallowed

63

all trace of the moon and only the uncertain stars in the west provided what light there was in the sky.

They walked back to the village without a word, surprisingly sober after the evening's drinking. When they reached the car, Potter said:

'Something I noticed about Nora Hession: her third toe is longer than her second.'

'She's an interesting girl.' said Gillespie. 'But wait till you see her sister.'

They said good night outside Roarty's and Potter drove home like a demon, keeping the near-side of the car so close to the hedges that the leaves brushed against the doors.

FIVE

'Can anyone be happy who thinks about happiness every day?' Roarty asked himself as he polished a pint tumbler.

It was just after opening time and the empty pub looked shipshape to his approving eye, the seats neatly ranged, clean ashtrays in the centre of the tables, the floor swept, the beer and stout shelves full, and a fresh bunch of ferns in the empty fireplace. He looked out of the big west window at an open boat running on lobster pots in the bay. It was Rory Rua's. He could just make out the red pullover of the owner on the stern thwart, and he wondered with satisfaction how many of the men who came into his pub could recognise a man on the other side of Ranny-weal. For that you needed a keener eye than most men, even most countrymen, could boast. He wasn't boasting but he could count the windows and parapets of the tower on the north mountain from this window. It was one of the reasons he was as good a shot as Dr Loftus, and Loftus was reckoned to be the best in the county.

His eye wandered over the fields by the sea where men in shirt sleeves were mowing and women in aprons were turning the hay with rakes. It was a bright morning; it would be another warm day. And the men bent over their scythes would be sweating and thirsty, imagining a pint of cool ale or stout at the end of the day. There was no denying it was a great summer for the trade. He looked up Gara's brae and sure enough Crubog was half-way down, keeping to the green selvage with irregular hops, avoiding the rough stones in the centre which bruised the corns and bunions of his old feet. He was always the first customer unless a commercial traveller came in for a quick one between calls.

'Can anyone be happy who thinks of happiness every day? Yes,' said Roarty. 'I am happy, and I think of happiness all the time.'

If he was happy, he could attribute it only to the murder, the perfection of which was a triumph of intelligence in the most threatening circumstances. And far from falling prey to Macbeth's rooted sorrow or 'that perilous stuff that weighs upon the heart', his perceptions had quickened, his joy in life enlarged. On the morning after, he had looked at a rose and felt himself being drawn into a dimension whose existence he had never suspected. The rose seemed to hint at worlds beyond his wildest yearnings yet entirely within his grasp if only... He brushed a petal with his forefinger and experienced a pleasure so rare and immediate that he felt it could only have come from having made the world safer for innocence. It was as if in ending life he had acquired a keener sensibility and a sharper and more subtle penetration.

It had been a week of potential catastrophe but because he had the perception of misfortune he was not unprepared; quite simply he had had the presence of mind to convert possible danger into actual security. On Monday Eales's mother rang from Dingle and he told her that Eales had gone without leaving an address. That was only commonsense; what was intelligent was his decision to tell McGing of the phone call so that when there was an SOS on the radio for 'Eamonn Eales who is thought to be travelling in south-west Donegal and whose father is dangerously ill' he could dismiss it without concern. He also took certain other precautions: he thoroughly washed the boot of his car and the spade and slane, burned the clothes and wellingtons, and cleaned the floor where Eales had fallen. However, he did not clean the whole bar because a pub without the barman's fingerprints would only heap suspicion on his head.

One result of the murder was that it prompted him to think about the world in ways he had not done since he left the seminary over twenty-five years ago. Arguably, therefore, it had made him a better man—if a thinking man is better than a non-thinking man. He supposed that a theologian or even a secular humanist would see the murder of Eales as evil but he could not for the life of him *feel* that it was evil. He saw himself rather as a benefactor of humanity; he could not find in himself the merest hint of regret or sorrow for what he had done. It was the blinding light of his conviction, this unaccustomed lack of shadow, that made him think. And he wished that he had his annotated copy of *De Malo*, with its simple distinction between moral and physical evil, if only to experience again the divine clarity of the Angelic Doctor. Would Aquinas, who saw the world with God's eyes, blame him for slaying Eales? Would he not concede that the murderous blow had been as involuntary as a patellar reflex? He went upstairs and looked in *Britannica* but there was no article on 'Evil', only a brief entry on 'Evil Eye'.

Susan Mooney, his new barmaid, came into the bar with a mug of black coffee. It was her second day, and already she was bent on pleasing, a willing girl who would be even better when broken in. She had come from Drimgallon in the outer mountains, the daughter of Mooney Mor, noted over three parishes for the potency of his poteen and his dexterity in outwitting McGing and his raiding men.

It was nice having a young woman about the house again. She moved in silence but wherever she went she left her mark. And apart from her work in the bar she scrubbed and cleaned and cooked in the kitchen. In time he would teach her the essentials of the drinking man's diet and how to make hot toddy in the mornings to drink in the bathroom as he shaved. He took the coffee and watched her vanish into the kitchen at the back. A definite improvement on Eales, she was sturdily built, wide in the beam with a round belly that protruded sufficiently to catch his middle-aged eye. A pity that he did not have the old hand pumps so that he might watch her breasts swelling as she pulled.

A hawk and a shuffle at the door told him that Old Crubog had arrived.

'So we live to drink another day,' said the old fox.

'It's the only pastime in this weather,' said Roarty, choosing a tumbler.

'There's nothing as heartening as the sight of an empty pub in the morning, the shelves full and everything spick and span before the barbarian hordes come in. Them that drinks bottles spoil the look of the shelves but draught is a different story—you never see the barrel going down.'

Crubog hoisted himself slowly onto a stool and placed his peaked cap on the counter to cushion his rheumatic elbow.

'Four thousand, two hundred and fifty,' said Roarty, putting a pint of stout before him.

'Is it on the house?' Crubog enquired while he fished in his pockets for loose change.

'It is, seeing that we're just the two of us alone. Four thousand, two hundred and fifty was what I said.'

'I hate to turn down a friend but four thousand, two hundred and fifty doesn't tempt me. You see, it isn't the money I'm after; it's a say in what happens when I'm gone.'

'You want to make history after your death.'

'Wouldn't we all if we could?'

'You're a contrary man. Your land is lying under the crows, and you won't lift a finger to—'

'Make me an offer I can't refuse.'

'I've made you as good an offer as you're likely to get.'

'I don't mean money, I mean a programme. What would you do with the land?'

'That depends . . . there's a limit to my capital.'

'It's an unholy nuisance, the self same land. I'd sleep sounder without it, there's no denying it. Offers on all sides and ne'er a programme.'

'What do you mean?'

'Last night Rory Rua came up with a bottle of whiskey to buy me out, lock, stock and barrel. He said he wouldn't leave till we made a bargain but he left empty-handed after two hours and without his bottle.'

'He's a mean man is Rory Rua. He bought Nabla Dubh's and Den Beag's and he's still not satisfied. Can't you see he's just a grabber. He doesn't see your land as special; he wants to buy it just because it's land.'

'And that's why he didn't get it. What I would like to do is sell to a young man with a young wife, a man that would husband it like the little holding it's always been and raise children that would in their turn look after it. If

I sell to either you or Rory Rua, God knows what will happen to it. You're a businessman and he's a fisherman with a mania for land. What I want is a hard-working farmer.'

Crubog was impossible. He listened to him with growing impatience until it was time for the other village codgers and pensioners to come in for their morning tipple. But even then there was no stopping him. He maundered on about his land as if it were the Duke of Buccleuch's estate, and Roarty wasn't sorry when he left to collect his pension.

Almost on the stroke of twelve McGing arrived for his only drink of the day.

'And what's on your mind this morning, sergeant?' Roarty asked as he poured him his black-and-tan.

'Ragwort and brucellosis. Here, would you mind putting up this poster.'

Roarty cast his eye over the oblong, yellow sheet: 'Brucellosis Eradication—Controls on the Movement of Cattle. Issued by the Department of Agriculture and Fisheries'.

'What about the ragwort?' he asked.

'Every field I clap eyes on is yellow with it. Some farmers seem to grow nothing else. They know it's poison: you'd think they'd do something about it without waiting to be pestered by me.'

'It's the way of fallen flesh,' said Roarty.

'It's a disgrace that a policeman of my experience should have nothing better to think about than ragwort,' said McGing, hooking his thumbs in the breast pockets of his well-filled tunic. He was a tall man, about six foot two, pink faced and heavily built. He was within a few years of retirement but he was still fresh skinned and light on his feet in spite of the miles he had walked over soft bogland in search of the ever-elusive still and worm. Among the glen people he had a well-earned reputation for officiousness for he was particularly severe on publicans who failed to clear their pubs in time. About ten years ago he summonsed Roarty for not opening the door to his knock at twelve, and he swore in court that he had heard the hum of drinkers' conversation and laughter inside.

'Did you hear the knock on the door?' asked the judge.

'Yes, your honour,' said Roarty.

'And why didn't you open it?'

'Because I was sure it was some drunk man trying to get in, and I wasn't having any of that.'

'And what about the hum of conversation?' asked the judge.

'Oh, that was me,' said Roarty. 'I always talk to myself when I'm washing up.'

'And what about the laughter?' asked the judge.

'That was me too,' said Roarty. 'I often laugh at the jokes I've heard during the evening. It's my way of unwinding.'

Sergeant McGing laughed so loudly and derisively that he was reprimanded by the judge who swallowed Roarty's story hook, line and sinker, and let him off without as much as a warning. From that day Roarty and McGing treated each other like two wary antagonists—with polite but distant respect.

'After a month of reminding farmers about their ragwort I sometimes wish I were in London with Scotland Yard solving rape and murder cases by the dozen.'

'But isn't it pleased you should be that we're all so law-abiding.'

'It's a policeman's paradox. His job is to prevent crime

71

't happy unless he's investigating it.'

'You might say that he encourages it by his presence.'

'Not in Glenkeel. In the country, I'm quite convinced, all crime is imaginary. People don't act out their fantasies as they do in the city. The last known crime in these parts (forgetting after-hours drinking which we don't mention) was five years ago, the Case of the Tumbled Trampcock.'

'With the torn knickers?'

'The very one. And who solved it, I ask you?'

'Every Glenkeel man knows the answer to that.'

'The other two guards blamed the two young tourists who were camping in the next field but I told them better. Do you know how I solved it?'

'No.'

'No semen on the knickers,' said McGing solemnly. 'Some of these young fellows know no forensic.'

'It was a tricky case,' said Roarty, beginning to enjoy the conversation from his position of unassailable security.

'It was an easy one for the right policeman. Look at the facts. Old Crubog wakes up one morning to find one of his trampcocks knocked flat, looking for all the world like a makeshift bed with a pair of torn knickers on top of it. It has rained heavily in the night and the hay is ruined, £10 worth, a tidy sum to an old-age pensioner. Young Garda McCoy investigates, finds footprints leading to the next field where two teenagers from Derry are camping in the rain. He comes back to the barracks thinking he has solved the case until I breathe the pregnant word "semen". "But maybe he took her knickers off before he laid her," says he. "Why should he tear them off?" says I, "if they're both camping happily together in the next field?" "A fetishist," says Garda McCoy triumphantly. "A practical joker," says I, "and a local man too. This was done to make Crubog think that the younger generation are sex maniacs. The lads are always filling his head with stories.'' And I put my cap on my head and went straight to the man that did it.'

'Cor Mogaill Maloney.'

'Imagination is what a policeman needs, not logic. A born policeman has a criminal imagination. The only difference between him and the criminal is that he uses his imagination to solve rather than commit crime.'

McGing took a long draught from his pint and winked at Roarty.

'A policeman,' he said, 'feels closer to the criminal than to the most law-abiding citizen. It's the tie between the hunter and the hunted. You're a sportsman; you would agree that a good hunter knows his quarry.'

'A good sportsman is first and foremost a naturalist.'

'And a successful policeman is first and foremost a criminologist. He gives his days and nights to the study of the criminal mind. Though I say it myself, it's a pity I never got a chance. Oh, if only there was a Moriarty in Glenkeel. I've got the nose, you see. But what's the good of a nose if there's no one to leave a . . .'

'Spoor,' suggested Roarty.

'Spoor indeed,' said McGing, shaking his head sadly.

There was a thud in the hallway as Doalty O'Donnell put down his postbag.

'You're late,' said McGing authoritatively.

'A heavy post. It took over an hour to sort,' said Doalty, untying the string on a bundle of letters.

'Let's see what you've got,' said Roarty.

'Nothing but bills,' said Doalty apologetically. 'It's something I've been noticing lately, the increase in official mail and the falling off in private correspondence.

A postman's pleasure is easily measured when all he delivers is bumf.'

Roarty looked perfunctorily at the brown envelopes. One from a bottling firm, one from the Electricity Supply Board, one from a record club, and a tatty envelope that had been used before and restuck with sellotape. He tore it open out of curiosity and felt his legs go limp as he read.

'Doalty is right,' said McGing. 'The telephone has murdered the art of letterwriting.'

Roarty mumbled a reply and placed a glass under the nearest optic, his mouth nauseatingly dry. He said 'That reminds me' and went out to the kitchen and asked Susan to mind the bar while he went upstairs. Sitting in a daze on the edge of his bed, he reread the letter, pausing unnecessarily over the large block letters written no doubt with a matchstick:

Dear Roarty: Eales is transplanted but not his magazine which I'm still enjoying. If you want to keep his whereabouts from McGing, pay £30 a week into Acc. No. 319 291, The Bank of Ireland, 34 College Green, Dublin 2. Pay in notes, not cheques. Begin in three day's time, August 13th, and oblige yours sincerely but seriously, Bogmailer.

SIX

Roarty was so shattered that he could not think. Until lunchtime he went about his business in a dream, pulling pints and giving change mechanically, making small talk without knowing what he was saying. He was relieved when Susan called him to lunch but he wolfed it down so quickly that when he had finished he could not tell what he had eaten. In the afternoon he left Susan in charge of the pub and went fishing to see if it would settle his nerves.

With his trout rod on his shoulder he climbed the hill towards the loughs, forcing himself to concentrate on the present, on the familiar features of the landscape: old ditches with lichened stones built in more straitened times, sheep pens and makeshift dipping troughs, clumps of ferns and rushes, a solitary foxglove sheltering in a river bank, pools of red water where he had fished for eels as a boy. The red water was the *ruamheirg* for which there was no English, and he listened to its piano music falling in a miniature cataract on smooth stones. Further up the river in another pool fronds of brown dirt wavered at the bottom among the pebbles while the surface was speckled with a red and gold and silver scum which formed a kind of iridescence. He walked along poached sheep tracks with heaps of sheepshairn like black peas which he tried to avoid; past a patch of kindly grass near an old lime kiln; past the mound of rushes where a snipe always rose; past spongy hollows among the firmer ground; past pools with thick foam churned brown between stones, clotted froth, swirling, swirling, froth which would give you warts or so his mother told him as a boy. And in the river pools here and there the stones were covered with a green alga *cál leannógach*, another word which formed part of the comic consciousness of the glen.

When he reached the top of the hill, he sat gratefully on a clump of heather. Beneath him the glen was spread like a feast of which he could not partake. He tried to recapture the delight he normally took in the scene but now he was a mere onlooker, not a participant. The bottom of the glen with its patchwork of fields; the north mountain irregularly dotted with whitewashed cottages; the village of Tork where he himself lived, a sorry straggle of houses, a blemish on the beauty of the landscape; the sickle-shaped strand in the west and the greeny blue of the sea beyond— all were so many disparate parts which failed to form a satisfying whole. A wild bee hovering over a heather clump prompted him to get up. He plucked a handful of moss and, putting it to his nose, inhaled the smell of newly cut peat which he remembered so well since boyhood.

The hilltop was a plateau of bogland on which his father used to cut turf before he took a bog in the Abar Rua, and it stretched before him like a carpet of light and darker brown streaked by washed-out green. The old bog where his ancestors had cut their turf was derelict, the sites of the old turf stacks like graves, mounds of peat mould overgrown with rushes and here and there a whitened stick of bog fir strewn among the heather and mountain grass. The old face of the bog was broken down by sheep's feet, rough weather and running water. Tufts of heather grew in crevices and the marks of the slane denoting the different spits were all gone, vanished into eternity, blown to dust by Atlantic winds. In a moment of lucidity he had a sense of centuries passing quickly while the long pull of his own desperate existence seemed never ending.

Ahead of him the ground began to dip, forming twin basins in which lay two lakes, the Lough of Gold and the Lough of Silver. He reached the Lough of Silver first, the larger of the two and the nearer to the sea. A west wind was ruffling the surface of the water, making the waves boil among the black stones on the lee shore, producing a continuous singing which differed noticeably from the rhythmic wash of sea waves. He walked out along a little causeway of stepping stones, watching a belt of sunlight traversing the water and a little inlet on the left full of white froth streaked with brown. On the right was a patch of water weed, the leaves pointing with the wind to the eastern shore.

On the far side of the lake was a solitary water bird, sailing before the wind, its black body high in the water, its black neck gracefully arched. He retraced his steps to the shore and sat down to watch the bird. It was too high in the water to be a cormorant, and it lacked a cormorant's nervous vigilance. It was drifting peacefully before the wind, looking to neither right nor left, its gaze fixed on the water below its breast. And he could not but feel that it was a strange bird seldom seen in these parts, perhaps a bird of ill omen. When it reached the eastern shore it rose against the wind and with slow flapping returned to the windward side of the lake. Then, as if whiffing for fish, it sailed back before the wind once more, only to repeat the performance when it reached the eastern shore.

Roarty pulled the letter from his pocket and spread it before him on the heather. The sense of nausea he experienced when he first read it had gone, and in its place was a dull ache of anxiety, a kind of tugging that distorted his thoughts, making all around him seem as unreal as the sense of impregnable security he had felt while talking to McGing that morning. His pattern of thought had crumbled into a thousand fragments, and now he knew that to survive he must pull himself together and decide tomorrow on a sensible course of action. The first thing he must do was to discover who wrote the note. This wasn't strictly necessary of course; he could make a decision without knowing. But he felt that he could decide more easily if he knew the temper of the enemy. He studied the writing but the anonymous block letters told him nothing. Any clues they contained must lie in the language, in the telltale turn or twist of a phrase. The writer was obviously intelligent, capable of expressing himself succinctly and with dry humour, capable of writing over fifty words with only one error. Or perhaps he had written 'in three day's time' rather than 'in three days' time' as a deliberate ruse to put him off the scent. The word 'transplanted' was another clue; it would come naturally to a country man but it could also come naturally to a city man who had met farmers. And what of the word 'bogmail'? He felt that here was the crux, that in this rather self-conscious attempt at humour lay the clue that would lead him to the enemy. The writer was probably a regular customer, someone who could have got his hands on an old business envelope with his name and address, someone who lived in Glenkeel and had a bank account in

Dublin. In theory such men were few but they were not at all easy to identify. Cor Mogaill? Gimp Gillespie? Rory Rua? Kenneth Potter? All of them were possibilities, not to mention three or four others that came to mind. On the internal evidence Cor Mogaill, Gimp Gillespie and Potter were the likeliest. All three had the type of humour which would have enabled them to write such a letter, while Rory Rua, though well read, was dour and unimaginative, not the kind of man who was likely to call himself a bogmailer. But on the other hand he was the most likely to have seen him burying Eales. He cut turf on the Abar Rua and it was known that he often got up early to see if he could catch the turf thief all the neighbours complained of. Potter was another possibility. He was a keen bird watcher, often on the mountain with his field glasses, but was he likely to be bird watching at three o'clock in the morning? Roarty felt that he was in a labyrinth from which there was no exit. He could spend the rest of the day on 'ifs' and 'buts' without achieving anything; the only real evidence he had was the letter. He read it again, hearing Potter's exuberant laugh on the other side of the counter. It was Potter, by God; he was just the man to find humour in a word like 'bogmail'. He would keep a weather eye on him, listen assiduously for the tell-tale phrase which would transform a harmless hunch into dangerous certainty.

Looking at the regal progress of the water bird, he wondered what was best to do. He could pay the £30 a week and hope that the blackmailer would not ask for more; he could go to McGing with the letter in outraged 'innocence'; or he could quite simply ignore it. As he considered the three options, however, he knew in his heart that the choice lay between the first and the last. He pulled off his hat and took a Connemara Black from the band. It was the best fly on a day like this with the wind blowing against the flow of the water where the stream left the lough in the south-west corner. His eye travelled over the popply surface, glinting with light from the afternoon sun, and he thought of brown trout lurking in the shadows of the peaty bottom, dark and mysterious like their unplumbed home. He attached the fly to the trace and picked up his basket, about to make his way round the edge of the lough to the far side. But as he turned, the water bird raised its head and looked him in the eye for a long moment before concentrating once more on its unobtrusive whiffing. The long moment changed his mind. He would not dare compete with such a seldom-seen visitor. He would simply cross the hill to the more sheltered Lough of Gold on the other side.

The wind blew stiffly in the heather and against the back of his legs, and then he was on the other side of the hill without a breath of air stirring. Below him the sheltered lake was a sheet of reflected blue with stooping reeds on one side and a patch of water weed, red and green, near the edge, flat, floating circles with missing segments. Just then his eye caught a familiar form: a grey, high-shouldered heron on a stone near the shore. And he dropped to his knees in the heather, his eye still on the skeleton-thin sentinel. He was not sure if the heron had seen him. If it had, it did not give the slightest indication, not even a tilt of its crested head. He stared at the long beak on the rough breast and gradually he became aware of the true meaning of immobility. In an instant he knew what he must do. Like the heron he would move neither head nor foot; while presenting a picture of intelligent vigilance, he would affect a masterly inactivity and possibly make Potter think again.

A devilish thought entered his head; he would test the heron's nerve as Potter no doubt would test his. He got to his feet and began walking straight towards the bird, determined to see how far he would get before she took flight. Would she turn on the stone and fly into the east or would she rise in the direction in which she was facing and turn on the wing? He picked his steps carefully over the rough ground, never once taking his eye off the stooped head. A sudden flap made him jump. Another heron which he had not seen rose from the reeds, and when his eye returned to the stone its companion had also risen. It would not have happened to him yesterday. His nerves were on edge; he was too easily distracted. He watched them fly off in different directions with powerful wing beats, their long legs trailing behind, and gradually converge over a hillock to the east of him.

'By your gimp I would say your basket is light.' The voice came from the hillside behind him but he recognised it with a tremor of apprehension as McGing's.

'There isn't a stir on this water,' said Roarty.

'Have you tried the Lough of Silver?'

'Yes,' he lied. 'They're rising short, the buggers.'

'Never,' said McGing. 'Not with the wind in this airt. It's the best airt there is.'

He watched the other man coming down the side of the hill, the deep heather brushing the sides of his wellingtons. He was wearing corduroy trousers tucked into the tops of his gumboots and a grey thornproof jacket with bulging pockets that made him look broader and more awkward than he was. His face was flushed, and when he came level Roarty could see a tear in his left eye from having been looking into the wind. They stood on the shore of the lough, two once powerful men now past their prime, and

Roarty felt that if they were to wrestle there was no telling which of them would win. But they would not wrestle. Any conflict between them would be one of alien intelligences.

'And what fly did you have on?' asked McGing.

'A Connemara Black.'

'I'll try a Zulu then. Either should be killing on the Lough of Silver with the wind and the sky as they are.'

'You can try what you like. I think myself that it was the black water bird on the other lough that put the evil eye on me.'

'A black water bird? You mean a *duibhean*.'

'It wasn't a *duibhean*. No cormorant ever kept her head so still.'

'It's nothing else,' said McGing. 'Didn't I see her myself last week, a big *duibhean*, as big as a swan.'

'But you don't find *duibheans* as big as swans.'

'Let's have a look then.'

They climbed the hill but when they came within sight of the other lough there was not a trace of the water bird.

'It's gone,' said Roarty. 'You might catch something now.'

'It was a *duibhean* all right. They come inland from the sea for a change of diet. Are you going to try your luck again?'

'No,' said Roarty. 'I won't wet another fly today.'

McGing's flat-footed attempt at humour had annoyed him, and he set off across the brown bogland with his mind racing before him. He was still apprehensive but now he had a sense of immediate purpose. This evening he would be as inscrutable as a heron but he would keep a wary eye on Potter.

SEVEN

Potter was waiting outside the priest's gate for Nora
Hession. He had met her in the village by accident four
days ago and when he asked her to come to the pictures in
Donegal Town to his surprise she agreed.

'Wait outside the gate, not outside the parochial house,'
was all she said.

In the meantime without seeming to, he asked Roarty a
few questions about her sister and then in the shape of an
afterthought a few questions about herself.

'They're a curious pair,' said Roarty. 'Both luckless in
love, ill-served by two undeserving men. Maggie, as I told
you, never recovered from her Highland gentleman, and
Nora hasn't looked at a man since she ran off to England
six years ago after a good-for-nothing scallywag who used
to manage the sugar beet factory in Glenroe. She was a
schoolmistress in Largyweal and only twenty-three when
she fell in love with him, but he was a light-headed young
pup, more interested in women than in a woman. He got
into trouble at the factory—he was accused of embezzling
wages—so he had to do a flit; but he hadn't landed in
London before Nora was at his heels. She was only six
months in England but whatever happened between them
she came back like a wraith, a ghost of her former self.

She was as thin as a rake and she couldn't face the teaching again. So she ended up as housekeeper to Canon Loftus. O, she's a sad girl. You can see it in her eyes when you meet her in the road on the brightest day in summer.'

He switched off the engine and watched a shower from the sea envelop the shoulder of the bluff on the north side of the glen. The shower passed along the mountain like a veil dimming the brightness of the landscape but only a few sparkling drops fell on the windscreen of the car.

The door of the parochial house opened and Nora Hession came down the avenue, stepping daintily in high heels with all the caution and sedateness of a heron. He experienced a momentary thrill at the comparison, seeing lakes and moors under an evening sun and a lone heron fishing. He leaned across and opened the door for her, and she filled the car with a fragrance that reminded him of crushed bluebells and a day in Derbyshire as a boy.

'Why did you ask me to wait by the gate?' he enquired.

'Your car is bigger than the Canon's. He has a worldly streak for a priest. He might just be envious.'

'Why should you wish to spare him envy?'

'Because it's one of the seven deadly sins. Though I'm paid only to look after his bodily needs, I consider it my duty not to lead him into temptation.'

'You're a serious housekeeper, not all domestic economy.'

He sat back and drove quickly through the village, narrowly missing a cockerel at the crossroads, then up the hill behind the houses while she told him what the Canon liked on his toast in the morning. Soon they were flying over the Abar Rua, the bogland stretching on each side with a blue lake and a yellow boat and the dark bulk of Slieve League on the right. The road was narrow and the hair-pin bends came up so unexpectedly that his hand was hardly ever off the gear lever. Then they left Glenroe behind and they were driving through more kindly countryside with small cottages at the ends of laneways and farmers and their sons making hay in the nearby fields.

The west coast of Ireland, he thought, was a landscape of harshness and exiguity, a million miles from the green and pleasant land of England. It was a landscape carved by a warped history, eaten to rock bottom by the forces of erosion, now almost irreducible in its barrenness. It was a landscape of green patches precariously struggling against the wildness of encroaching heather; drystone walls instead of hedges; stunted trees bending before wet winds; futile roads winding towards long-abandoned homes and bare hilltops; and lonely beaches among black rocks and the tormenting crash of the sea. It was an alien land but he liked it. It was here that he had found the image that brought him, he thought, to the very quick of the country: a solitary fisherman in a boat on a mountain lough and night falling, darkness in the hollows of the hills and streaks of broken light on the dull water. The man and the boat were a mere silhouette, darkly outlined against the play of the water, the surrounding landscape vague in the thickening light. When he saw this silent figure, an angler no longer fishing, he was moved as he had not been by anything else in the country. And he carried this image with him until he chanced on a more potent one: a grey heron fishing knee-deep in a stony moorland tarn, solitary, statuesque, timeless, making him realise that a country has a life of its own, deeper, more mysterious even than its people. He felt that he had peeled off a further layer of onion, and it seemed to him that he had discovered not so much a paradigm of Ireland as a paradigm of life, of the

85

dread and desperate loneliness at the heart of it. He looked at Nora Hession, at the faint lines that branched from the corners of her mouth, and he wondered if she dreaded the night.

'Have you ever thought about Irish villages?' he asked, wishing for a more ingenious topic of conversation.

'No, I've just lived for most of my life in one.'

'They are the ugliest feature of Ireland, warts on the face of the landscape. In England villages improve the countryside; they embody for most Englishmen an ideal of life. In fact their most implacable enemies are the towns-people who drive for miles every Sunday to have tea in them. I can't imagine the most confirmed conservationist driving to have tea in one of these hungry straggles. They are all the same, one street with a row of grey houses on each side: a church, two shops, a petrol station, a police station and six pubs. Now, in England we ring the changes; we have "square" villages as well as "street" villages, villages built round a green where people once gathered to play cricket. It's a simple device, yet no one seems to have thought of it here.'

'I think the main difference is that Irish villages have a history of deprivation, and if there's one thing more deprived than an Irish village it's an Irish town.'

'Have you ever seen an English village?'

'No, my six months in England were spent in London.'

'That was a mistake. You didn't see England.'

'I saw the Serpentine.'

'And what did you think of it?'

'I cried when I compared it with the Lough of Silver. It was so small, so artificial, so crowded with people heavy after Sunday lunch. It seemed to me that all the ugliness of humanity was there.'

He glanced at her serious face, and it occurred to him that he did not wish to talk to her about villages or the Serpentine but to walk with her on the shore of the Lough of Silver and show her perhaps the stillness of a heron.

'I take a different view. I think that the one cannot be truly appreciated without a knowledge of the other. It is in opposites that we find ourselves.'

'It is my fate to be taken to the pictures by men with a taste for sophistry.'

'And who is the other sophist in your life, may I ask?'

'Canon Loftus. He has the knack of making me feel positively simple-minded.'

When they reached Donegal Town, he parked the car in the Diamond and they had a drink in the small lounge of the Central Hotel.

'What film are we going to see?' she asked, sipping her dry sherry too daintily, sipping it like a girl who would have preferred to drink it. She had crossed her legs and had twisted one foot round the leg of the table, which made him feel she was not so much at ease as her conversation had led him to believe. He would, he thought, have to do better.

'I'm afraid I don't know,' he said. 'I had meant to look it up but it completely escaped my mind.'

'You have gone native already. It's what I would expect from an Irishman rather than an Englishman.'

'You must stop expecting me to be typical. I came here merely to be myself.'

They finished their drinks and strolled across to the Four Masters' Cinema, pausing on the way to look into shop windows.

'My God, it's *My Fair Lady*,' he said. 'It follows me everywhere.'

'I've always wanted to see it,' she said, suddenly excited.

'I've seen it four times already because of girls like you and I've seen *Pygmalion* twice. Let's forget about it and have another drink in the Central.'

'I want to see the film.'

'Surely you don't want to spend a lovely evening like this in a stuffy flea pit. If you come back to the Central with me, I'll sing you "The Rain in Spain" and I'll do the Cockney better than they do it in the film.'

'No, thank you.'

'Is there another cinema?'

'No.'

They arrived in time for the main feature, and he sat in the dark cinema wondering if he would pass through middle age as gracefully as Rex Harrison. He was annoyed at having to watch *My Fair Lady* for the fifth time, and at his fate of meeting girls whose tastes passed his understanding. His wife was another example. She had seemed reasonable when he first met her but over the years she had sunk increasingly into her Irish background. He tried to follow her to the extent of reading a few books on Irish history but a rudimentary knowledge of the genealogy of Brian Boru and the exploits of Niall of the Nine Hostages gave him little leverage in their domestic disagreements. Homesick, homesick; that was her trouble. Homesick for the oppressive constrictions of the village life of Dublin.

She had failed him beyond question. In his London job he was a busy man with little time for such symbols of culture as books and records. His wife on the other hand spent most of her time reading and listening to music; but though he could see the input, there was no visible output. After listening to Beethoven's thirty-second piano sonata she would merely sigh and say nothing. And if he asked her whether she had enjoyed it, she would merely say yes. She would never say how or why, and this reluctance to translate experience into language irritated him beyond measure. If only he had a woman who would share her life with him and in so doing enlarge his own. Though she was 'cultured', she was of little help to a busy man caught up in suburban cultural infighting at week-ends. Once when she booked tickets for a concert in the Royal Festival Hall, they arrived too late to get a programme, and when he asked her the name of the orchestra and the soloist she said she had forgotten. It was the kind of thing he'd expect any well-organised wife to know, the kind of thing his secretary would have known without trying. A good wife should be among other things a good secretary, and Margaret had failed dismally in her secretarial functions. In the dying stages of a suburban party when Scotch had begun to play havoc with his memory, she could never supply the missing word in his conversation. If he said 'To see a World in a grain of—' and snapped his fingers, she would more than likely say 'salt'. He had learnt to live with her but though they were married they were not man and wife. They did not 'grow' together; their lives did not entwine like the branches of two contiguous trees. And now he realised that it was his failure to understand her that had driven him here.

'We'll have supper in the Central,' he said when the film ended.

'I don't think I should. I'd be back too late. The stairs in the parochial house are old and when they creak they wake the Canon.'

'I don't see why we should allow the Canon to spoil our evening.'

'He hasn't spoilt our evening. At least he hasn't spoilt mine. I'll tell you what we'll do: we'll have fish and chips in Garron on the way back.'

'But aren't fish and chips a trifle sordid after the dream world of *My Fair Lady*?'

'Not as they're cooked in Garron. The fish will have come off the boats this evening, still tasting of the sea.'

He did as he was told. He stopped in Garron and they both went into the fish-and-chip shop in front of the harbour and joined the queue which extended almost to the door.

'I'm not so sure that I'm going to enjoy this,' he said, looking at noisy teenagers on each side.

'We don't have to eat them here. We can take them to the car if you like.'

They drove round to the other side of the harbour and he parked the car on the water's edge. They sat in silence for a time eating their fish and chips from a newspaper, looking at the pale moonlight on the waves.

'To me there's nothing more asymmetrical than a moon four days past the full. It looks as if someone clipped the top off it with a shears,' he said.

'Look at the water. It's lovely. Canon Loftus always takes me here after the pictures. He was born in a fishing village, and there's nothing he likes better than boats.'

The lights of the town surrounded the small harbour, and looking at the water you would think that there was another town under the waves. It seemed to him that he was living in a drowned city, looking from a distance at the life above, observing himself with uncanny objectivity, a sensation which he felt he owed to Nora Hession.

'Do you have fish and chips with the Canon?' he asked, watching the forest of masts on the other side of the harbour and a faint light in the wheelhouse of the nearest vessel.

'We always have fish and chips here on the way back from Donegal, and we sit in the car and watch the lights on the water.'

'So our evening has been a replica of all the evenings you've been out with the Canon.'

'Not exactly. Tonight the conversation is different, the feeling that time is passing more pronounced.'

'What sort of man is the Canon? Is he as gruff in conversation as he sounds in his sermons?'

'He's gruff with men but not with women. Though he says in his sermons that women are the root of all evil, he treats them with wary gentleness.'

'It's a wise man who respects his enemy.'

'You know, I do think he sees me now and again as an enemy or at least in league with the Enemy.'

'If you're his enemy, why does he pay you to remain with him?'

'Because he likes my cooking. He says that I'm the first cook who's ever been a temptation to him. Before he met me, he says, he ate only to live.'

He looked at her profile in the dark, trying to make out if she were being serious, always a problem in Ireland. Though her comments were never less than acute, there was an innocence in the way she expressed herself that gave to her conversation the quality of originality.

'What does he talk about when you're with him?'

'He's like you; he asks me questions all the time. Though you wouldn't think it to see him farming, he's a very holy man. He always closes his eyes when they're kissing on the screen. We have an unspoken understanding about that. I give him a nudge when it's safe for him to look again.'

'I wonder why he doesn't want to watch kissing.'

'I think I know,' she said slowly. 'He was a man of strong passions in his youth.'

Impulsively he put his arm round her and drew her dark head onto his shoulder. Her hair was soft against his cheek, and the warm fragrance of her body mingled with the smell of fish and chips in the car.

'I'm glad you don't smoke,' he said. 'I can't stand the stink of women who do.'

She raised her head to look at him, and he hugged her with both arms and kissed her on the lips. Something tickled his cheek, and when he put his hand to her face it was wet.

'Do you always cry when you're kissed?' he asked, giving her his handkerchief in puzzlement.

'I cried the first time but that was ten years ago.'

'Why did you cry now?'

'I think it was because of the Canon. It was so strange being kissed like that after fish and chips in Garron.'

They drove home without saying much while Potter pondered the strangeness of a mature woman who cried on being kissed. Was it because of her reluctance to peer out of her shell after six empty years of denial? Or was it because she sensed the tenderness he felt when she had half-expected to be hurt by him? Perhaps she had seen the parochial house as a refuge from the world and everything else, including himself, as mortal danger. The Canon was a man and yet not a man. She could share his house, cooking and washing and ministering to his whims in safety, and he would never make a demand she could not meet. Now she was faced with a different beast, a man who would hold a mirror to her face and perhaps surprise her into self-discovery.

Talking to her now, Potter was conscious of choosing his words with care. He was treading cautiously like a man with a brimming cup between his hands because at any moment he might trip and cause it to spill. He was aware of a life of inviolable boundaries, more terrifying in its privacy than any he had encountered. And he realised how lacking in shadow was his relationship with his wife, for without shadow there could only be the blindness that comes from excess of light.

He stopped at the priest's gate and pressed her hand.

'I'll make you flower. Wait and see,' he said. 'From now on you will feel only the warmth of the sun.'

She laughed lightly at the foolishness of his self-confidence and said: 'The sun is never warm here. Even on the finest day there's a breeze from the sea.'

EIGHT

Roarty slept little in the fortnight after he received the letter, and whenever he did sleep he was troubled by the same dream. He would see himself against a dark brown landscape with a head of flowing hair, thick at the roots with wriggling maggots that scurried over his scalp, burrowing under the skin, tapping on the hard bone of his skull. This would go on for what seemed like hours, and whenever he tried to scratch his head he would find that his hands were tied with sea wrack behind his back. Then in a moment of unspeakable terror he would realise that what he had experienced was nothing. What if the maggots should tunnel through the bone and eat the very marrow of his skull, the brain pith that gave meaning to life and motion? His hands still tied behind his back, he would run wildly with the wind till he came to a tumbling stream and put his head under the icy water so that it flowed healingly round his ears and over his skull. Meanwhile he would look out between his legs at the upside-down landscape and the upside-down cow at the pool below drinking the floating maggots from his clinging hair.

Looking out at Rannyweal from the west window of the bar, he wondered how long the nightmare would last. He had decided to ignore the letter but forgetting it was not quite so easy. It was for ever at the back of his mind, a reminder that among the men who laughed at his jokes in the bar was one who . . . He listened carefully to every word and every nuance of conversation but the moment of certainty that he craved escaped him. After a fortnight he was left with the suspicion he had begun with, that Potter was the man to watch, and with the fear that McGing would call one morning with the blackmailer's evidence. He could bear for a while the fear and uncertainty that tugged at his peace of mind. What was more difficult to endure was the loneliness of suspicion, the loneliness of a mind that sees all through the wrong end of a telescope. It was a pity that it had to be Potter because Potter was potentially a friend. He was an unknown man, as mysterious in his ways as the wildlife he watched through his field-glasses, but he must make friends with him, extend a hand across the deep ravine of human loneliness that threatened constantly what creature comforts man could muster. He would invite him out for an evening's fishing in his boat, and perhaps as they laughed and talked something of mutual comfort would emerge, a glimpse perhaps of the shared darkness behind the confident smiles. It would be a far-sighted act to make friends with him because, if it ever became necessary to 'delete' him, a friend would be the last to come under suspicion.

He turned to Gimp Gillespie, his only customer.

'Is it true that Potter is courting Nora Hession?' he asked.

'So they tell me,' said Gillespie without interrupting his contemplation of his glass.

'He's a rare man is our Potter,' Roarty said in an effort to elicit Gillespie's opinion.

'He's upright and reserved, nothing if not a straight shooter.'

'Have you ever seen him shoot?'

'What I meant was that he knows his mind and speaks it.'

'He's very English. He has no sense of indirection—he comes to the point too quickly.'

'That I haven't observed. What I would say is that he comes from a class of men who absentmindedly acquired an empire and later lost it rather self-consciously. Not an easy burden to bear.'

'Like all of us he has his faults,' said Roarty piously.

'What faults?' Gillespie asked quickly.

'Oh, minor faults, I would say. His greatest is that he never lounges. He is for ever on guard, even when he laughs, and he never laughs longer than he considers necessary. I once heard him say that laughter interrupts the breathing, that a yawn is better medicine.'

'He said that ironically to take the piss out of Cor Mogaill. He's too intelligent not to recognise the therapeutic value of a laugh.'

'Have you ever noticed how he speaks?' Roarty asked. 'Not like you or me. You could write down everything he says without changing a word, as if he'd thought it all out in advance.'

'He speaks as you or I might walk on thin ice, picking his way cautiously between words. It's a habit I've noticed in men who have no natural way with words.'

'It may be an English trait,' said Roarty.

'Not a bit of it,' said Gillespie. 'Nobody can murder the language with the same philistine insensitivity as a middle-class Englishman. I don't see Potter as typical of a class, though. He may be English but he was taught by Jesuits.'

'It's a potent combination,' said Roarty thoughtfully.

He turned to the window and placed a hand on the casing. Canon Loftus was coming up the avenue with a load of hay behind the tractor and he stopped as Nora Hession came out of the house. She ran across to him, they spoke for a moment, and she continued down the avenue to the gate. Roarty watched her climbing the hill to the village in flat shoes and a cotton dress, swinging her empty shopping basket, the very picture of quiet self-possession in the empty road. A rare girl. Had she at last found the man for whom she had been waiting? A potent combination. He would see him this evening and mention the boat. They might even make a habit of going fishing together. There was nothing more natural on this coast than an accident in a small boat.

'Good morning to you.'

'Good morning, sergeant. You're a bit early. It's only eleven, you know,' said Roarty, reaching for a tumbler.

'No, don't get me a drink,' said McGing. 'I'm here on duty. I want you to come with me to the barracks to make an identification.'

'Of what?' asked Roarty, his mouth going dry.

'If I knew, would I be asking you to help me?' said McGing.

'If you wait a minute, I'll get Susan to look after the bar while I'm gone.'

Roarty went into the kitchen for Susan, cold sweat prickling his forehead. When she had gone to the bar, he went to the dresser and got out the gin, Guinness and ginger beer. He poured a quadruple shot of gin into a pint tankard, then the half-pint of Guinness, and finally the ginger beer, his hands trembling so much that he noticed them. It was an elixir he kept in reserve for catastrophe, and he drank half of it at a draught in case sipping might dissipate the effect. He had decided to go with McGing without further question. McGing was a headstrong man who liked having his way even in the smallest things, and now was not the time to cross him. His treatment of the local tailor last Hallowe'en was all too typical. The mummers stole the tailor's smoothing irons as a joke, and the tailor reported the theft to McGing.

'The mummers, they've stolen me two geese,' he said solemnly.

'How fat were they?' asked McGing, pulling out his notebook.

'I don't mean birds. I'm talking about me smoothing irons,' said the tailor in exasperation.

'You're talking about gooses then, not geese,' said McGing.

'No, geese I said, and it's geese I meant.'

'I'll gladly look into it for you,' said McGing. 'If it's geese you've lost, it's missing birds I'll investigate. But if it's gooses, then that's a different matter. Now, which do you think you've lost, gooses or geese?'

'Gooses,' said the tailor in bewildered resignation.

The incident had once amused Roarty but the recollection of it failed to amuse him now. He put the half-empty tankard on his head and, passing the back of his hand over his brow, returned to the bar.

'Is there a story in this for me?' Gillespie was asking McGing.

'It could be the biggest story that's ever broken in these parts. Mark my words, we'll have the Dublin dailies down here before tomorrow evening.'

'I'd better come along with you then,' said Gillespie.

'Not now,' said McGing firmly. 'Duty before journalism is what I always say. But if you come down to the barracks this evening at seven, I'll give you a statement. You'll be the first with the news, I promise.'

'What is all this?' asked Roarty.

'I'm not going to prejudice you by telling. I want you to see for yourself.'

McGing left his bicycle outside the pub and drove with Roarty to the barracks, about a quarter of a mile to the east of the village. Roarty drove with care and in self-conscious silence, preferring to say nothing than risk saying the wrong thing. He kept telling himself that there was nothing to worry about, that McGing was behaving like an ass, but he was relieved when they had reached the barracks door.

McGing led the way into the kitchen and sat down at the bare table in the centre of the floor.

'What now?' asked Roarty.

'Take a look in the fridge,' said McGing, pushing his cap back from his broad forehead.

Roarty opened the door but as far as he could see the fridge was empty.

'There's nothing here,' he said, wondering what on earth McGing was up to.

'In the ice box,' said McGing from the table.

He looked in the ice box, at the white polythene bag, and then at McGing who was observing him in an attitude of exaggerated relaxation.

'Open the bag and look inside,' commanded McGing.

Roarty had begun to feel foolish but when he opened the bag he felt positively ill. It contained a frozen human foot, severed three inches above the ankle.

McGing got to his feet, took the bag from Roarty and put it back in the ice box. Weak at the knees and with his tongue sticking to the roof of his mouth, Roarty sat at the table and began filling his pipe without first raking out the dottle.

'What do you make of that?' asked McGing.

'Maiming or maybe murder.'

'Did you recognise it?'

'What?'

'The foot of course.'

'How should I recognise a foot?'

'It's the foot of a friend.'

'What friend?'

'Eales,' said McGing with self-conscious superiority.

'And how do you know?' Roarty asked, less from curiosity than a desperate desire to keep the conversation flowing.

'There was a luggage label tied round the ankle. It said: "Eamon Eales, passenger to Hades via Sligo".'

'A grim humorist,' said Roarty.

'But a humorist who's left a clue or two for me to follow.'

'His handwriting?'

'He wrote with a matchstick and in capital letters, and I suspect with his left hand. But he spelt "Eamon" with one "n", the way Dev used to spell his name. Now, in Donegal most people would spell it with a double "n" because that's how it's spelt in Irish. And which farmer would call Hell "Hades"?'

'I don't know about that,' said Roarty slowly. 'The young curate often calls it Hades in his sermons since the bishop ordered priests to stop preaching hell-fire.'

'Be gob, you're right,' said McGing. 'Two heads are better than one, even a good one. But now I want you to think carefully. Was there anything distinctive about Eales's feet?'

'They stank. He was a great one for lotions and perfumes but he never did manage to drown the smell of his feet. Whenever he walked about the bedroom in his socks in warm weather, the smell would seep down into the kitchen like heavy air.'

'And what did they smell of?' asked McGing, pulling a notebook from the breast pocket of his tunic.

'Over-ripe gorgonzola on the better days and rotten fish after a week without a bath.'

'Would you care to smell the foot in the fridge?' said McGing, getting up. 'After all, identification by smell must be as acceptable in law as identification by sight.'

'I think there is a limit to a citizen's duties in helping the police. I draw the line at smelling dead men's feet.'

'Very well. But I smelt it myself in the interest of science and I can tell you that it's odourless.'

'It may not be Eales's foot after all.'

'No, you're on the wrong tack. The reason it doesn't emit the characteristic odour of putrefaction is that it's been frozen. My guess is that it was sawn off soon after death and that it's been in the freezer since. Another clue, you see. It isn't everyone who's got a fridge round here, and even fewer have got freezers.'

'That limits the list of suspects for a start,' said Roarty, beginning to get the flavour of his pipe.

'We can limit it further,' said McGing. 'We can limit it to men—or possibly women—who live on their own.'

'Why is that?'

'Because only a man living on his own could store the foot in the house. What if he had a wife and she found it in the ice box when she went to get out the Sunday joint?'

'A good point.'

'Somehow I feel that I'm dealing with a pretty sophisticated intelligence, possibly an Irish Moriarty, a man who thinks he can trick me with red herrings like "Sligo". Yet this subtle humorist cut off a man's foot. He's two men in one, civilised but brutal.'

'Just what I've been thinking,' said Roarty, realising that the sergeant in his flat-footed way could possibly have been describing Potter.

'The pity is that we've been sent a foot rather than a hand. A hand, you see, would have been of more interest to a forensic scientist. It could have grasped a button or a few fibres from the attacker's clothes. A foot by comparison tells fewer tales. But it will tell enough tales when the forensic boys get going. It will tell how long after death the body was mutilated. I know myself, and I'm no scientist, that he didn't die of carbon monoxide poisoning.'

'Well, I must be getting back,' said Roarty. 'Susan will want to put on the dinner.'

'And I'm going to ring the homicide squad. No doubt they'll want to talk to you. After all you're the last person who saw him alive.'

'I don't think I can help much.'

'You've helped me without knowing it. You helped to clear my mind. This could be the making of me, Roarty. Do you realise that? I've got the nose and now at last I've got the spoor I can smell the murderer in the air. All I need is to trace the features of his face.'

McGing raised his head and smelt the air between himself and Roarty.

'Incidentally, how did you come on the foot?'

'I wondered when you were going to ask that. After all it's the obvious question. It was hanging there from the door knocker when I got up this morning.'

McGing grasped Roarty by the sleeve and held him in the hallway.

'A final word before you go. If you'd killed a man here, where would you bury his body?'

'I have no idea.'

'Think. The success of this murder hunt may well depend on your answer.'

'Murderers on the whole are not very intelligent. In murder they show their failure to solve their personal problems rationally. I'd say for that reason that whoever did it would go no farther than his back garden.'

'We'll start with your back garden then.'

'Thank you very much.'

'No offence. We'll search every garden in the village, and in the glen if necessary.'

'Feel free to begin with mine,' said Roarty, getting into his car.

'Don't tell anyone about what you've seen. I don't want the news to get round till I've phoned the homicide squad.'

So far, so good, thought Roarty with relief. He had concealed his anxiety from the sergeant and, while appearing to be helpful, had given nothing away. But the real test was now to come: the investigation and the questions which would follow. He parked the car outside the pub and waited for Doalty O'Donnell who was coming down the street with a sheaf of letters in his hand. He gave him a tatty, brown envelope stuck with sellotape, and Roarty went straight upstairs and sat on the edge of the bed. At length he opened the envelope and read with mounting nausea:

Dear Roarty: The trotter is just an antipasto. If you wish to be spared an entrée, pay £50 a week (note the higher tariff) in banknotes into Acc. No. 319

103

291, The Bank of Ireland, 34 College Green, Dublin 2, by September 1st. Otherwise I will arrange for McGing to find a severed head (just the thing for brawn) in your garden. Your far from sleeping partner in devilry, Bogmailer.

Roarty made for the bathroom and bent over the wash-basin, retching in painful spasms but no vomit came. He wiped the tears of stress from his eyes and returned to his bedroom, waiting for the wave of nausea to pass.

Judged on the internal evidence the letter was more of a conundrum than the previous one. A local man would surely have said 'crubeen' for 'trotter', and neither would he have said 'antipasto'. Both 'trotter' and 'antipasto' pointed towards Potter, but not 'brawn' which was more likely to come from a rustic than a bon viveur from the London suburbs. On balance, therefore, it was Potter; but whoever it was had to be stopped immediately. The only way to keep his mouth shut until all the fuss had died down was to pay. He would put the first £50 in the post tomorrow, and thereby purchase the time he needed to extirpate the bastard.

He lay on the bed with his eyes closed and for the first time in years thought of Dusty Parker, a student he knew as a young man in London. He was working in a pub in Bloomsbury at the time, and the student used to come in at week-ends to help in the saloon. He and Roarty were of an age, and soon they were the best of friends. They would go to Continental films together, and Parker would turn up at Roarty's digs at all hours, laughing drunkenly and waving a bottle of cheap wine. Then they would sit up till the early morning, drinking and talking, the student telling story after story so that Roarty could only marvel at such a treasure-trove of experience in another human being. He himself had come straight from the seminary but he began to think like the student, sensing the dark ambiguities of a life he had yet to live. And when Parker would laugh with devilish glee and tell him that Dante conceived the idea of Beatrice in a moment of cunnilingus with a slut, he would not know if he was horrified or overawed by the student's emancipated intellectual world, so wide and unrejecting compared with the Jansenist narrowness of his own.

Parker had told him that he was studying French at Bedford College but it seemed to Roarty that he studied nothing but Rimbaud. He quoted him, or claimed to be quoting him, a hundred times an evening, and whenever he had too much to drink he would translate for Roarty because Roarty knew no French. One night Parker told him that he had made a discovery which would ensure his literary reputation and possibly his fortune. Rimbaud, he said, had disappeared into the heart of darkest Africa at the age of twenty-one, never to return to France again.

'He died there in 1891, the year Conrad returned from the Congo. Does that mean anything to you?' he asked.

'No,' said Roarty.

'It's simply this. Rimbaud met Conrad in the Congo and became Mistah Kurtz in the "Heart of Darkness". Nobody suspects it but me,' said the student with professorial assurance. 'As soon as I've published my thesis and made my name I'll vanish one day like Rimbaud, reject the world with a laugh and never be seen again.'

Not long afterwards that was more or less what he did. He disappeared one week-end after cleaning out the till, and Roarty never heard of him again. For months afterwards he was lonely beyond description. He could hardly believe that one man could pine so keenly for the company of another, and he still stayed in the same digs, hoping that Parker would turn up in the night with a drunken laugh and a bottle of Spanish wine.

Years later he came upon a life of Rimbaud in a public library and he could not resist the temptation to read it. But to his amazement he discovered that Rimbaud had spent his time abroad in Ethiopia, and that he returned to France before he died. He could not believe that such an elementary fact would have escaped a student of his poetry. Was Parker a student at all? Or was he a fantasist who found in a naive Irishman the eager audience of his dreams? And what of his claim about Dante? Was that imagination too?

The student had marked his life though. Since then he had never had a friend. But in many ways Potter reminded him of the student. He had the student's frosty objectivity and a reductive capacity that enabled him to scotch the imponderable with the chop of logic. He wondered what it must feel like to be Potter. He did not wish for his form, the slope of his shoulders, the thrust of his chin, or the look he had of being pampered by history, remote from the brute centre of himself. No, what he wished for was his detachment, and he could not have that without amputating the part of himself that nagged and nagged, wasting his every thought on the commonest trifles when he should be reclining like a god, contemplating the tides of life with a Jameson in one hand and a Peterson in the other.

'If only I could be friends with Potter,' he muttered, going down the stairs to the kitchen.

NINE

Potter was leaning over the parapet of the Minister's Bridge, looking at the breakwater splitting the flow between the brown stones. The river came down the glen out of the mountains, those melancholy mountains that seemed to sit brooding over one another even on the brightest day of summer. He crossed to the other side of the bridge and looked again at the stony river winding to its estuary and at the solitary angler working the left bank.

It was evening. The Angelus bell had just sounded in the meagre village above him, and the air was heavy with the savour of peat fires and the fragrance of gorse blossom from a nearby hillock. It had been a warm day and he had spent it by the sea cliffs with his field-glasses watching guillemots, blackbacks, cormorants, gannets and any other species of bird that flew his way. A swath of summer mist had come in from the sea and was travelling across the face of the north mountain so that the crest was visible but not the middle. An eerie scene which the half-forgotten William Allingham had observed before him:

> With a bridge of white mist
> Columbkill he crosses,

On his stately journeys
From Slieveleague to Rosses;

A sandpiper came up the river, flying low over the water, and disappeared under the arch of the bridge. He heard a whistle behind him and, turning, saw Cor Mogaill and his dog Sgeolan coming up the road.

'What are you looking at?' Cor Mogaill asked.

'The stones in the river. The peaty water has washed them all a uniform brown.'

'I've been carrying hay to the road since eight o'clock this morning, and I'm buggered for want of a drink. Would you be coming for a jar?'

'I had intended going out to the loughs for an hour before sunset. Roarty tells me that there is a strange water bird on the Lough of Silver.'

'I remember five years ago I went out to the loughs and came back again. And it was a very cold day.'

Potter looked at Cor Mogaill's sad grey eyes and the black hair on his forehead matted with the sweat of the day. They both stepped aside as an old man with an ass-cart of turf and a bag of flour on top passed with a clacking of iron-shod wheels.

'I'm buggered with the drouth,' said Cor Mogaill. 'I'll be lucky if I make it to Roarty's.' And off he went up the hill, whistling after his yellow sheepdog.

'I remember five years ago I went out to the loughs and came back again. And it was a very cold day.' What could he have meant by it? Did the incident have a significance in his life which words failed to convey? Or had he in the extremity of his thirst omitted unwittingly the main point of the story? So much that happened between these two ranges of hills was a mystery, he thought, watching the angler playing a trout and trying to catch the whirr of the reel. But though there was mystery and melancholy, there was also spiritual peace. Never before had he been so close to the true centre of himself, so aware of half-thoughts and intimations and the vague nudgings of the unconscious in the blood. But perhaps that was something he owed to Nora Hession.

Canon Loftus's car came round the corner, powdered with the dust of mountain roads. It pulled up beside him on the hump of the bridge and the Canon looked at him through the open window.

'Are you the Englishman who's in charge of the prospecting?' He had a rough voice like that of a farmer who is hoarse from hay dust.

'Yes, I'm Kenneth Potter.'

'How do you do. I'm Canon Loftus, your parish priest while you're here.'

'So I see,' said Potter, aware of the force of the other man's scrutiny.

'You're going out with Nora Hession, I believe.'

'Correct.'

'Do you know that she is my maid?'

'I have no objection to maids,' Potter laughed.

'That is not what I meant.'

'She has already told me that she is your housekeeper.'

'That's a complication, a factor to be considered. Have you considered it?' asked the Canon, thrusting out a stubbled chin. One of those men, Potter thought, who should shave at least twice a day.

'You mean that if we should decide to get married you would have to find a new maid?'

'No,' said the Canon with annoyance. 'I mean that I'm responsible for the girl and therefore an interested party.

109

Are your intentions serious?'

'What do you mean?' Potter asked quickly, aware of rising anger.

'Do you intend marrying the girl?'

'How should I know? I've only known her a fortnight.'

'She's a sensitive girl and I won't have her hurt. Are you a Catholic?'

'You know I attend your church, so why do you ask?'

'But you're an English Catholic, a different species from us Irish. You've got different standards. Are you married?'

'What is this? The Inquisition?' Potter laughed incredulously.

'Most Englishmen are married by twenty-five, and you will never again see forty. I must be satisfied for the girl's sake that you are bona fide.'

'Your question is an unpardonable impertinence.'

'A typically English stance. No Irish Catholic would dream of speaking like that to his parish priest.'

'In England there would be no need. English rectors mind their own business which, if they're good rectors, is God's.'

Canon Loftus flushed a deep crimson and a blue vein rose like a knot in his trunk-like neck. Potter felt pleased that he had roused him.

'Don't try to teach me my business,' the Canon spluttered. 'As an English Catholic you're in no position to. You belong to a rump, less than a minority, a sect with neither temporal nor spiritual power, remote from the ideals that give life to the English nation. And yet you, one of these rag-tag Irregulars, come over here and tell me, a Regular, how to behave in my own parish. I call it cheek, damn cheek.'

'What on earth are you trying to say?' asked Potter who

had begun to see the Canon's funny side.

'The English genius is a Protestant genius, and therefore the only proper Englishman is a Protestant. Just as the only proper Irishman is a Catholic. The rest in each case is the rag-tag and bob-tail. To be English and Catholic is almost to be counterfeit. Tell me this and tell me no more: what have English Catholics contributed to English culture?'

'Well, we've had Alexander Pope and Gerard Manley Hopkins to name but two.'

'They wouldn't be missed if they'd never written a line. The trouble with you English Catholics is that you lack backbone. You are sunk in respectability, a namby-pamby respectability which is only an expression of your unconscious awareness that you are aliens in your own country.'

'You speak like a man who has never set foot in England.'

'I don't have to. The history of the Catholic Church in England is one of my subjects. Rest assured that I'm well informed. I know enough of England to know that your typical Englishman thinks the confessional is a place where the confessor takes vicarious pleasure in the penitents' sins; that Catholics *adore* the Virgin; that the transubstantiation is hocus-pocus; that priests are either latent homosexuals or dirty old men in black macs. And doesn't living in such a society fill you with a proper sense of defilement?'

'The short answer to all that is "no",' Potter said, baffled by the sacerdotal venom he had unwittingly aroused.

'A word of fatherly advice in your eye. Go back to England and take up Protestantism. It may interest you to know that it's the first staging post on the highroad to agnosticism.'

'You wouldn't say that in front of your ecumenical bishop,' Potter smiled.

'I say it before my God.'

'You know that His vengeance is more considered these days, possibly a deal slower than a bishop's. Don't pretend to be braver than you are. Incidentally, you are holding up the traffic, padre.'

'Don't call me padre. I don't like it.'

'It's a term of manly camaraderie but that may not be the response you as an Irish parish priest wish to invite.'

'It's barrack-room insolence but if you had fought with the Chindits I might have taken it from you.'

'There are three tractors behind you waiting for you to move.'

'I know.'

'And not one of the drivers has the courage to blow his horn.'

'Faith overcomes even courage.'

'How typical of Irish Catholicism! What these wretches need is the cheek of English Lollardism, a stage you have still to reach in this priest-infested country.'

'Let's keep them waiting for another three minutes to test their faith. Have you ever considered what might have happened to English Catholicism if you'd had a Cambridge rather than an Oxford Movement?'

'As a Cambridge man myself, I obviously have,' said Potter with covert irony.

'It's a measure of the aridity of English Catholicism that such a question can be taken seriously.' And with a puff of black smoke and a crunch of pebbles, the Canon, having had the last word, was gone.

He's burning oil, thought Potter as he climbed over the sod dyke by the bridge. He set off along the river bank towards the sea, his pleasure in the evening perceptibly diminished. Though he was amused by the Canon's idea of what constituted a 'proper' Englishman, he was vexed by his impertinence. The Canon was a local 'character', the kind of man who naturally inspires apocryphal anecdotes, and now he could see why. He was a horse of a man, tall, craggy and powerful in every limb. More farmer than priest on week days, he was a pastor only on Sundays. He would spend the week among his cows and bullocks, driving the tractor which was his latest toy while he left the parish work to his enthusiastic curate. A local farmer in a moment of diagnostic acuity said that he had foot and mouth disease because of his reluctance to visit the sick and preach on Sundays. However, he always marked the Lord's Day in his own way. At ten o'clock he would drive to the village and toll the bell for five minutes to warn those who lived in outlying townlands that it was time to get up for eleven o'clock Mass, a practice he was said to have adopted after a mountain man told him that the sexton's toll could not be heard behind a newspaper. The Canon's great strength was evident in the force of his bell-ringing which did not go ding-dong, ding-dong, but dong-bling, dong-bling, dong-bling. Like the interpretation of English history the art of campanology was beyond him. He could never manage a single stroke. It was always a double, and a double of such power that the sexton lived in dread that he would pull the bell down on top of him. After the first bell on Sundays he would go home to fodder the cows but he would return at ten minutes to eleven for the second bell which was, as he put it, for the benefit of those who were nearest the church and farthest from God.

In the pulpit his appearances were brief but telling. With enormous fists tucked like breasts underneath his chasuble, he would preach a five-minute sermon with all the confidence of a seventeenth-century parson. He not only told his flock what to do but also where they would end if they did not do it. He had two heroes among the popes, Julius II, whom he revered as a builder, and Leo XIII whom he admired as a writer of encyclicals. One Sunday he went as far as to say that the prose style of *Rerum Novarum* was superior to that of *De Senectute*, and he said it with the confidence of a man who neither brooked nor feared immediate contradiction. Though he never said it in so many words, he believed that the miseries of men were to be laid at the door of womankind, and one of his favourite axioms was that 'whenever a man falls, you may be sure that a woman has fallen first'. Needless to say, the men of the parish held him in high respect. They called him a man's man, and most certainly a man's confessor. Where he would give a woman five rosaries as penance for fornication in a haystack, he would let a man off with six Our Fathers and a warning. Understandably, the women seldom entered his confessional; they went instead to the effeminate young curate who was said to have a more sensitive understanding of their spiritual needs.

The Canon's ambition was to go down in the history of the parish as a great builder. When he came to Glenkeel six years ago his first thought was to replace the old chapel with a new one. As his parishioners were far from wealthy, collecting the money for the undertaking was an uphill task, but the Canon was not deterred. 'God did not make you rich,' he told the menfolk of his congregation one Sunday, 'but he made you sound of heart and strong of limb. If you cannot give money towards the building of your new chapel, give your time and labour.' And that was how the new chapel was being built. By 'voluntary' labour.

The Canon got a Dublin architect to design what he called a post-Vatican II church to meet the requirements of the new liturgy. It was a building of forbidding blue-black brickwork with a flat roof surmounted by a cone which horrified everyone except the Canon and the schoolmaster. As it took shape under their hands, the glen farmers and fishermen regarded it with amazement and incredulity but the Canon told them that it conveyed the austerity of true spirituality, something of the spirit of early Irish coenobitism, and that the cone was an ingenious attempt to translate into modern idiom the corbel-vaulted stonework of renowned Skellig Michael.

Potter had come within sight of the sea. The tide was at low ebb and the shore was bare. He took off his shoes and socks, rolled up his trousers and walked out over the furrowed sand to the little lagoon of slack water on the landward side of the sandbank. He paddled in the lukewarm water, listening to the crash of the Atlantic on the other side of the Oitir. He had the lonely sea and the shore to himself, and he stood with his back to the sun looking at a farmer in the triangular corn field above him bent over the shearing sickle, touched by the gold of the evening light.

'He must be taught a lesson,' he said aloud. 'A priest who talks like that to a compatriot of John Wycliffe is deficient in a sense of history let alone temporal reality.'

He walked back up the beach and wiped the sand from his feet with his socks.

'I must talk to Roarty,' he said firmly as he laced his shoes.

TEN

Roarty was late. He had said that he would be at the slip at six, and it was now half-past. Potter sat on an old up-turned boat, looking at the twisted rocks that surrounded the cove, grey-blue beach stones, lengths of rope and bleached timber, heaped nets, rusty anchors and the debris of broken crab shells at his feet. It was a lively evening with the wind from the south and a slight swell on the sea, enough to give the impression of rise and fall even though it was now slack water. On a narrow ledge of the green bank above him a ragged goat was straining its neck to reach a kindly tuft of grass. He wondered how the goat had climbed down to the ledge because there was no path, and his wonder increased when he considered how it would climb up again.

Roarty came down the path in waders carrying the out-board engine, a blue reek rising from his pipe.

'Sorry I'm late,' he said. 'A commercial traveller called just as I was about to leave.'

'I spent the time trying out my new fishing rod. It casts well.'

'Solid fibre glass and a multiplier reel—just the thing.'

Roarty clamped the outboard on the transom and went back to the car which he had parked at the top of the path. When he came down again he was carrying a fishing rod, rifle and woollen pullover.

'What are you going to shoot?' asked Potter.

'I don't know yet, but I like having my rifle at the ready.'

'I can't think of anything you could shoot at sea at this time of year.'

'We'll see,' said Roarty.

They pushed the boat down the slip into the water. Potter jumped in first, sat on the centre thwart and prepared to get out the oars. Roarty gave the boat a shove and climbed nimbly aboard, and Potter rowed out through the inlet which was wide enough to take the oars with a yard to spare on each side. As they cleared the mouth, the wind caught the bow, and Potter had to pull harder with his left oar. Roarty stood up in the stern, wound the starter cord round the flywheel and pulled. On the first pull the engine spluttered. On the second it started and immediately they were under way.

Potter shipped the oars in a sudden surge of happiness. Roarty and he had never before been together in a boat and, though no word had been uttered, each performed his task as if rehearsed to perfection. His happiness came from the knowledge that he was a practical man in the company of one of his peers, someone who could be trusted implicitly to do the right thing in a tight spot. For some curious reason he thought of Margaret to her ankles in the sea at Killiney. And it came to him that a man who lived without the company and conversation of a woman missed half the pleasure of life, but that a man who did not enjoy male camaraderie and manly pursuits missed the other half.

They headed down the bay, the wind astern and white

clouds above them racing into the north. The glen seemed to open up before them so that they could see roads and houses which were not visible from the shore.

'I always have a feeling of freedom on the sea,' Roarty said.

'It would be a lovely evening for sailing.'

'She'd run faster than she'd motor this evening. If we weren't droving for pollack, I'd put up the sail. Pollack, you see, like a slow-moving bait.'

'There's nothing slower than rowing,' said Potter, getting ready to cast.

'It's too much like work for a man who is past his best. I wouldn't begin yet if I were you. We're still over the bare sand. Wait till we're above the wrack; that's where the pollack feed.'

They were approaching a blunt-headed rock that rose darkly out of the waves underneath its white cap of sea-bird droppings. Potter thought that they were making straight for it until he saw that they were about to enter a narrow channel between it and the land.

'This is Éalach na Mágach, the Channel of the Pollack,' said Roarty. 'If you don't stick in one here, we'd better go home.'

Roarty took the way off the boat and set up his fishing rod against the gunwale with his foot on the butt so that the feather jig he was using as a lure trolled behind them. He then put the drag on the reel so that it would not yield line except to a hooked fish. Potter cast his lure astern and sat again on the thwart with his rod over the gunwale while Roarty opened the throttle gently so that they went through the Éalach at the right speed for pollack whiffing. As they emerged at the other end without a bite, Roarty said:

'With the tide beginning to flow, it could be that they're feeding deeper.'

He released the drag and paid out more line while Potter did likewise.

'We'll go down north,' said Roarty. 'If nothing else, we'll enjoy the scenery.'

Just as he spoke, Potter's rod dipped and the reel whirringly responded to the rush of a pollack. The power of the dive electrified his wrist and concentrated his mind on the fight and the moment.

'It's a monster,' he said through his teeth.

'You'd be surprised how much fight there is in a small wrack pollack,' Roarty said slowly. 'He's making for the wrack. I should have warned you that the bottom here is snaggy.'

'I've got the bastard,' said Potter, turning the fish's head.

No sooner had he spoken than Roarty's reel sang out, yielding line to a diving pollack. Each of them concentrated on his own fight, countering dive after dive until they brought their fish to the boat simultaneously.

'Two good-sized pollack,' said Roarty, flinging his own in the bottom of the boat.

Potter unhooked his catch more slowly as the hook was buried deep in the fish's gullet. He watched the pollack gasping for air on the floor of the boat, and he could not but acknowledge a sense of life's imperfection. It was a handsome fish with a dark-green back and olive sides and just a glint of reddish-brown which showed more clearly as it came up out of the water. Then he noticed the perfect curve of the lateral line and the long lower jaw moving pathetically with each gasp, and he felt, perhaps a trifle piously, that a sportsman's life is not made simpler by his love of his quarry. However, he did not take his thought seriously enough to reel in his line.

'The pollack is a bonny fighter if you take him near the surface,' said Roarty. 'If you hook him in deep water, he puts up less of a struggle. After the first dive he's exhausted because his swim bladder inflates if he's hauled up too quickly. The only way to fish pollack for pleasure is with a light tackle—it makes the struggle less unequal.'

They were now out of sight of the glen and the scenery had become wilder and more magnificent. The sea cliffs towered above them, great striated faces of dark and creamy rock with contorted seams that spoke of mighty upheavals. Potter, as he looked at them, experienced a rare sense of exhilaration as if the cares of life lay full fathom five beneath him, and the perpendicularity of the cliffs made him breathe more deeply as if he could not get enough of the salty air.

They continued northwards for another two miles until they came within sight of a hamlet on the other side of the mountains but neither got as much as a bite. Potter felt that it did not matter in the slightest; he was enjoying the sun and the wind on the green-blue water and the dozing seagulls and vigilant cormorants on every side. Roarty spent the time pointing out rocks and coves and recounting the legends enshrined in their names, and Potter listened with the kind of attention he might have given to the Ancient Mariner.

'We'll try driftlining for a bit,' Roarty said finally as he cut the engine. They allowed the boat to drift with their lines trailing on the tide, and Roarty meanwhile filled his pipe and stretched his legs, one on each side of his rifle, as if he were savouring the comforts of heaven.

'What did you make of the murder hunt?' he asked after a while.

'It's all been rather unreal. For a start I can't believe it happened, not here in remote Glenkeel, and the superintendent who interrogated me took the same view, I suspect. A few perfunctory questions was all he had time for.'

'And yet there *was* a human foot. I saw it with my own two eyes.'

'I heard about that, a frozen foot in good condition. McGing was puzzled to know if it constituted a sufficient proportion of the human body to warrant Christian burial. He said he was going to ring up the bishop after Canon Loftus denied him a straight answer.'

'McGing is a fool—worse, an officious fool.'

'This is meat and drink to him. He's been waiting all his life for a mystery only he can solve.'

'If he doesn't solve it, no one else will. The homicide squad have gone back to Dublin. We've seen the last of them, I'll warrant.'

'What I can't understand is why a murderer who had presumably committed the perfect crime should stir up trouble for himself by presenting the police with his victim's foot,' said Potter.

'The ways of the criminal mind are strange.'

'He may have wanted to leave McGing with a mystery he would appreciate as a change from ragwort and brucellosis. Who knows, the foot may be a first instalment. A hand or head may follow.'

Potter was aware of Roarty's scrutiny against the sharp evening sun, a pensive stare while he puffed at his pipe and moved his rod to give the lure a semblance of life in the water.

'It's difficult to understand why one man should wish to kill another,' said Roarty.

'There are men who are evil and men who are not.'

'It isn't man who is evil. It is God,' Roarty said with surprising vehemence.

'In the sense that he created man and is therefore ultimately responsible for his actions?'

'If we accept the idea of God, we must be prepared to lay the imperfections of the world at his door.'

'You say that God is imperfect because his creation is imperfect. You refuse to believe that the imperfect can emanate from the perfect.'

'A reasonable assumption.'

'You underestimate God,' said Potter. 'He is more complex than you imagine, not merely a "flat" character in a Dickens novel. He embraces at once both good and evil. He is at war with himself, which is why his whole creation is at loggerheads and man, his greatest work, is never at peace. His much-vaunted ecological system of herbivores eating plants and carnivores eating herbivores makes sense only to scientists. Consider it for a moment as a sentient being and it becomes an obscenity.'

'Are we saying the same thing?'

'No, you say that God is evil but I say that he is good and evil. While you merely see the disease-bearing viruses I also see the benign micro-organisms which by making among other things strong beers and delectable wines provide you with a livelihood and enable you to spend your evenings in alcoholic bliss.'

'If God isn't wholly good, why do you find it necessary to believe in him? Surely, if you don't accept the God of the theologians, you should consider expunging him from your life.'

'Though I believe the will is more or less free, I don't consider myself free to expunge him. He would raise so many unanswerable questions by his absence that I could no longer be myself without answering them. A godless world is for simple souls, men who live by mensuration, men without a sense of the numinous which ultimately is a sense of poetry. Do you lack a sense of poetry?'

'No,' said Roarty, galvanised into life by the whirr of his reel.

Potter watched him as he played the fish with all the unobtrusive skill of a man who has done something more times than he can remember. He had half-turned on the thwart and was puffing at his pipe as if he were back in the bar, as if a tussle with a pollack was no more arduous than pulling a pint of stout. There was a glint of red in the water, and the exhausted pollack came over the gunwale to beat a weakening tattoo on the floor. It was a large wrack pollack, seven pounds if it was an ounce, and Roarty looked at it with lofty appreciation.

'He was a stout fighter,' he said. 'His first rush was like a bullock at the end of a tether.'

'We had come a long way from Eales's foot in our conversation,' said Potter.

'So we had,' said Roarty, picking up his rifle and taking aim with lightning speed.

Potter just had time to turn and see a bull seal slide off a flat rock about sixty yards off the starboard bow while the shot seemed to rock the boat.

'A heart shot,' said Roarty. 'He didn't feel a thing.'

'It was rather unnecessary,' said Potter, taken aback.

'If God is evil, why be good? For a moment I felt that I was he, remote, capricious, death-bestowing. What happened to the seal happens every day to innocent children except that they suffer before they die.'

Potter was perplexed to discover a side of Roarty which he had not previously observed. He had not regarded him as a man of lightning impulse; he had seen him as unhurried and considered in thought and movement.

'It was far from godlike,' he said. 'However impressive the marksmanship, it entirely lacked reason and purpose.'

'It was a fair cull. And I did it from the highest of motives, to improve the flavour of the cod you and Nora Hession eat on your way home from the pictures in Garron.'

'What nonsense.'

'It may interest you to know that the cod on these shores are seriously infested with parasites that hatch from the eggs of worms in the stomach of the seal. Next time you have fish and chips in Garron think of that.'

'Blarney and balderdash,' said Potter, getting to his feet. He unbuttoned his flies and faced downwind, ready to send a virile spray over the gunwale. But the boat was bobbing, and every time he tried to pass water the dip of the boat made him tighten his grip on himself.

'I can't do it. It seems ridiculous but every time the boat dips I tighten.'

'There's a knack in pissing in a swell. Here, sit on the thwart and do it into the bailer.'

Roarty handed him a rusty tin can. Potter faced forward and held his penis in one hand and the bailer under it with the other, but try as he might he could not pass a drop.

'It's no good,' he said.

'We won't be going home for another two hours. I had better put you out on a rock.'

Potter rowed across to the flat rock where the seal had been and Roarty gripped the side while Potter climbed out

124

of the boat. He stood on the north edge of the rock with the wind on the back of his neck and pissed with relief into the froth-flecked water. It was a strange sensation standing on a rock the size of a dining-room carpet with the sea all round and tentacles of sea wrack rising on the tide. At the edge of the rock was a small pool of drying blood, and Roarty, a baldheaded man in a boat a hundred yards away, was playing another fish. He looked at the bird droppings at his feet and realised that the rock he was standing on would be awash before high water. He looked at the bare cliff tops with no one in sight and at the top corks of the lobster pots about three hundred yards away. At dawn the fishermen would lift them, and by then the rock would be bare again with the bird shit and seal blood washed away. He remembered a story he once heard about Cornish criminals being given a jug of water and a loaf and left on a rock at low water to wait for death by drowning, and in a moment he knew what it must be like to watch a rising tide without the possibility of rescue. Roarty unhooked his fish, looked over his shoulder and waved. Potter watched him row to the rock with deliberate ease, and again sensed the overwhelming freedom of the evening.

'The human mind is a mystery,' he said to Roarty as he got into the boat. 'For a moment on that rock I experienced the desperation of a marooned man who sees the tide rising and not a boat in sight.'

'You're a lucky man, Potter.'

'Why?'

'You have what I call the perception of catastrophe, and I think I've got it too. Without it you can go through life as if it were an acre of garden with a six-foot fence. But with it the experience of all human life is yours.

Without leaving your hearth you have been with the Persians at Salamis, with Leonidas at Thermopylae, and with the Highlanders at Culloden.'

'You make it sound like a coward dying many times before his death.'

'No, with this capacity you can forestall disaster by seeing it on the horizon. You can foresee another man's mistake before he makes it. Good lord, have you noticed that *gliobach* of sea fowl? They seem to have come down out of the empty sky.'

'What are they diving on? It can't be pollack.'

'Mackerel. They're really after the small fry the mackerel force to the surface.'

'Let's not hang about,' said Potter.

'Mackerel are not much sport with our tackle but if you want to try your hand, you're welcome.'

In a moment Roarty had restarted the engine and they were making straight for the cloud of screaming sea fowl. Suddenly the water around them was boiling with playing fish and glinting with the silver scales of ravaged sprat. Roarty skirted the school, steering round the outside so as not to drive them under and so that Potter could troll on the inside. Within seconds he felt the double tug of the first mackerel and glimpsed the metallic side of the fish sheering in the water as he reeled it in. It was entirely different from pollack fishing because the mackerel came at the lure with the speed of an arrow, surrounded by scores of open-mouthed rivals.

'You're not going to try your luck?' he asked Roarty when he had killed about three dozen.

'There's no need for luck here. They're practically leaping over the gunwale. What are you going to do with them? There's a limit to the number you can eat or souse.'

'I'll take them to the pub and any of your customers who wants one for his supper can have it.'

'It'll work wonders for my trade.'

'You're an unfathomable man, Roarty. You'd kill an uneatable seal and turn your back on a juicy mackerel.'

'My forefathers may have killed to eat. I kill for sport, and the essence of sport, be it with rod or gun, is skill. There's no skill in killing mackerel except with light trout tackle. On an evening like this you'd kill them with a bare hook. The only thing that determines the size of the catch is the speed with which you unhook them. Now a seal is different. Would you be ashamed of a heart shot from a rocking boat at sixty yards?'

'I shouldn't be ashamed of the shot. I've culled deer in the Highlands, and I think I know what I could do at sixty yards. But in culling deer the shot that kills comes at the end of a long and skilful stalk. It is the logical outcome of perhaps a whole afternoon's endeavour. But shooting a seal while he's sunning himself on a rock shows no sense of fair play.'

'But it shows a sense of humour,' said Roarty, pulling a hip-flask from his pocket. 'Will you be having a swig?'

'No, thank you. I don't drink Irish whiskey and besides I've had the forethought to bring my own!'

'The perception of catastrophe. You've got it, all right.'

Roarty cut the engine and they both enjoyed the contents of their flasks while the ravenous mackerel and terror-stricken sprat played round them.

'Have you put any water in yours?' Potter asked after savouring the last mouthful.

'I always put in equal amounts. What about you?'

'Just enough to bring out the flavour. The influence of my Scottish grandmother, I always think. Only men with jaded palates drink Scotch neat.'

'I'd swear it tastes stronger out here. It must be the air, heady with the smell of fish oil.'

'I've seldom enjoyed an evening such as this.'

'And it isn't over yet. With the thickening of the light we'll go back to Éalach na Mágach when the pollack are feeding on the surface.'

'So the light-shy pollack turns pelagic in late evening.'

'I had not thought of *Gadus pollachius* as a British heresiarch.'

'Pelagic, not pelagian.'

'Touché,' said Roarty.

The sun was going down behind them and the wind had acquired an edge which made Roarty put on his Aran pullover.

'Look at that cumulus; there are weeks of fine weather ahead of us,' he said, picking up a mackerel and taking a knife from his hip pocket. He held the mackerel in his left hand and cut a long thin strip of skin with the edge of the knife held towards the tail. Then he took a cork from his trousers pocket and laid the skin side of the strip downwards on the cork so that it looked like a silver tadpole, semicircular at the head and tapering to a tail. Finally he put the point of the hook through the thin end of the strip and handed the cork and knife to Potter.

'You think a lash of mackerel is what they're waiting for?'

'It will be very killing in about twenty minutes.'

Roarty restarted the engine and they both trolled their lines on the surface without the leads as they made for Éalach na Mágach. When they reached it, the sun had already gone and the darkening water flickered uncertainly in the afterglow.

Roarty was right about *Gadus pollachius*. He was ravenous, and by the time light had begun to fade fast they had killed eight or nine each, most of them good-sized fish, weighing between five and seven pounds.

Potter had a profound sense of relaxation as he reeled in and Roarty headed for home with open throttle. The shoreline in front of them was dark, the village lights were on, and the last dregs of pinkish light in the west were draining away.

'There is something I've been meaning to bring up,' said Potter after lighting his pipe. 'Everyone I meet here has one thing on his mind, the new chapel. Everyone thinks it a disgrace, a cube surmounted by a cone in a village which should have a traditional church with a spire. We've had crude geometrical architecture in London for the last forty years, and Londoners have learnt to live with it. But London is not Donegal. A man who spends the morning in a City office totting up figures can hardly be surprised to find himself surrounded by crude geometrical shapes when he emerges into the street at lunchtime. But a man who makes his living on land and sea, in step with the swing of the seasons, has a right to better. Londoners have been brutalised by an anonymous bureaucracy which has fallen prey to every current and eddy in fashionable architectural "thinking", but here we live in a place whose only connection with the world of ideas is your *Britannica*—'

'The 1911 edition,' Roarty emphasised.

'Here the villain is not faceless but large as life. And we—you and I—can bring him to heel. The cube and the cone are already standing, and now it is too late to pull them down. But we can do something about the altar which is still to come. The wooden altar in the old church is good enough for the new. It was carved by craftsmen in an age of craftsmanship, so why must we have an expensive block of cut limestone? Only because the Canon says so. The wooden altar was installed in the middle of the Famine with money which could have been used to buy food for the dying—I am only quoting local gossip—yet this landmark to the inhumanity of organised religion is to be put on the fire while a slab of polished limestone—a convenient *tabula rasa*—is to be erected in its place. Everyone knows this, everyone says this, but no one has the courage to say: "Enough!". This is where we come in. We must insist that the old altar be preserved if only as a reminder of more austere and possibly truer times, as a memorial to craftsmen who lived on diseased potatoes. There is plenty of feeling. There is plenty of tinder. All we need is to set a match to it.'

'I'm with you,' said Roarty. 'But have you considered the Canon?'

'He is the villain. It is his mania for building and his obsession with Pope Julius II—'

'the employer of Bramante, Raphael and Michelangelo as he calls him—'

'that has made the village of Tork look like a Bauhaus exhibition.'

'He's a crafty old fox. We'll have to tread carefully.'

'That's why I've spoken to you. I'm a stranger here. If I organise the opposition, he will brand me as an English communist and discredit what we're trying to achieve. I'm only too willing to help but I mustn't be seen to lead.'

'And what would you like me to do?'

'Call a meeting and get everyone who drinks in your pub to come to it.'

'We'll need a committee.'

'We'll ask Gimp Gillespie, Cor Mogaill—I wish you had more pronounceable names—and Rory Rua.'

'I don't think Rory Rua would be a good committee man. He's too self-opinionated; he thinks no one reads anything but himself. He calls himself a fisherman but he couldn't tell the difference between a cunt splice and a futtock plate.'

'You mustn't dismiss him on that account. There's many a Cambridge professor who'd fail the same test. We're not all students of *Britannica Eleven*, you know.'

'Leave it to me,' said Roarty. 'I'll whip up feeling with every pint.'

Roarty cut the engine and Potter rowed slowly into the dark cove. After winching up the boat they put the fish into two sacks and carried them up the steep path to the road.

'I'll see you at the pub,' said Potter as he drove off.

He felt satisfied with the evening's work. He was confident that he was now on the way to giving the Canon a comeuppance in accord with the reforming spirit of English Lollardism.

ELEVEN

After closing time Roarty and Susan Mooney cleaned the
pollack in the kitchen. Coming from the depths of the
mountain, she had never cleaned a fish before, but she was
quick to learn and before they had finished she could
dispose of a backbone and swim bladder almost as readily
as Roarty.

It had been an instructive evening for Roarty too. He
was now sure that Potter was his man if only because
of his reference to a hand or head as a further instalment,
which accorded with the threat in the blackmailer's second
letter. It was a pity, because he liked Potter. He was an
intelligent and entertaining conversationalist, and conversationalists were sufficiently rare to make one reflect
before reducing their number. He was afraid, however,
that their number would have to be reduced simply
because he could not afford to pay £50 a week for ever
more. He had considered staging an accident should the
opportunity arise but Potter's perception of catastrophe
might make an 'accident' difficult to contrive. He could
have left him on the rock if it had been closer to dark;
but to have done so with two hours of daylight still left
would have been nothing less than stupid. A sheep farmer
might see him from the cliff tops, and anyhow the villagers

knew that they had gone fishing together. He was fully aware that expunging Potter was not an easy matter. He could not poison his drink without risk of exposure, and he was unlikely to find an opportunity to hit him over the head with the twenty-fifth volume of *Britannica*. He suspected that the murder weapon would have to be a rifle or shotgun, and because bullets bore rifling marks and cartridges the mark of the firing pin he would have to find a gun other than his own. Perhaps it would be better to wait for a few weeks until the shooting season began in earnest.

He was pleased, however, about Potter's interest in the old altar though he could not imagine how it had arisen. He did not believe for a moment that Potter merely wished to commemorate 'craftsmen who lived on diseased potatoes', nor did he believe that he was striving out of the goodness of his heart to save Donegal from the fate that had overtaken London. But whatever his motives, Roarty welcomed his interest. He recognised immediately that involvement in the impersonal was what he needed to take his mind off McGing. If he became immersed in committee work, he would have less time to brood over his dreadful secret. He would be engaged with other men in a common pursuit which would knit his life to theirs and alleviate the isolation he had come increasingly to feel.

His feeling of isolation had been reinforced by the murder investigation, an ordeal which he would not willingly re-endure. First came question after question and then the repetition of questions he had already answered, while McGing took down everything in a black book and the detectives dusted the bar for fingerprints and scoured every room for blood prints. 'Keep looking,' he had heard McGing say to one of them. 'All we need is a milligram of dried blood and we're there.' He could see that he was under suspicion though the detectives had assured him that their questioning was routine. But there was nothing routine about the way they let loose their Alsatians in his garden, nor in McGing's pompous talk about trace elements, somatic and molecular death, and the effects of refrigeration on hypostasis (whatever that was). The homicide squad stayed in the glen for four days, interviewing everyone Eales had known, poking in back gardens, dredging loughs and rivers, examining fridges and freezers, and scouring the wild places in the mountains. McGing travelled with them wherever they went, ostensibly to guide them over unfamiliar terrain but in reality to pester them with suggestions and urge them to greater efforts in the interest of criminology. When they left defeated, he took it as a personal affront. He told Roarty over his morning drink that he believed the murder had been committed out of a desire to tantalise him. 'Why else should the murderer send me his victim's foot?' he asked. 'He is not content with having committed the perfect murder; he must let me see that it has been committed. Well, he is making a mistake. I have three more years before retirement, and I intend devoting every day of them to solving a crime that has defeated the experts.' Roarty believed him; there would be no peace, no let up, while McGing was on duty.

All was not ill-luck, however. He was fortunate, for example, that the letter for Eales had not arrived while the homicide squad was on the premises. As the envelope was typewritten he was tempted to take it straight to McGing, but curiosity prevailed and he steamed it open to discover that it was from Cecily, asking Eales what had happened, demanding to know when he was coming to England. He was glad that he had opened it. If McGing had seen it, the motive for the murder might have been laid bare. He burnt Cecily's letter but not the envelope as he knew that the postman might well tell McGing that there had been mail for Eales. To avoid further suspicion he took a brochure for cat meat which Eales had had some months before and put it in the envelope and resealed it before giving it to McGing the following morning.

'Would you care for a nightcap?' he asked Susan Mooney when they had cleaned the last of the fish. He was feeling lonely and deflated after the excitement of the evening, and he thought it might be soothing to put his feet up and talk to Susan before going to bed.

'I'll have a gin and tonic,' she said brightly. 'It will be nice to have a drink in peace and quiet.'

He went to the bar humming 'The March of the League of David against the Philistines' and came back with a tray of drinks and a bowl of peanuts. Susan was sitting on the old settee, and he sat down wearily beside her and poured her drink into a tall tumbler. She did not drink much as a rule, just a bottle of stout in the morning which made her burp like an archbishop and two or three gin-and-tonics in the evening which made her giggly and giddy. She was an innocent sort of girl who never asked awkward questions. She was always affable, always willing to help, with always a calming word for tricky customers. She was only twenty and perhaps because she was plain she had no boyfriend. Possibly she had never been kissed except once or twice in the dark on bonfire night or maybe on the way home from a winter ramble in the wildness of the mountain, and then by a silent sheep-farmer with the rain making runnels in his stubble. A young man might say that she was ugly because her face was distinctly

135

asymmetrical and her nose turned up flatly at the tip; but a middle-aged man, fatigued by the familiarity of his wife's figure, might overlook the face for the sturdy body with its muscular calves, protruding belly and overflowing breasts. He might say that though she was ugly she was attractively ugly, one of those women who beckon men at least into the penumbra between the known and the unknown. Such a man, Roarty thought, must surely be as perceptive as himself. Any man could lust after a clear-skinned, fair-haired girl of eighteen but it took talent to treasure a girl whose rump was to be measured not in roods but acres and whose breathing was as heavy as a cow's after a long day in summer aftergrass. He handed her the glass and wondered about the truth of the couplet in his mind:

> And fifteen arms went round her waist
> (And then men ask, Are barmaids chaste?)

She smiled at him as she took the glass and said:

'Whenever I drink gin-and-tonic I think I'm by the sea on a bright day in summer with a cooling breeze coming over the water. But when I drink stout, I do burp.'

'And which do you prefer?'

'Each has its time and place. In the mornings I like to burp but in the evenings I like to think of the sea.'

'I think I know what you mean. After a night's sleep and perhaps a breakfast you don't really fancy, there is nothing more fulfilling—if that's the word—than a rift of sour wind, what Dr McGarrigle, God save us all from his attentions, calls a "judicious eructation". But in the evenings after the sun has gone down you need something to release the imagination from the cares of the day.

The imagination, you see, is at its strongest in the night; it is then that we are closest to the vegetable state, and if we are to realise the darkest depths of ourselves we must dull the flighty mind with the fumes of alcohol.'

'I never dreamed that drinking a gin-and-tonic could be so complicated. Is that why you drink whiskey?'

'I drink whiskey to maintain the correct alcohol level in the blood during the day and to re-experience lost innocence in the evenings.'

'You must drink a lot over a long summer day.'

'That's because I'm a man. Women, you see, are closer to the vegetable state than men, which is why you don't have to drink so much to be happy.'

'I don't think I understand you.'

'That's because you haven't had enough to drink. Here, have another dash of gin in that tonic.'

He poured the gin, regretfully aware that there was nothing he desired more than to lay his head upon her breasts. She was wearing a low-cut cotton dress, and as she moved on the settee the light and shadows played delicate games along the curves of her breasts, a dark shadow in the valley between and lighter shadows on the top of each globe disappearing imperceptibly into the whiteness of her throat. He tried to think of a joke that would make her laugh so that he could watch her breasts heaving like two great jellies and re-experience that helpless feeling below the midriff. He told her why Budgeen Rua was so-called, how Crubog got his name, and how Potter pronounced 'Cor Mogaill' but she merely smiled with the whitest of teeth, perfect for the most ravenous gobble-gobble, and never heaved a breast at all.

'Are you right handed or left handed?' he asked.

'Left handed.'

He took her right hand, her destiny hand, and ran the nail of his forefinger along the line of life at the base of her thumb.

'You will live to be a great age,' he said, 'but I cannot see where.'

'What are you doing now?' she asked.

'I'm feeling your mounts. You've got seven of them but the most interesting is the Mount of Venus. It's very fleshy, a sign that you have love and music in abundance.'

'Where is my Mount of Venus?'

'There,' he said, pointing to the base of her thumb, inviting her to feel it for herself.

'It's very fleshy. Perhaps you're right.'

'Believe me, it's true.'

'You gipsy!' she laughed, her breasts like a cornucopia of fruit spilling from her low-cut dress.

He drew her head onto his shoulder and placed his right arm round her neck so that his hand rested on her right breast. It was not in the least jelly-like to touch: it was round and full, firm as a grapefruit, with a strong nipple that thrust against her dress. No wonder Potter called his pub 'The Bristols Bar'.

'Tell me about the mountain,' he said, caressing her breast, his fingers inside the light cotton.

'It's lonely. When you look out the window, all you see is one hill behind another and white roads running over them and maybe a house here and there with six or seven sheep grazing behind a ditch with their backs to the wind.'

'But surely it isn't all that different from the glen.'

'It's more silent. You could spend a morning without hearing a thing except the wind whistling in the heather. Here there are more sounds and they're all overpowered by the deeper sound of the sea.'

'But it's people, not sounds, that make a place.'

'I prefer the glen to the mountain because life is kindlier here, but I'd sooner have mountain people. My father used to call Tork the metropolis, and now I know why. Everyone in the village thinks he's a cut above the rest of the glen.'

'You're right,' he said. 'Put six houses together in a row and you change the nature of the people who live in them.'

Pressing the tip of her nipple as if it were a doorbell, he bent over her and kissed her slippery lips, inhaling the smell of fried liver, bacon and onions and gin-and-tonic from her breath.

'It's the first time I've been kissed by a man with a beard. It isn't as different as I thought it would be. It's nice and soft, nothing like as rough as a stubble.'

'You've been giving the matter some thought,' he laughed.

'There is many a strange thought that comes into a body's mind.'

He placed a kiss in the valley between her breasts and she wriggled with pleasure or perhaps because of the tickling of his beard. He opened her dress at the back and slipped her arms out of the sleeves, revealing two white breasts with brown nipples inviting the maddest of kissing.

'You don't wear a bra.'

'I like to let the air cool them in summer,' she laughed, and he could tell that she was as proud of them as he used to be of his large penis.

She lay on her back on the settee and he lay between her legs and kissed one breast after the other, licking the erect nipples and going from one to the other like a man who cannot make up his mind where the greater pleasure lies. Meanwhile she caressed the back of his neck with her strong fingers and scratched his head behind the ears as she might do to a cow to get her in a mood for milking. And he thought that she was nothing if not sweet-natured, so different from his late wife with her scrawny tits and her will-power and scraggy haunches, for all the world like a tinker's mare. He felt the adrenaline running in his stomach as it always did at the thought of his wife, and to regain his calm he put his hand up Susan's dress and ran his fingers over the short hair on her other Mount of Venus. She raised her leg to give him freedom of action and he felt her moist pussy, ripe as a peach, all shipshape and Bristol fashion as Potter would say, making him sharply conscious of the great quiet in his crotch. He fondled her clitoris, imitating with his forefinger as best he could the action of a penetrating penis until she clung to him like a waif in a storm, thrusting her mons veneris against his thigh and wriggling to find relief with a low moan that bespoke as much pain as pleasure.

'It was hard work,' she said.

'I'm dog tired,' he answered, allowing his head to sink heavily onto her arm.

She held his head to her bosom and he began to breathe heavily, pretending to be asleep, not wishing to face her obvious puzzlement. As he began to 'snore', she put her hand down inside his trousers and felt his limp penis all along its length which, he was still pleased to think, was quite considerable. He groaned like a dreaming dog and she left the room and came back with a bedspread which she laid lightly over his shoulders. His eyes still closed, he heard the click of the door handle and her heavy tread on the stairs.

On the verge of sleep, real sleep, he tried to hold a picture in his mind: fishing cod in the Sound on a windy evening in March, a leaden sea sploshing against the bows, the sky a blue-black cupola of low cloud and an opening in the west above the horizon where an invisible sun shot feathery cloud with golden light. It was such a contrast, the blue-black above like grim night descending and the window of gold over the water providing what light there was in the evening. Somehow it seemed to him to be an image of his life, and he bent stoically over the gunwale to haul a cod, but when he raised his head again the strip of light had gone and all was blue-black like premature night.

He woke and shivered though the night was warm. It was three o'clock by his watch, and he realised that he must have slept, that the tiredness he had been at pains to feign was real. He picked up the bottle of whiskey and his empty glass and quietly climbed the stairs so as not to disturb Susan. Without switching on the light in his bedroom he went to the window to pull the curtains. As he raised his hand, a movement on the other side of the street caught his eye. Someone was standing in the shadow of a gable, looking across at the house. He moved to the corner of the window without taking his eyes off the figure, wondering who it could be. He did not have to wait for long. As the church clock struck three, a man moved out of the shadow and walked slowly up the street. It was McGing.

Roarty was shaken. He knew that McGing had vowed to catch the murderer but he had not realised that he himself was to be the quarry. He was not imagining things; there was no other earthly reason why McGing should keep the house under surveillance. And regrettably, therefore, there was only one thing to be done: to take McGing's mind off the murder by giving him something more urgent to think about. He looked at his watch. He would give him half-an-hour to get back to the barracks and his bed. Then he would strike.

He put the Rhenish symphony on the gramophone and poured himself a drink, half aware of an unresolved crux in the music and in his life. His hands were shaking but they usually shook first thing in the morning and it was now only two hours from sunrise. He sat on the bed with a pillow between his head and the wall, consciously striving to expunge McGing from his thoughts. He thought of Potter pissing on Carraig a' Dúlamáin, almost a trusted friend compared with McGing. And he thought of Cecily playing *Papillons* with a lightness that had promised invincible innocence, now a grown woman writing in desperation to a debauched bugger from Kerry, her purity of heart overcome by the primacy of the clitoris. And finally he thought of the woman who had brought her into the world, and he could hardly marvel at the transformation that had overtaken her daughter. Her mother was a prize bitch, and no doubt Cecily had gone through the first toll gate on the highroad to a monstrous middle age. But try as she might she would never equal her mother in bitchiness, wilfulness and feminine hard-heartedness.

In a way he owed his wife to the mysterious student of Dante and Rimbaud, Dusty Parker. When Parker disappeared, a nondescript girl called Florence Kissane took his place in the pub. It was a difficult time in Roarty's life. He had left the seminary a year before, and he was still trying to convince himself that in leaving he had taken the right course. He could have taken an office job, he supposed, but he was driven into a pub because he saw it as a crossroads of life where the good meet the bad and in the encounter get to know more of themselves. He felt that after six years in a seminary he needed the experience of everyman to eradicate the enervating feeling that he himself was a prize exhibit at a public fair. He needed to lose himself in a field full of folk, and he reckoned that a London pub was the twentieth-century equivalent. For his first year outside the walls he lived without women, having decided that he would not surrender to the urge of the flesh except for beauty. It had not been a difficult decision; he merely thought that to give up the priesthood for anything less would have been unworthy. He waited and waited, however, wondering about the effect of the kiss of a truly beautiful woman (healing or searing?) and realising with every day that passed how few of them there were in the world. When Florence first came to the pub, he hardly noticed her. She had come from Tipperary, from the Golden Vale as she called it, still smelling of milk and buttercups, a rare enough achievement in the fug and stink of a Bloomsbury pub. As the weeks went by he spoke to her from time to time, noting the efficiency which he thought the landlord must have sensed when he took her on. She was the best barmaid he'd met, quick on her feet, quick to pull pints, quick to give change, and more quick-witted than necessary with drunken litterateurs. The landlord was the opposite, an ass of a man with a phoney accent who got from one day to the next simply by laughing. He laughed at everything from 'Good morning, gov' to 'A pint of bitter, please'. And one evening when an uncharacteristically sober journalist said in his hearing that his pub was the worst-run in London he laughed even more than usual. Hearing him, Florence looked over her shoulder from the till, and in her glance Roarty saw that he had found his future wife. She was far from beautiful but somehow beauty had suddenly lost its pre-eminence. He was pleased that he had found her, and it was a pleasure that remained with him until years later, when he discovered that it was she who had found him.

The early and unselfconscious years of their marriage were something only a little less than heaven. They were both bent on going back to Ireland and they began at once to save for a place of their own. After a year a small pub in Roarty's home village came on the market and they bought it with all the confidence of a couple with 'London experience' setting up shop in Donegal. It was only a shebeen but soon they had made it into a comfortable pub, a natural place of congregation for village wiseacres as well as a natural place of rest for any Bloomsbury litterateur who might find himself on holiday in Glenkeel. They were both thrifty and efficient without being too niggardly to enjoy the pleasures that country life affords. And they might have continued to enjoy them until old age or even death but misfortune struck one night when at the age of twenty-eight Roarty discovered that he was impotent. He had been worried for months before, sensing his sexual urge ebbing like a tide from an estuary, conscious that he no longer looked at girls' breasts with a feeling of unutterable tenderness in his chest. This was different, however. For the first time in five years of married life he had failed. Aware of the frightening quietude in his loins, he lay facing his wife, his penis on his thigh limp as Adam's in Michelangelo's depiction of the Creation. But the memory of the physical beauty of that particular penis gave him little comfort. Florence, always a girl to take the initiative, tried to give him a helping hand out of his difficulty but he ejaculated weakly against her palm before he had even got an erection.

'Not my night,' she said, turning her back on him with

a final shrug of the shoulders.

They tried again the following night but also in vain. By now he was more than worried and so was Florence. Her diagnosis, however, was simple and unanswerable. 'You've got brewer's droop', she said, 'and the cure is total abstinence'. He told her that he was drinking only half a bottle a day, chicken feed for a man of his physique, but nevertheless he went on the wagon, knowing that though moral blackmail is a woman's most common weapon in marriage it is also the deadliest. The cure, however, failed to match the simplicity of the diagnosis. After a week without drink he began getting the occasional tremor of desire, followed by a beguiling show of the flag at half mast. He would begin making love to Florence, knowing how badly she needed a rub of the relic, and when she was all shipshape and Bristol fashion his erection would collapse with a trickle on his thigh. The irony was that now as a teetotaller he was showing the classic symptoms of brewer's droop as enunciated by the Porter in *Macbeth*: 'much drink may be said to be an equivocator with lechery; it makes and mars him; it sets him on, and it takes him off; it persuades him, and disheartens him; makes him stand to and not stand to . . .' And far from being amused at this most common of male jokes he was so worried that a normal approach to his wife was now impossible. At the best of times sex caught him as it does all self-aware men at his most vulnerable and most ridiculous but now the complications of failure were so great that it was simpler and more sensible not to begin. Florence readily agreed, saying that it was cruel to set her on only to leave her high and dry with a sleepless night to follow, and she would not let him touch her with his hand.

At first she betrayed moments of understanding but

her understanding soon turned into the sour milk of long-suffering. They took to separate bedrooms and to eating breakfast in belligerent silence. Previously he alone had taken the business decisions but now he found that she had begun to order extra barrels of stout without consulting him. Just because he had failed to trigger the ritual spasm in her gleety vagina he had dwindled within a month from a landlord to a cipher. But there was method in her audacity. She was taking the opportunity to chat up draymen, excise men, weights and measures men, commercial travellers and every stranger in trousers who came to the pub. She was not pretty. She was not the type of woman at whom men naturally made a pass. She was the kind of sensible plain Jane who would have to flash her crimson knickers at least three times before anyone except a sex maniac would take a blind bit of notice. She must have done precisely that because one day about six months after his first failure she said over dinner:

'I can't stand this any longer. I need a poke, and a good one at that, to keep my sanity. But I won't shame you by going out with one of the locals. Instead I'll have a sly one with MacSwilley's drayman on Thursday. I'm telling you in advance because I don't want you to think I'm being unfaithful.'

He was taken aback by the brutal feminine logic, and he wondered why there were no great women philosophers.

'I appreciate being told,' he said with unobtrusive irony. 'I'll go shooting to make things easier for you.'

'And who will look after the bar?'

'I didn't think the bar was on your mind.'

'You'll stay here. Everything must go on as usual so that the customers don't suspect.'

'You have a nice sense of the appropriate,' he said, almost choking over a gristle in the scrag end of neck she had just overcooked him.

As was her wont in those days she got her way. He sat uneasily in the bar making conversation with Crubog while a drayman in wide shoes drank tea in the kitchen and plunged on the bed upstairs. But the incident gave him an insight into women which was almost blinding in its simplicity. Man's relationship with them, when all the talk of Michelangelo was done, could be reduced to a simple formula:

$$H = E + P + S$$

when H = Happiness; E = Erection; P = Penetration; and S = Spasm.

$$\therefore S = H - (E + P)$$

which for men with poor memories could be expressed in the mnemonic SHEP. If only he had seen this truth before! What fun it would have been in the days when he used to give her two spasms on a single stalk. But it was typical of the School of Life that what it taught you was no longer of use. Only an impotent man, he thought ruefully, could realise the full force of the truth he had just seen plain.

'There's a run about the rocks today,' he said to Crubog, trying to regain his grip on common, quotidian perceptions.

'The sea can do only one of two things, rise or fall,' said Crubog sagely.

The drayman came and went and a commercial traveller in cigarettes took his place. Florence became more civil as she became more unfaithful. She would make small talk about customers and humorously promise to give him oysters to cure his droop, but he could not respond. The joy and self-forgetfulness had vanished from his life. He simply could not understand how a woman could turn her back on five rare years of happiness and treat the man who had helped make them like a discarded dildo. If he had been morally culpable, he would have understood, but he was no more to blame for the failure of his erection than for the fact that the axis of the earth is inclined about 66°33′ to the orbital plane. It was typical of a woman, even an intelligent one, that such a basic perception should be beyond her. He went through the motions of living, watching her sprightly return from Donegal Town every fortnight and wondering why the hell he did not wring her fucking neck. He continued to wonder while doing nothing, and one day when she told him that she was pregnant he laughed as though it were a dirty joke. She took her pregnancy seriously, however. She gave up seeing the man who had sown her and spent the days of turgescence on the settee in the sitting-room, reading light novels and eating Turkish delight. Dr McGarrigle came to see her, felt her belly, and told Roarty that there was danger of a premature birth. She was rushed to Donegal Hospital and in case the neighbours should suspect discord he went to visit her. There had been complications, he discovered. A baby girl had been born by caesarean but the mother was at death's door. She opened her sunken eyes and took his hand, and somehow he knew that she would never take it again.

'We've had some good times, Tim,' she said weakly. 'We've come a long journey together. You will never know how much you shortened the first hundred miles.'

What could he say? Her words bore the full gravity of

life's tragedy and no repartee of his could cheapen them. In dying as in living she had defeated him.

He looked after the child as best he could, somewhat grudgingly in the beginning and then tenderly as she came to recognise his stooping form over the cot and joyously as the first miraculous words brought new life to the house. She was a lovely little girl, dark haired and dark eyed, her oval face bright with innocent intelligence. Within a year she had transformed his life. She was not only his daughter, she was his little woman too. He taught her to read and write long before she went to school. He took her for walks and told her all he knew about the flowers and small animals of the glen. He drove her seventeen miles to Garron twice a week for piano lessons with the best teacher in the area, and when she was thirteen he sent her to the best convent school in the county. She was not his flesh but she was the apple of his eye. And because she was not his flesh he was driven to mould her to an extent which no ordinary father would attempt. He was for ever at pains to provide the tilth of experience in which her young personality could grow, and grow it did in purity and health as only her playing of *Die Davidsbündlertänze* could show. Her holidays from school were heaven. Then the house would flow with piano music and he would eat everything she cooked and ask for more. And then Eales came and transplanted her to a putrefactive tilth, the midden of life where nothing grows but black-gilled toadstools. A fortnight ago he had written to tell her that she had won a university scholarship, imagining her joy and the urgency of her return, but he still had not heard from her. Instead he had had her pathetic letter to Eales. He sighed. The symphony had ended, leaving him with a sense of life's, and perhaps Schumann's, ambiguity. His thoughts hung on the trinity of Eales, Potter and McGing, and he could not help feeling that they were one and the same person, the creation of his own insatiable demon. Day after day these three persons tortured him with their ubiquity until he longed to cleanse his mind of all trace of them. But he had to admit that if he should succeed in doing so, he would no longer be himself because the obsessive nature of his thoughts coloured his experience of life and provided the very core of his personality. We are all in love with ourselves, he thought. Even if we could be reoriented and streamlined at a stroke, we would no more desire it than a lover of Schumann would wish to see his music rescored by a composer with a finer sense of orchestration for the simple reason that it would no longer be Schumann.

He tiptoed down the dark stairs and let himself out by the back door. He took a pair of gardening gloves, a cold chisel and a hammer from the garage and followed the west road out of the village. At the crossroads he turned north and doubled back through the fenced fields until he was just north of the high-walled churchyard. A salmon rolled in the river, and the sudden soss made him hold his breath. He squatted on his hams and held up his finger but he could barely see it. The sky, which had changed since sunset, was cloudy and starless, pressing like a black cope on the shoulders of the hills.

He climbed over the unmortared wall of the churchyard and lurked for a moment behind the dark mass of the belfry. When he was satisfied that all was quiet, he stole forward to the sacristy window and raised the bottom sash with a heave, pleased that the catch was not working. He put on his gloves and climbed inside without a sound, remembering as he found his way in the dark the five years he had served Mass as a boy. He stood in the sanctuary doorway, watching the flickering of the sanctuary lamp and the uncertain shadows that darted along the walls with each upward leap of the flame.

He walked down the nave to the porch and in a moment he had prised open the poorbox which stood inside the door. Without a moment's delay he stuffed the money in his pocket and within fifteen minutes he was back in his bedroom.

He felt pleased with himself. The investigation which the Canon would order would keep McGing busy for a week or two. It would be a baffling case if only because it was difficult to imagine a man who would sacrilegiously steal ninety-four pence from the poor. He felt a little guilty but he would expiate that tomorrow by sending £1.88 to the St. Vincent De Paul Society in Dublin. After all it was common knowledge that the urban poor were more deserving than their country cousins.

As he fell asleep McGing seemed to recede into the dark but Potter loomed larger with his extraordinary description of the Famine as representing more austere but truer times.

TWELVE

'Has everyone got a drink?' asked Roarty.

He had locked the street door and taken the till from the bar so that, if McGing knocked, it would appear that he was having a social drink with some friends.

'Let the meeting begin,' said Cor Mogaill from the depth of the armchair by the fireplace. His thin face was sharp with eagerness, the face of a man who had dreamt of revolution and could not believe that he had lived to see it. He kicked his knapsack away from him and, resting his weary feet on it, inhaled the smoke of his cigarette so deeply that Roarty felt it must have reached his toes. An innocent young man, he thought. A Marxist perhaps but the salt of the earth nevertheless. Not a man to cut through another man's tibia with a hacksaw.

Potter and Rory Rua were sitting on the settee and Gillespie was seated at the table with a writing pad in front of him. Potter, in a well-cut corduroy jacket, open-necked shirt and cavalry twill trousers, looked the picture of suave urbanity at ease in the country. Sun-tanned and fine-featured, athletic and self-confident, he stared with handsome eyes that betrayed an icy coldness for all their wholesome blueness. A thoroughbred, thought Roarty, compared with whom Rory Rua is a Clydesdale. Potter offered his tobacco pouch to Rory Rua who took it with the awkwardness of a man who has no sense of ceremony. His hair looked redder than usual and the freckles on his face and hands were so large that they seemed like the blotches of some rare skin disease. As he tamped his pipe with broken finger-nails, Roarty could not help noticing the raw-red saltwater boils on his wrists and he shivered as if he himself was in danger of catching them, as if Rory Rua was somehow less than human. 'I'm becoming far too sensitive,' he thought, taking a therapeutic swig from his glass.

'You all know why we're here,' he said, sitting down opposite Gillespie. 'Until we have elected a committee I'll take the chair. I think the first thing we must do is elect officers, and I propose Kenneth Potter for president and chairman.'

'I second that,' said Rory Rua.

'I appreciate your faith in me,' said Potter, 'but I feel that I must decline. I'm a stranger here, suspect in the Canon's eyes and therefore a liability in any negotiations with him which may ensue. I feel that the executive committee should be above criticism. While I am willing to give all the help I can behind the scenes, I believe that I should not hold elective office. I therefore propose Mr Roarty for president. He is a respected figure among us and, I feel sure, broadly acceptable to the Canon.'

'I second that,' said Gillespie.

It was put to the vote and Roarty was elected.

'Thank you,' said Roarty. 'Is it the wish of the meeting that I should remain in the chair?'

'Yes,' said everyone except Cor Mogaill.

'Can't we have an informal meeting over a few jars without carrying on like a drove of schoolteachers at their

AGM?' he asked. 'Is all this fiddle-faddle about proposing and seconding necessary among boon companions?'

'We will now elect the secretary,' said Roarty, ignoring him.

'If we must elect a secretary, I propose myself for the job,' said Cor Mogaill.

There was a second's silence while the others looked at one another and then at the self-promoting Cor Mogaill sitting back in his chair, staring challengingly and holding a pint of stout on the arm.

'I don't think that would be a good idea,' said Rory Rua. 'We can't have a self-confessed Marxist as secretary. We must elect men who go to Mass on Sunday and receive the Sacraments regularly. I propose Gimp Gillespie because he fulfils those two conditions and because he's used to writing and in a position to give us necessary publicity in the *Dispatch*.'

'I second that,' said Potter.

A vote was taken and Gillespie was elected with Cor Mogaill abstaining.

'Now for the treasurer,' said Roarty. 'May I have a nomination?'

'I am sure that Gimp Gillespie will make a good secretary,' said Cor Mogaill. 'But I think I would make an equally good treasurer. I don't mind going to Mass and the Sacraments while this project of ours is in motion. Will someone nominate me then?'

'Where are your Marxist principles?' asked Rory Rua.

'I'll define my position after I'm elected. I must be elected without interrogation or not at all.'

'No reflection on your honesty, Cor Mogaill, but I think that a man who has admitted to robbing the poorbox should not be in charge of the finances of what could become an epoch-making society in the history of the Church,' said Rory Rua.

'I didn't rob the poorbox,' said Cor Mogaill.

'Then why did you admit it to the Canon and McGing?'

'I did it as a joke on McGing. When he accused me of breaking and entering and robbing the poorbox, I thought it would be a good jape to admit it and later deny it. Just to show him up for the jackass he is. But when he took me to the Canon, and the Canon asked me if it were Marxist doctrine to rob the poor of their coppers, I thought that the opportunity to confuse him with Scripture must not be missed. I told him that the New Testament says quite clearly that gold and silver are infected and that I robbed the poor box and threw the money into the sea so that it might be cleansed before the poor received it.'

'Cor Mogaill, you are quite mad,' said Roarty. 'Everyone in the glen now believes that it was you who stole from the poorbox. Why did you blacken your name by admitting to something you now say you didn't do?'

'You're all sunk in embourgeoisement. What does the opinion of capitalists, even tuppence-halfpenny capitalists like you, matter to a Marxist revolutionary? I don't give a stuff whether you believe I robbed the poorbox or not. I've promised to mend the box and "return" the money, and this I am going to do. I think it an excellent jape against Church and State. Loftus and McGing are happy in their ignorance, and the real culprit might be encouraged to commit a more serious crime in the hope that I'll take the rap again. In this way I'm a true revolutionary, undermining society by seeming to take its sins on myself.'

'It's a Christ-like rather than a Marx-like gesture,' said Potter.

'Anyhow, we can't have you as treasurer,' said Rory

Rua. 'You're too confused in your thinking to seek high elective office.'

'Shit and cock and balls,' said Cor Mogaill.

'I nominate Rory Rua for treasurer,' said Gimp Gillespie.

Potter seconded the proposal and Rory Rua was duly elected.

'And what are Potter and myself to be?' demanded Cor Mogaill.

'We'll make you both honorary officers,' said Roarty, going to the bar for another round.

He was both angry and annoyed. How could he keep McGing busy if Cor Mogaill was going to put a spanner in the works? He would have to think of something more serious, something that Cor Mogaill would not wish to 'confess' to, something a little more indictable than robbing the poorbox. Thanks to Cor Mogaill, McGing was free to devote himself to the murder again. He must not let the grass grow under his feet, and he still had to devise a way of dispatching Potter. He was enjoying the meeting, however. It was a new venture and would help to obliterate the insistent pattern of consciousness which dogged him night and day.

'Next we must think of a name for our society,' he said, returning with a full tray.

'Surely, you're putting the cart before the horse,' said Cor Mogaill. 'Let's first talk about what we aim to do.'

'A name is important,' said Rory Rua.

'I propose a straight-forward name,' said Roarty. 'The Society for the Preservation of the Wooden Altar.'

'It lacks imagination,' said Gillespie. 'We need a name that will catch the public ear because it makes a pronounceable acronym like Unesco. We must think in terms of public relations. We must see ourselves from a sub-editor's point of view, and there is nothing a sub likes better than a snappy title. The column width of the *Dispatch* is only twelve picas, in layman's language two inches. You therefore need a short name for headlines, which is why I propose the Wooden Altar Society. It provides, you see, the catchy acronym WAS.'

Cor Mogaill flung his head back and hooted into the ceiling. 'I think we should call it the SFB,' he said. 'The Society for Bullshit because it's what you're all talking.'

'I agree with Gillespie,' said Potter. 'What we need here is the x-factor.'

'And what is a fucking x-factor? More bullshit?' asked Cor Mogaill.

'It's the unquantifiable. It's what made John XXIII a universally loved man though he was pope and it's what made Wellington, Nelson and Winston Churchill great leaders against the odds. This x-factor could make us by its presence or mar us by its absence. With it we could be the instigators of a revolution, a liturgical counter-revolution that will put the clocks back to pre-tridentine times.'

'Let's not lose our sense of proportion,' said Cor Mogaill.

'Our aim is to preserve the wooden altar,' said Rory Rua.

'And possibly to remove Canon Loftus,' said Cor Mogaill. 'Let's not pretend to an innocence which as children of the dark we don't possess. If we raise enough stink over the altar, the Bishop of Raphoe will want to know why Loftus isn't keeping his parishioners in line. There will be questions over the brandy and possibly a change of scene for our Canon.'

'We must not be led into cheap Marxist anticlericalism,' said Rory Rua. 'We must not show the slightest hint of personal animus. We must all appear to be upright men, occupying the front seats at Mass on Sunday. We must reform from within, not without.'

'Rory Rua, you scoundrel, hypocrite and would-be flatterer,' roared Cor Mogaill.

'If we keep sniping at each other like this, we'll deserve to be called the Altercation Society,' laughed Gillespie.

'A man who perpetrates a pun like that should be strung up by the privities and shot with a ball of his own dung,' hooted Cor Mogaill in high-pitched aggression.

'We may talk lightly,' said Gillespie, 'but our meeting could be a turning point in the history of the Church. We are not merely saying "no" to a limestone altar; we are also saying "no" to a table altar, the centre-piece of the new liturgy. This, as Kenneth says, could be the genesis of the counter-revolution.'

'You've mentioned the x-factor,' said Roarty to Potter. 'But you haven't told us the title that's got it.'

'It's quite simple,' said Potter. 'The Anti-Limestone Society.'

'It sounds like a society for cranks, a geological variant of the Flat Earth Society,' said Cor Mogaill.

'Precisely,' said Potter. 'We need something that isn't too solemn, something to show people that we have a sense of humour as well as a knowledge of theology.'

'I do believe you're right,' said Roarty. 'We'll put it to the vote. Hands up all who vote for the Anti-Limestone Society.'

They agreed to adopt Potter's title and Roarty turned to the next item on the agenda.

'We must now discuss tactics,' he said.

'Wouldn't it be better to discuss strategy?' asked Cor Mogaill.

'We'll discuss both,' said Potter.

'Our immediate objective,' Roarty said, 'must be to hold a public meeting to which the majority of the glen people will come. But first we must do something to show that we mean business, something that will make us a topic of conversation in every chimney corner.'

'I think we should do something at once painless and outrageous, like threatening to stop paying in collections or withholding our voluntary labour,' said Cor Mogaill. 'That's what would hurt the Canon most, and show the bishop that he has lost all control of his flock.'

'No,' said Rory Rua. 'We must be reasonable. The farthest I'd go is to paint slogans on walls and hang banners across the village street. Then, when we have organised public support, we'll present a signed petition to the Canon with a carbon copy to the bishop.'

'A good idea,' said Gillespie. 'A picture of banners with slogans is certain of publication in the *Dispatch*. The questions is, Which slogans? I propose the slogan "We Want Wood" because in headlines it could be abbreviated to "WWW" or "W3".'

'You are obsessed with subbing,' said Cor Mogaill.

'I suggest "Wood v. Limestone: Where Do You Stand?",' said Rory Rua.

'A slogan is a good idea,' said Potter. 'But it must be more than a slogan. It must be a battle-cry which, thanks to Mr Gillespie, will soon be known from one end of the county to the other. We'll paint it on walls and display it on stickers in the rear windows of our cars. We'll even place a prominent ad in the *Dispatch*.'

'It all sounds very promising but you haven't told us the

battle-cry,' said Cor Mogaill.

'HOOA! HOOA! HOOA!' said Potter, raising his clenched fist.

'What does it mean?'

'Hands Off Our Altar!'

'I don't like the sound of it,' said Cor Mogaill. 'It's neither Irish nor English. It's like a battle-cry from one of the emergent countries of Africa.'

'Get stuffed or stewed, whichever is the less convenient,' said Potter urbanely.

'I think Potter's idea an excellent one,' said Roarty. 'We'll make banners and stickers. HOOA! I can see it become a national watchword.'

'I know something of lettering,' said Potter. 'I'll make some banners and stickers at the week-end.'

'And we'll put up the banners in the middle of the night,' said Roarty. 'That way they'll have the maximum effect on Loftus when he sees them on his way to say Mass in the morning.'

'No,' said Potter. 'We must not come like a thief in the night. We must act in the blaze of noon so that everyone knows who we are.'

They talked for another hour until Cor Mogaill, assuming the role of chairman, began to rebuke them for repeating themselves. At two o'clock Roarty went outside and looked up and down the street to see if it were clear; and then they left by the back door, one after the other. Potter was the last and Roarty gripped his elbow at the door.

'What about a *deoch a' dorais*?' he asked.

'A what?'

'One for the Strasse.'

'If it were any other night, I would. I've had three late nights in a row, and I'm absolutely knackered. I really must get to bed.'

'I think we can be pleased with the night's work,' said Roarty.

'It was a very Irish night, no offence.'

'And you were the most Irish of all,' laughed Roarty.

'*Hibernicis ipsis Hibernior.*'

'You're not the first, but I think I should tell you that the precedents have not been all that happy.'

'It is something to bear in mind.'

He watched Potter vanish into the night, an elusive, chameleon-like figure, yet undeniably effective among men. He had declined to be president but he influenced the discussion more than anyone else by appearing so detached that his opinion unfailingly commanded attention. It was a pity he would not stay for a drink because a chat when the mind is weary from Scotch and the business of the day might cast a shaft of light on so much that was dark.

'A difficult man to corner,' he thought, climbing the stairs. 'I'll just have to run him into the open, I suppose.'

He went to bed but his mind was too active for sleep. After lying in the dark for half an hour he put *Fünf Stücke im Volkston* on the gramophone and looked up the article on Aqueducts in *Britannica*. Pablo Casals's cello playing and the drily technical language of the encyclopedist gave him a sense of comfort he had not previously felt that day. It seemed to him that the most subtle luxuries of life were his, that his greatest temptations were intellectual.

THIRTEEN

Roarty could see the parochial house from the west window of his bedroom, and now he could see Nora Hession closing the front door and coming down the avenue between the trees. Canon Loftus, who was on retreat in Letterkenny, would not be back until Saturday, and while he was away Nora slept at her sister's or possibly with the ambidextrous Potter. The parochial house would now be empty until morning, and he would have time to do what he wanted. And what he wanted to do would give McGing plenty to think about, take his mind off the murder which he now talked about to the point of pathological obsession.

Roarty sighed with what he realised could be premature relief. All through September he had felt harried as a hare. He felt as if every wisp of his every thought were known to McGing, and his discomfiting sense of self-exposure was accompanied by a psychological impotence which kept him from thinking about anything let alone doing anything to the purpose. Cecily had written to say that she wished to remain with her aunt in London, that she would not be going to university in spite of the scholarship, but he was so self-absorbed that he gave her decision scarcely a thought. Far from going to London to take her back he merely wondered with indifference at the distance he had strayed from his former self. There seemed to be no escape from the tangle of his anguished preoccupations. He was pinioned by thoughts of Potter and McGing to the point where his health had begun to suffer and he had begun to fear for his sanity. Even with the help of a bottle of whiskey a day he could hardly get one hour's untroubled sleep at night. He would toss between recurrent dreams of criminal investigation, complex cross-questioning, and sitting down to a meal with Potter at which the entrée was thick brawn made from a severed head; and he would wake in the morning with the black thoughts of the night clinging to him like suffocating cobwebs. He would stagger wearily into the bathroom but he would first have to drink three hot toddies before the tremble left his hand and it was safe to shave. And then he would note with hypochondriac horror that his stool was streaked with blood, and conjure up visions of surgeons like white vultures bent on a colostomy.

> I noticed I was passing blood
> (Only a few drops, not a flood)
> So pausing on my homeward way
> From Tallahassee to Bombay
> I asked a doctor, now my friend,
> To peer into my hinder end,
> To prove or to disprove the rumour
> That I had a malignant tumour.

How anyone could make fun of cancer was more than he could understand but nevertheless he went to see Dr McGarrigle more in jest than in hope.

Dr McGarrigle lived in Glenroe but he held a clinic in Glenkeel on Wednesdays. He was a large, likeable man, an indefatigable womaniser who fancied his chances with young and old provided they were of a certain social standing. The secret of his success with his women patients was that not one of them would dream of complaining of an unwanted advance. To be the object of a pass by Dr McGarrigle was considered to be a cachet of respectability, and to be 'cured' by him was a pleasure not unknown to several widows in the glen whose complaints had been proof against the ministrations of more orthodox doctors. But in spite of his readiness to indulge himself in the clinic, he seemed to take his duties as a doctor seriously. A heavy drinker in the evenings, he would often go up to a patient in a pub and say: 'Don't you realise that if you finish that whiskey you may be shortening your life by as much as a year. I'm not telling you to put it down; I'm merely ensuring that you'll enjoy it all the more by drinking it in the full knowledge of its side-effects'. Not surprisingly he was liked by all, even by husbands whose wives had been cured of what he described as menopausal melancholia by one or two visits to his clinic. But the quality that endeared him most of all to his patients was his tendency to treat a large proportion of them for the same condition no matter what their symptoms. A few winters ago, when he was treating most of those who came to see him for septicaemia of the foot, Old Crubog went to him about rheumatism in the left shoulder only to be told that it was a referred pain originating in his big toe, simply a question of metastasis, or metathesis as Crubog reported. This year by all accounts he was treating most people for gout, and the funny thing was that none of his patients seemed to mind. In fact those suffering from 'septicaemia of the foot', 'gout', or whatever disease was most prevalent in his clinic that winter were rather proud of their status because they took it to mean that they need not worry. It had long since been observed that only those patients who were treated for more common diseases actually died. For this reason, Gimp Gillespie had evolved the theory that McGarrigle had what few doctors can be accused of—a professional sense of humour. He simply treated all patients suffering from imaginary ailments for the same condition on the principle that a placebo for septicaemia of the foot was as good as a placebo for rheumatism.

Roarty had been wondering what he would say to him but his curiosity was soon satisfied.

'What can be ailing a fine big fellow like you,' the doctor asked.

'Blood in the rectum,' said Roarty, pleased that unlike most of the doctor's patients he knew the word 'rectum'.

'Rectal bleeding,' said McGarrigle 'Not as uncommon as you might think. Let's have a quick look at the seat of the trouble, no pun intended.'

'You're not going to poke something up my arse?' enquired Roarty, so alarmed that he forgot the word 'anus'.

'That may be necessary.'

'Would you mind warming it in your hand first. I'm rather sensitive behind.'

'You sound like a condemned man making a last wish.'

Roarty bent forward with his trousers round his ankles, and thought of Edward II, King of England between 1307 and 1327.

'Mm!' said McGarrigle.

'What?'

'I just said "Mm!", a noise that doctors make to assist diagnosis.'

'Well, what is it? Gout?' asked Roarty hopefully.

'Why do you think it might be gout?'

'I eat a lot and drink a lot. I thought it might be a possibility.'

'It isn't gout,' said McGarrigle firmly. 'Hold out both hands in front of you.'

Roarty watched his hands tremble though he tried to keep them still.

'How much do you drink a day?'

'No more than a bottle.'

'Stout or whiskey?' McGarrigle asked humourlessly.

'Whiskey.'

'I think a bottle is enough.'

After that McGarrigle gave him a thorough examination and sat down at his desk as if he were suddenly weary of life and death.

'What's the verdict?' asked Roarty. 'Haemorrhoids?'

'No, it isn't piles, not precisely. It's something more shadowy, lurking in the no man's land between the psyche and the soma.'

'And what does that mean?'

'I think it's a symptom of stress, mental stress.'

Roarty laughed as if the doctor had made a bad joke.

'I'm going to have you admitted to Sligo Hospital for examination. It's probably nothing to worry about but the modern GP is usually tempted to leave the verdict to a higher court. Could you drink less without putting yourself out?'

'I don't think so.'

'Well, don't force yourself then.'

He watched McGarrigle write a prescription for sleeping tablets and thought that it was a psychiatrist he needed, not a doctor. What would McGarrigle say if he had told him of his more alarming symptoms: the enfeebling dreams of macabre feasts with Potter or sisyphean struggles with an eagle in red knickers? In many ways the latter was more harrowing because he invariably woke from it in trembling exhaustion. He would see a downy eaglet in an eyrie transformed before his eyes into a golden eagle of fearsome strength and majesty that stared at him with predatory curiosity. He would fling a spear at the great bird which would catch it nonchalantly with its wing and fling it back at him. The single combat between bird and man would continue for what seemed like hours until Roarty in desperation would pick up the spear and drive it straight through the bird's furcula. But the eagle would pluck it from its breast and drive it in again, laughing with aquiline remoteness. Finally it would turn double somersault, revealing to Roarty a pair of knickers under its thigh feathers red as a summer sunset.

'I'm wearing red knickers,' the great bird would crow. 'I'm utterly impregnable, you impotent half-wit.'

He would wake from sleep, sweating with exertion as if he had undergone a real struggle with a real bird. Though he could not tell the significance of the red knickers, he felt that the dream symbolised his daily torture by Potter and McGing which seemed Promethean in its inexorable continuity. It was the red knickers that haunted him during the day, however, impressing on him the extent of the darkness within that threatened to disrupt his very light and reason.

He took McGarrigle's sleeping tablets for a week but bad dreams, he found, were preferable to a thick head in the morning. The rectal bleeding concentrated his mind with every visit to the lavatory, after which the best relief was a walk in the garden and a moment of communion with the withered conifer. It was no longer dying. It was now dead, but still he continued to feed the roots before breakfast. He would carry bucket after bucket of water to the bottom of the garden and feel the dust-dry needles that crumbled between his fingers as he plucked them, brown as snuff. Yet in the deepening twilights of September the perfect silhouette of the dead tree gave it the very outline of life. He thought of Cecily in a foreign country, impressionably vulnerable, a prey to a kind of soft talk for which her experience had not prepared her. And he thought that life as he had known it had come to an end. All that was left was the outline, days of going through the motions while his thoughts were coloured by a baleful light invisible to all except himself. He had become a piece of furniture in other men's worlds. They came into the bar, shook his hand, and whispered a joke in his ear; and he smiled, pulled pints, and took money with as much conviction as a puppet. Where would it end? Suicide or imprisonment? Further murder or a life not worth living? Quite simply, in destroying Eales he had destroyed himself. But his instinct was still for life and it grew in him as he watched Nora Hession take the fenceless road to her sister's cottage or possibly to Potter's.

He went downstairs to help Susan in the bar and noted with interest that Potter was missing. The evening went by slowly because he had decided to limit himself to six whiskies, and he was glad when the last of the regulars had left and he and Susan could begin the washing up. At a quarter past twelve he said good night to her and climbed the stairs to his room. As he could not begin the night's work for another two hours, he lay on the bed listening to Schumann's piano quintet and reading the article on Alchemy in *Britannica*. But the transmutation he most desired was such wishful thinking that he put down the volume and closed his eyes, suddenly alive to the spontaneous clarity of a young man's music. He had first heard the quintet on his honeymoon in London and immediately realised that it was the music of a man in love. Years later he discovered that Schumann had written it in the first blissful weeks of his marriage to Clara Wieck; and though his own marriage had turned to bitter aloes he was grateful to Schumann for confirming his perception of a reality which he had found all too fleeting. He was also grateful for these few moments of brightness in a world which had become so opaque. He picked up a tattered biography of the composer and opened a page at random near the end:

Suddenly on the night of February 10 the final dissolution of personality began. Previously Schumann had been distressed by aural illusions. Now what had formerly been a noise became a persistent note. As sleepless night followed sleepless night, the sound grew into music, 'a music more wonderful and played by more exquisite instruments than ever sounded on earth'. In the disordered mind whole compositions appeared to compose themselves.

* * *

After Dietrich left the house Schumann quietly collected a few effects and asked Clara to send for Dr. Böger in order that he might be taken into an asylum. He feared the night. 'It will not be for long,' he said. 'I shall soon come back, cured.'

Unlike the egomania of Nietzsche, the madness of Schumann flowed from an oversensitive nature which was capable of the most exquisite self-knowledge. There was mental instability in his family, and Schumann himself had experienced symptoms of mental disorder by the time he was twenty-three. After such knowledge he must have lived from one year to the next with the fear of insanity like a storm cloud over his head until the hammer blows of experience finally put him down. Suffering was the surest way to self-knowledge but suffering was not enough. One needed a nerve of steel to survive long enough to profit from it, for what was the use of suffering that snuffed out the sufferer? Who suffered more, Beethoven or Schumann? The answer, if suffering could be measured in a unit like ergs, might conceivably be Beethoven, yet he had the will and stamina to survive to compose the Choral Symphony, the Missa Solemnis, the Diabelli Variations and the last five string quartets while poor old Schumann had already succumbed to the stress of living by the time he was forty-four. There was no doubt in Roarty's mind which of the two had his most profound sympathy.

He remembered a spring day when he was eight, a day of fleecy clouds that made him think of open fields and fishing under weeping willows on the way home from school. A big, white ambulance was stopped in the village and mad Lanty Duggan was sitting in the back clutching a spray of bluebells to his chest, shaking his big, empty head until the sparse ringlets of grey hair swept his shoulders. Roarty and the other boys peered through the open door of the ambulance and listened to Lanty crooning the word 'Kruger' over and over again. He looked at them with dismay in his big, red eyes and flung the bluebells in their innocent faces. Then an old-timer called Dúlamán came up behind Roarty and said:

'Say good-bye to Lanty Duggan. You'll never see him again.'

'Why?' asked Roarty, not knowing what to make of Dúlamán.

'Because he's your uncle even though you may not want to know it.'

Lanty Duggan's ringlets shook like sleighbells and he neighed like a horse and grabbed Roarty by the elbow.

'Ask your good-for-nothing father if his fingers smell in the morning,' he hooted.

'Is Lanty Duggan my uncle?' he asked his mother when he arrived home.

'Who told you that?'

'Dúlamán.'

'Dúlamán should be saying his prayers.'

'Is Lanty Duggan your brother, Mammy?'

'He was my brother when we were growing up.'

'And why are they putting him in the asylum?'

'Because he's too sick to look after himself.'

'He told me to ask Daddy if his fingers smell in the morning.'

'He doesn't know the meaning of what he says. But don't mention it to your father; he might not like it.'

Roarty knew little of Lanty Duggan except what he had gleaned from overheard gossip and in later years from his mother, but he gathered that Lanty had been a black sheep from the beginning. When he was nineteen, he took a religious turn which manifested itself in an extreme distaste for women. He had never gone with a woman himself, and he was determined to make it impossible for any other Glenkeel man to go with one either. He would lie in wait for courting couples and belabour them with an ashplant or, having put the man to flight, he would tear off the girl's knickers before letting her off with a warning. In fairness it must be said that he was not a common fetishist because instead of storing his trophies to help while away a winter night he would climb the nearest telegraph pole and nail them to the crossbar as a reminder to passers-by that Lanty Duggan had been there.

His family were so horrified by his exploits that they paid his passage to Glasgow and promised to send him three pounds a week for as long as he stayed there. But the life of a remittance-man was not for Lanty. After two months he arrived back in the glen with a new-found knowledge of Scottish poetry and a crooked staff which, he claimed, once belonged to the Ettrick Shepherd. However, his detestation of women seemed to have abated. He began to lead the life of a quiet vagrant who knows every cranny and nook of his hinterland. In summer he lived in a tent which he carried on his back and pitched in a roadside field wherever night overtook him; and in winter he would take up residence in an empty byre or hayloft and emerge during the hours of light to warm himself over a fire of turf and brushwood under a rock or in some sheltered corner.

He saw himself as the last of the Fianna, leading the life of Oisin after all the comrades of his imagination had gone. It was a romantic image which was not borne out by the reality. He would spend the day begging for milk, eggs, fish, potatoes, turnips and cabbage as well as turf on which to cook them. In his way he was something of a gourmet. He would never eat baker's bread. He insisted on having soda bread and home-made butter, and not every housewife in the glen could make those very special commodities to his liking. It was little wonder then that he was made welcome in those houses where the housewife took his begging as a complimentary comment on her cooking. On these occasions he would say that there were two things in the world which not every woman could make—soda bread and butter—and that half the secret was to know how much soda to put in the former and how much salt in the latter. Though he was regarded as a half-wit, he was seen as a prince of beggars because he never accepted money. Drunken farmers in pubs on fair days would thrust pound notes under his nose but though he would accept as much stout and whiskey as he could hold he would never sully his hands with cash. For this reason many of the glen folk saw him as a saint, albeit a saint who neither washed nor shaved and who allowed his hair to grow in greasy ringlets round his shoulders. His saint-hood might have achieved formal recognition from the Church if the grand climacteric had not unbalanced him. In his sixty-third year all sense of shame, as the locals put it, deserted him. He would sit on the roadside with his flies undone, sunning his cock and scrotum and saying to passers-by that his was the only sun-tanned cock in Christendom. But worse was to come. He began taking an interest in little girls. He would wait for them as they came home from school and offer them butterscotch in return for what the schoolmaster called 'intimate personal services'. One afternoon the parish priest found him bouncing a nine-year old girl on the shaft of his erect penis, and that ended the exploits of Oisin. The parish priest had a word with the sergeant and the sergeant had a word with the doctor, and before Lanty Duggan knew where he was the ambulance had whisked him to the asylum. It was a sad end for a man who had meant no wrong, especially since the girl on whom he had tested the strength of his erection grew up to be a big, jolly, well-adjusted woman with a family of fourteen, the eldest of whom became a Jesuit and the second youngest a gauger.

Dúlamán was right. Lanty Duggan never left the asylum. He died in a straitjacket a year later, shouting his head off for beautiful women. Roarty had a vision of a smelly old man in the back of an ambulance clutching a bunch of bluebells, and suddenly he feared for himself. It seemed to him that far from being short life was longer than he cared to contemplate. Day after day reached into the distance like a dusty plain that must be traversed by the traveller unaided; and each day was a lifetime in itself, full of encounters and conversations that smothered the spirit in deadly fungus. If only he had not been blessed with a vivid memory. Though it afforded him the pleasure of learning by heart whole articles in *Britannica*, it was a curse in that it preserved old hurts and sores that were best forgotten. His consciousness was largely the product of his experience, and the force of his experience could only be attributed to his unusual memory. If only he had the power to control his memory, to suppress what he most wished to forget and to remember only those things that brought a warm glow. With his vivid memory went a vivid imagination which in normal times enriched his life but now forced him to seek meaning without end where none may have been intended. He could not hear a sentence from Potter without repeating it to himself like an actor, changing the inflexions and recasting it to see if by some linguistic alchemy it might expose the Englishman's dread secret. And he could no longer pass the time of day with McGing without sensing the brute single-mindedness of the hunter who is half in love with his quarry. If only he could anaesthetise himself against the force of these encounters; if only he could have one day of innocent self-forgetfulness without having to pour a bottle of whiskey down his neck to achieve oblivion by the evening.

He put Schumann's piano concerto on the gramophone and thought that he detected a foreshadowing of madness in the evanescent darkness of the first movement. But it was only a moment's intimation, shattered by flashes of heavenly light, and try as he might he could not discern the lack of mental robustness which he so eagerly sought.

At half-past two, when the moon had set, he crept downstairs, got a hold-all from the kitchen, and stuffed into it a small bag of blue till which he had taken from a quarry on the mountain a few weeks ago, a pair of thick woollen socks, a pair of gloves, a torch, a cold chisel, a club hammer and a box of cigarette butts, cigarette ash and charred matches from the waste paper basket in the bar. He then left by the back door and took the west road out of the village, ready to jump behind the ditch if the rays of headlamps should warn of an approaching car.

He lurked briefly under the trees by the parochial house gate, listening for an unusual noise, but all he heard was the fluttering of a roosting bird which he had disturbed and a groan from a spancelled donkey in the next field. He looked at the stars through the threadbare roof of branches above him, noting that the wind was due west and that clouds were gathering over the sea. With a tremor of antici-pation in his hands he opened the hold-all and put on the gloves and pulled the woollen socks over his shoes. Then keeping to the shadow of the trees, he sidled towards the house and nimbly crossed the lawn to the back.

With a tap of the hammer he broke a pane in the kitchen window and retreated quickly to the garden to listen. He waited for ten minutes, ready for the slightest stir on the road or in the house, but all was silence. He stole forward again and in a moment he had opened the window and climbed through. As a member of the parish council who had business with the Canon from time to time, he knew the house so well that he went straight to the little door under the stairs. Inside, the Canon kept his vintage claret and his guns which he was in the habit of showing to visitors of social consequence. He took out the two shotguns, put them standing against the wall in the hallway where Nora Hession would see them in the morning, and put two bottles of claret in his hold-all for his Sunday lunch. He then took out a leather leg-of-mutton bag which he knew contained a .22 Remington rifle belonging to Dr Loftus, the Canon's brother who came to Glenkeel to shoot from time to time. He opened the bag and pleasurably balanced the rifle on his hands in the dark. A fine weapon by the feel of it, and he knew it to be in beautiful condition. He gripped the small of the butt with his right hand and felt for the trigger with his trigger finger. Then pushing the safety catch over and bringing the rifle up, he took aim at the centre of the fanlight above the front door. He pulled the trigger and listened appreciatively to the decisive click of the striker pin. Very satisfying, provided the right man was at the other end of the barrel. It would have to be a heart shot because he did not believe in causing a fellow-sufferer unnecessary pain. A professional job, cold and unfeeling, sharp and sure as the death of the seal on Carraig a' Dúlamáin. He put the rifle back in its case and went into the sittingroom, scattering the blue till on the floor and trampling it into the carpet. He filled an ashtray with cigarette ash, cigarette butts and burnt matches and spilt some of the ash on the Canon's mahogany table. Finally he went to the sideboard and shone the torch on the bottles. His eye passed over the Bushmills and rested on an unopened bottle of Glenlivet. He poured out half a glass of the whiskey and, without tasting it, poured half of what was left down the kitchen sink, praying God to forgive the unforgivable waste. Then he put the bottle beside the glass on the table and placed a chair and a pouffe alongside. It would make a perplexing sight for McGing when he was called to investigate in the morning. He would take it as a personal affront that someone should have had the audacity to break into a house within half a mile of the barracks, steal a rifle, smoke nine or ten cigarettes, muddy the carpet, and drink half a bottle of the Canon's best Scotch before leaving. It was not the kind of thing that happened in the best policed parishes, Roarty thought with pleasure.

He could not help laughing as he climbed out of the window with the hold-all and the rifle. He walked down the fields to the river, crossed the Minister's Bridge, and walked along the north bank to a culvert he remembered from boyhood. He had little trouble finding it in the dark, and after pushing back the rushes at the mouth he crawled inside and hid the rifle in the uppermost and driest part. Coming out, he pulled the socks off his shoes and after filling them with stones flung them into the river.

It was a splendid exploit, and he felt the better for it. His head had cleared and the black anxiety that had been gnawing at him for weeks had gone without trace. Clearly he was a man of action who had chanced on unsuitable times. Instead of enjoying the camaraderie of the officers' mess or the campfire, he was living the life of an idle publican, condemned to mete and dole unequal pints unto a savage race.

When he reached home, he scraped the labels off the claret bottles with his penknife and slept soundly until morning.

FOURTEEN

Potter was reading a book about bogs which Margaret had sent him from Dublin. It was, he felt, typical of her childish sense of humour to find the idea of bogs amusing, and it was typical of her narrow, suburban soul to expect him to share her prejudices. Though she might be surprised to hear it, he had read the book with interest and in the knowledge that he was quickly losing his innocence. He now knew that the bogs on the west coast of Ireland, unlike those in the central plain, were classified as blanket bogs; and he could never walk over one of them again without remembering this and possibly comparing it with *Hochmoore, Niedermoore, Übergangsmoore* or even bogs of the ombrogenous or soligenous varieties. It was altogether typical of Margaret to complicate his life in this totally unnecessary way.

He put down the book and went to the north window of the kitchen. It was the last week of October and most of the garden trees were bare. Day after day over the past month he had watched them change colour, seemingly at random, to olive green here and light yellow or brown there. And he had watched the leaves falling in twos and threes, floating to the ground on the still air every five minutes or so. He would get up in the morning expecting to find that a wind in the night had blown them all to the ground but the nights remained calm and most of the leaves remained on the trees. Then at the week-end the weather turned cold, bringing a still, dry chill that pierced the walls of the house, and he woke on Sunday morning to find that most of the garden trees had shed their leaves, as if the cold of the night had nipped their attenuated stems.

A big thrush lit on a mountain ash whose red berries had gone except for an out-of-reach cluster at the tip of a drooping branch. Remembering summer mornings and birds breakfasting, he watched the fern-like leaves, some sickly yellow, some faded green, looking as if they belonged to different trees. His eye travelled to the weeping willow at the bottom of the garden, to the drooping branches waving to and fro like ribbons sweeping the black, sticky earth on which nothing grew. A single leaf fell from a sycamore and stuck in the wet clay beneath, a cheerless sight that made him sense the cold sting of the breeze in the top branches.

Day was fading from the sky. Ink-black clouds crowded over the north mountain while in a corner of the west a shaft of crimson light pierced a rack of cloud above the sea. It was beginning to rain, and with the rain a sadness descended on him which made him hum an adagio from an early Mozart symphony which Margaret was in the habit of playing on Sunday afternoons.

He had enjoyed the past two months. As he predicted, Nora Hession had flowered. In the space of a few weeks she had brightened into a laughing, happy girl who had only rare moments of doubt about the reality of what was happening to her. She came to the cottage to cook him meals on the open peat fire, simple meals with flavours as

179

fine as her own sense of humour. And she first came to his bed with a semblance of both reluctance and longing which reminded him of his adolescence and made him feel closer to her than he was. Later she was open and loving, meeting him as an equal partner with the power to jog him into moments of self-mockery and happy self-discovery. Altogether he never before had such a sense of freedom in a relationship. He took her to Matlock House for drinks, to the pictures in Donegal Town, to Garron for fish and chips, and for walks on the mountains and along the sea cliffs where she shared his field-glasses and soon came to recognise the rarer species in which he was interested. They talked about everything except their relationship, and this pleased Potter because he saw it as too fragile to stand the strain of self-conscious conversation.

When he was not at work or with Nora Hession, he was immersed in the affairs of the Anti-Limestone Society. He felt that he was devoting too much time to it but he knew that without his constant urging it would have died a natural death. The executive committee, provided it had enough to drink, would talk the hind leg off a donkey, but not one of the members, except possibly Cor Mogaill, knew the meaning of action. Roarty seemed willing enough at meetings but he was not a self-starter. He was preoccupied and absentminded and had to be nudged at every turn. Rory Rua was sensible and sharp-witted but too unwilling to offend the Canon. Gimp Gillespie was a man of words rather than deeds, and the words with which he described their meetings in the *Donegal Dispatch* read like a mischievous parody of the affairs of the Irish Countrywomen's Association. Only Cor Mogaill matched words with deeds. He and Potter made banners which they hung across the village street, and stickers which they distributed to every car owner in the glen. They visited every house in the parish, collecting signatures for a petition which they delivered to Canon Loftus with a copy for the bishop in Letterkenny. They organised a well-attended meeting in the local hall but in spite of their apparent success in getting the parishioners on their side the Canon sat tight. They had expected fulminations from the pulpit but he never said a word. They had expected at least a letter of acknowledgement from the episcopal palace but not a scrap did they receive. The silence, as Gimp Gillespie said, was as suspicious as it was deafening. Potter did not believe for a moment that Loftus would allow himself to be bested without a fight, and he felt that they must show at all costs that they had not run out of ideas. For this reason he prevailed on Roarty against the counsel of Rory Rua to call a public meeting next week to discuss the possibility of withholding financial support from the new church unless the Canon gave in. And he urged Gimp Gillespie to write a lively piece for the Dublin dailies because the bishop was said to be sensitive to adverse publicity. Gimp Gillespie, however, had his own ideas about his proper role. 'I'm a Donegal man writing for Donegal men,' he said, 'not for semiliterate Dublin jackeens, skittery asses who never saw a square meal'. Potter was angry. He saw in Gillespie's refusal to put himself out an all-too-frequent manifestation of the cussedness of the Irish character. He liked the Irish. He thought them distinctly more attractive at home than abroad—like their national drink they did not travel well. What he could not understand was their readiness to be taken in by conversation. They firmly believed that if you talked about something for long enough it would come to pass without the need to raise a hand or foot. As an attitude it might be excusable if the quality of the conversation was high, but he had come to the conclusion that the superiority of Irish conversation was a myth put about by reticent Englishmen. The Irish, he had come to recognise, are not great conversationalists in the sense that Dr Johnson was; they are great talkers who brogue away over pints of stout, constructing verbal castles in the air without as much as a thought for matter or meaning. If the essence of conversation is communication, then the Irish failed the test, dealing as they did in evasion and obfuscation. Irish conversation was like one of those Celtic designs in the Book of Kells made up of a simple form like a serpent that tied itself into a thousand ornamental knots before finally eating its own tail. He wasn't sufficiently narrow to wish to tell the Irish how to converse but he did think that he had shown a few of them how things are done. And now he would have another word with Gillespie, just to show him once for all the folly of his ways.

He drove to the village in the gathering dark with great raindrops splashing on the windscreen and drumming on the roof of his car. He was taking Nora Hession to Matlock House for a drink at eight, and the prospect of talking to her alone in the comfort of the hotel lounge by the big peat fire with the big tongs sent a thrill of pleasure up his spine and down his arms.

Gillespie's cottage was at the top end of the village. It was a low, pink-emulsioned, thatch-roofed house with great eaves that had deepened over two centuries. Potter parked his car in the road and went in without knocking as was the local custom. Gillespie was hunched over his desk with two long fingers poised over his antiquated typewriter and a pair of steel-rimmed spectacles on his nose that gave him the look of an owl in a nursery book.

On the shelf above him were the tools of his humble trade
—Brewer, Bartlett, Chambers and Fowler—and along the
walls were great stacks of dusty newspapers, old copies of
the *Donegal Dispatch* which he plagiarised unashamedly
when news was scarce.

'What are you writing?' Potter asked.

'Next week's notes for the *Dispatch*.'

'Don't you even wait for the news to happen?

'I know it already,' said Gillespie, handing him a typewritten sheet.

Potter sat at the table and read with the sense of utter
disbelief he always experienced when confronted with
Gillespie's prose:

> A gentle, kind and charitable member of the Balti-
> more community has passed to her eternal reward in
> the person of Miss Caitlin Cunningham. News of
> her death cast a shadow of gloom over Glenkeel last
> week though the deceased had not returned to her
> native Tork since emigrating to America towards the
> close of the last century. She had just celebrated her
> ninety-sixth birthday and was for many years head
> cook to General Eisenhower before he became Presi-
> dent.

> The potato crop in mountainy townlands is the best
> in living memory. The moist, boggy land coupled
> with the long, hot summer and no blight accounts,
> farmers are agreed, for the prolific crop. In particular
> it has been a vintage year for Aran banners.

> Glenkeel shopkeepers are reporting an early demand
> for Christmas cards this year with stronger emphasis
> than usual on religious themes. This early demand is

regarded as highly significant. One surprised shop-keeper told your correspondent that people are either disregarding rising prices and high postage or have decided that their decision not to send cards last year was too Scrooge-like to be worthy of a people who walk in the footsteps of Saint Patrick.

'But there isn't a word of truth in what you've written!' said Potter. 'There is no gloom over Glenkeel. There are no queues for Christmas cards. Dammit, man, it's only October. And I heard a farmer from the mountain complaining the other day about the smallness of the potatoes this year. He didn't even call them potatoes. He called them ...'

'Scideens.'

'Then why have you written this pack of lies when you could have tossed off a column of the truth about the business of the Anti-Limestone Society? Or are these seemingly idiotic notes an allegory for something else? All I can say is that when you sit down to a typewriter you lose all touch with reality.'

'You fail to realise that there is a received style for the "Donegal Notes and News". When someone dies, a shadow of gloom invariably falls over the area. A dead man is always described as being of sterling character and from a highly esteemed family, and a dead woman as gentle, kind and charitable. If ever these time-honoured epithets were omitted, the relatives of the deceased would want to know why. I've heard of a correspondent from Garron who got two black eyes for mis-spelling the word "sterling".'

'I'm not complaining about the style. I'm complaining about the subject. Why not write what everyone is talking about in the pubs: bestiality in Ballyhoolahaun; the meeting to stop paying in church collections; the theft of the Canon's rifle and claret? If you were on a Fleet Street paper, you'd be sacked on the spot. They wouldn't even have you on *The Times*.'

'I write what people expect to read. And they don't expect to read about bestiality in Ballyhoolahaun.'

'This is an unselfconscious society. If it has a voice, it is you. Your notes are the only reflection of themselves that people see from one week to the next. They don't read books and they don't watch television. All they read is your notes, and this is what you give them!'

'You don't understand, Potter. They read my notes simply because they know what they will find in them. They don't seek the new or the sensational; they seek reassurance in repetition. They don't want to read about the Anti-Limestone Society; they want to read about foxes killing lambs in spring, shoals of mackerel off the coast in summer, bumper crops in the autumn, and impassable roads in winter. My notes are not meant to represent the reality of this society. If you wish to know how this society represents its existence to itself, don't read my notes but go down to Roarty's and listen to the conversation in the bar. It's the nearest thing to art that this society creates.'

'No, Gillespie. You go down to Roarty's and listen to the conversation in the bar. Then come back and write your notes.'

'Have a drink, Potter. You are taking all this far too seriously.'

'I don't want a drink, thank you. I came to ask again if you are going to write a few wise words for the Dublin dailies about the Anti-Limestone Society. I've taken some pictures of the church and the banners and I'll let you have them.'

Gillespie went to the dresser and came back with two bumpers of whiskey.

'I'm sorry it isn't Scotch. All I have is Irish.'

'You had better give me plenty of water. Neat Irish gives me the most vicious heartburn.'

Gillespie vanished into the kitchen and returned with an enormous jug of water which he placed on the table beside Potter.

'I'm still waiting for your answer,' said Potter.

'Why the hurry? Can't you sit back and stretch your legs, have your drink and let your mind hover over pleasantries.'

'If you don't do it, I will.'

'Well, what's stopping you?'

'Can I borrow your typewriter?'

'Yes, provided you return it in time for next week's notes.'

'I'll do that.'

'Potter, you are a changed man. When you came here first, I thought you had a sense of humour, but this Anti-Limestone business has taken you over lock, stock and barrel.'

'Talking of lock, stock and barrel, you should do an exposé of McGing. The man is mad. He practically accused me the other day of stealing the Canon's rifle and claret.'

'As Roarty says, the law as personified in McGing is not merely an ass but an egregious ass. But why did he pick on you?'

'He said that the burglar obviously had a knowledge of the parochial house which I could have had from Nora, that he left what he called "blue till" on the carpet and that there is a quarry of the stuff near where we're prospecting. He also said that the burglar drank half a bottle of Glenlivet and left a full bottle of Bushmills untouched, something apparently that no self-respecting Irishman would do.'

'And what did you say?'

'I said that I was not in the habit of carrying "blue till" on my shoes, that I have a perfectly good Winchester of my own, that I have two cases of better claret than the Canon's, and that Glenmorangie not Glenlivet is my drink. I think he took the point.'

'McGing reads too many crime stories. Believe it or not, I once heard him say quite seriously: "My methods are based on the observation of trifles".'

'And what are you going to do about it?'

'Me?'

'Are you going to expose him in the local press for a dangerous lunatic or are you going to write about potatoes?'

'You want me to write about the flower of a single summer. I want to write about the rhizome that's hidden in the soil but puts forth again.'

'Gillespie, you are impossible,' said Potter, rising to go.

'Where's your hurry? Stay until the bottle's empty and we've fulfilled ourselves in philosophical conversation.'

'I must go, I'm afraid. I'm taking Nora Hession to Matlock House.'

'As a bachelor, what can I say? The way of an eagle in the air; the way of a serpent upon a rock; the way of a ship in the midst of the sea; and the way of a man with a maid. They are four things which I know not,' Gillespie laughed.

'Come up to my place for a drink tomorrow evening.

I've got a full bottle of Scotch and I'll get some Guinness to help out.'

'And we'll continue our discussion of the flower and the rhizome.'

Potter drove down the village street and parked outside Roarty's. He wanted to have a word with Roarty about the meeting and he thought that a large Glenmorangie might help to cool his throat after the fire of the Irish whiskey.

'I've got news for you,' said Roarty. 'The Canon has asked all of us on the executive committee to come to the parochial house for a meeting on Friday at eight. He has bitten at last, the devil.'

'I wonder what's on his mind,' said Potter.

'You can be sure it's nothing wholesome,' said Roarty.

Potter drank his whisky with lingering appreciation and discussed with Crubog whether snipe should be drawn before roasting. As he was about to go, Roarty, who was collecting glasses, caught his arm.

'I heard you on about snipe. Are you game for a snipe shoot the morning after the next full moon? If the night before is clear and calm, they will be sitting close, just right for a shot.'

'There's nothing I'd like better,' said Potter, determined to get the bigger bag.

FIFTEEN

An evening without whiskey was a trial to Roarty, and for that reason he usually avoided places without a ready supply of what Potter called the 'amber elixir'. Needless to say, he was not looking forward to an evening of near-abstinence in Canon Loftus's parlour. He was confident that the Canon would be sufficiently politic to offer them a drink, but it would be 'a drink', not drinks, not enough to wet a drinking man's gullet. As it was now seven, he had only an hour to introduce sufficient alcohol into the blood-stream to ensure a glow of comfort for a further two hours. He had now poured his sixth double of the evening and he was still on edge; he still felt that contraction of the muscles or the nerves or something that left him with a pervasive sense of discomfort. He could relax neither standing nor sitting, and everyone who entered the bar impinged on him with painful immediacy. Even Susan was getting on his nerves. Ever since the night he put his hand up her skirt she did nothing but angle for more. She would brush slowly against him in doorways and stand too close to him in the bar when there was no one around. She would allow her breast to brush his shoulder as she took his empty plate away at dinnertime, and she would linger in the bathroom whenever she brought his hot toddy in the mornings. Her ever-impending availability and his own inability to enjoy her without humiliation irritated him so much that on more than one occasion he almost told her to 'bugger off' back to the mountain. He probably would have done so if he were not so preoccupied that she had ceased to have meaning for him. More and more he was conscious of living in a world of innominate fears, fears which usually showed their true colours only in sleep but which were starkly brought home to him that very morning. He was standing outside the pub, looking idly at the butcher's van coming up by the Minister's Bridge, when suddenly he felt an apprehending hand on his shoulder. He looked round and there was Flanagan, the lightkeeper, coming down the street in full uniform. He must have seen him out of the tail of his eye, and because of the uniform had associated him with the law. The incident was an eye-opener, showing him the eroding sense of insecurity with which he had been living for the past two months, a feeling which the latest letter from Potter did nothing to mitigate. It read:

> Dearest Roarty: Knowing why you stole the Canon's Remington puts me one move ahead. I've left a sealed envelope with my solicitor which is to be handed to the police if anything unnatural should happen to me. Nuff said? Bogmailer.

Though he had read the note five or six times, he was not impressed. It was a clumsy attempt at bluff, clumsy because dead men do not tell tales. Potter could set down in black and white that he had witnessed the murder, he could give the location of the body and the name of the murderer, but he could not ensure conviction. Admittedly, there would be suspicions and questions but with luck he could survive them. And since he was paying the blackmail in cash, not by cheque, there was nothing to connect him with the blackmailer. Though Potter might feel secure, he would get a rude awakening, if 'awakening' was the word for something that was more akin to a sleeping draught. But though the solution seemed to be within his grasp, Roarty's mind refused to rest.

He was glad of one thing, however. The burglary of the parochial house was keeping McGing fully occupied. He had practically forgotten about the murder; he talked of nothing but the stolen rifle.

'If only I were given the tools of the trade, I could solve this crime in a day,' he told Roarty over his morning black-and-tan. 'There are ways and means,' he nodded knowingly. 'The thief, careful though he was, left a trail of electrostatic footprints on the carpet. All I need do is sprinkle polystyrene beads on the floor. They will stick because of the electrical charge left by the feet, and the magnetised beads will show the size and shape of his shoes. And then there are the cigarette butts and ash. I sent them off for analysis but so far I've had no co-operation. No one wants to know about a stolen rifle. Only murder makes them sit up and scratch their heads.'

'What about finger-prints?' asked Roarty.

'There weren't any. I dusted every inch of the room but the only finger-prints belonged to the Canon and Nora Hession. We're dealing with a cunning intelligence, as I say, a veritable Moriarty. He probably had the foresight to wear gloves.'

'If you could catch him, your name would be made,' said Roarty.

'I'm convinced that if I catch him I'll also have the murderer. Oh, he's a cool one, drinking half a bottle of malt Scotch and smoking nine cigarettes before leaving the scene of the crime. My policeman's instinct tells me that there's worse to come. But what worries me is the amount of time I'm devoting to him.'

'Why is that?'

'I was reading an American book on criminology the other day and it said that detectives spend less time on the cases they solve than on those they don't.'

'You mean that the more time you spend on a case the less chance you have of solving it?'

'I mean that a case that is capable of solution will be solved quickly.'

'In other words only easy cases are solved.'

'But what constitutes an easy case?' asked McGing, lingering over his black-and-tan, enjoying the interest of his interlocutor.

'An easy case is one where the identity of the criminal is obvious.'

'But an easy case for one policeman might stump another. Horses for courses is the secret ... policemen for criminals. A criminal will go scot free for years until he happens to meet the right—or for him the wrong—policeman.' McGing looked at Roarty as if he had said too much.

'What do you mean?'

'A policeman with the right affinity, a man who can see into the dark convolutions of his mind, who can anticipate his next move. The great Sherlock Holmes solved his cases by logical deduction but I have a theory that he was short on intuition. In the perfect detective, what criminologists call the cognitive and the intuitive are perfectly balanced. One nourishes the other, and a man who is deficient in one is therefore deficient in the other.

I hope I'm not being immodest but I think I've got more intuition than Holmes.'

'You'd need it in this parish,' said Roarty.

'That's why I'm discussing this with you. You've just given me a new line of enquiry.'

'What is that?'

'I mustn't tell you,' said McGing, straightening his cap and leaving with a wave of the hand.

At five minutes to eight Roarty and Potter left the pub for the parochial house. The Canon himself in sombre canonicals opened the door and ushered them into the parlour where Cor Mogaill, Rory Rua and Gimp Gillespie were seated on a sofa with small glasses in their hands. The Canon, tall, craggy and red-faced, with a noticeable economy of phrase and gesture, offered them a seat and a choice of beer or whiskey. They made small talk about the weather while he poured them a drink but he showed his seriousness by saying nothing. He sat in the armchair by the big peat fire and stretched his legs so that his white woollen socks showed beneath the turn-ups of his black trousers, and then he put the fingers of both hands together as if he were about to deliver himself of a prayer. Silence fell on the company as the slow-thinking Canon stared at his thick fingers, not the silence of embarrassment but the silence of expectation which came from the rarity of the experience.

'Will you open the proceedings, Canon, or shall I?' enquired Potter, so impatient that he broke the Canon's spell in smithereens.

The Canon stared at him and then at the others before clearing his throat as he would in the pulpit before a sermon. Roarty sipped his whiskey and wished he had taken his hipflask. After all it might be possible later to nip out to the lavatory for fortification as opposed to evacuation.

'You know why we are nere,' said the Canon, tne commonplace sentence coming as a disappointment after the prolonged silence.

'I didn't ask you to come to preach to you. I asked you here to share with you some of my thoughts on the new church so that as reasonable men in God we might part in agreement. When I first came here six years ago, I saw that the old church, which had served since the beginning of the last century, was in need of replacement or repair. The roof was leaking, the seats were worm-eaten, the floor was holed, and the rotting windows were letting in the rain. I thought and thought, whether to renovate or rebuild because I knew that either way the burden of the cost would be heavy. But one evening as I was walking by the sea I looked into the west, into the clouds above the sunset, and I saw a modern church, a simple structure, a cone on a cube, and I knew that I had my answer. I won't say that it came from heaven but I will say that it came from a lifetime's thought and experience. Of course I knew that there would be difficulties. I knew that there would be those who would be horrified by the sight of a church without a steeple as there were those who vilified Pope Julius II for introducing Michelangelo's *terribilità* into the Sistine Chapel. But I went ahead after due consultation with the parish council and employed one of the best church architects in Ireland. I told him three things the first day he came to see me. "I want a simple church," I said. "I want an austere church, and a church that won't cost more than my parishioners can afford." You all know the result because all of you except Mr Potter have had a hand in building it. You have now got a simple church built from simple materials, a church which conveys something of the austerity of the lives of our saintliest coenobites. This did not happen by accident. It happened because I've had a life-long belief that a church should be a place of spiritual rather than physical comfort. Too familiar surroundings dull the senses, lull us, if we are not careful, into deepest sleep. Your new church was designed to keep you awake, to augment your awareness of yourself and of God by placing you among the unaccustomed. I know that I have my critics. The secretary of the Women's Sodality, a devout and prayerful woman, said to me only yesterday that she could not understand why I put large windows in the west aisle reaching to the floor and overlooking the graveyard. "When you look across from the east aisle," she said, "you'd think the tombstones had invaded the church." But this is precisely the effect I wished to create. As you kneel on Sunday to worship your Creator, I want you to feel the imminence of your end as a physical sensation, as real as the wood of the seat underneath your elbows. I did not want you merely to remember death but to fear death, to realise the force of *Timor et tremor* and of William Dunbar's best-known poem:

> Our pleasance here is all vane glory,
> This fals warld is bot transitory,
> The flesche is bruckle, the Fend is sle:
> *Timor mortis conturbat me.*

I need not explain because the English of Dunbar, thanks to the Ulster Plantation, is near enough the dialect you all speak—all except Mr Potter. But to continue. The cut limestone altar is a necessary part of my plan. It is an altar of stern austerity in keeping with the bare brown brickwork of the screen and the bare concrete blocks of the inside walls. The old wooden altar, fine though it must have been in its day, is too elaborate, too baroque, and above all too familiar to find a place in our new church. It was beautifully carved but it is now worm-eaten beyond repair. It is so bad that the dust from the holes falls into the wine in the chalice when I uncover it during Mass.'

There was a moment's silence during which Roarty sipped his whiskey and Potter looked round to see who was going to step into the breach.

'You have made an eloquent case for your new church and altar, Canon,' he said, realising that the task had fallen to himself. 'I accept that your motives have been the purest, but I don't think your arguments meet the fears and doubts that drove your parishioners to found the Anti-Limestone Society.'

'A handful of my parishioners.'

'Like me you are a stranger here, not through your own fault but because priests are birds of passage wherever they go, at the beck and call of a bishop with other ideas. They may be well-meaning but they do not have to live a life time with their mistakes. That is the lot of the parishioners they leave behind when they are moved to the next parish But it isn't for me to tell you these things. Those who have been born in the glen and spent their lives here are better qualified to remind you of what the altar means to them. And I think Tim Roarty can do that better than any of us.'

Roarty had been watching with fascination how the Canon's face turned a deep crimson as Potter spoke. The blood rose into his cheeks and spread down through his jowls and neck to disappear beneath the tight, white collar. It was the face of a man who resented being spoken to, and who saw in Potter an injurious threat to his pastoral autarchy.

'The wooden altar,' said Roarty, 'is not a priceless treasure like the Cross of Muiredach or the Chalice of Ardagh, but it is a piece of local history, carved by local craftsmen whose great grandchildren are still coming to Mass on Sunday. It has seen four generations of glen men, their baptisms and marriages and finally their funerals. It has become part of our common experience, and the carved saints that stand on each side holding a canopy over the tabernacle are not in the Church calendar. They are local saints, unheard of outside this parish, and now they are to be replaced with a nondescript "table-top" altar of the kind you see in every nondescript town in Ireland. We are being robbed of part of our local heritage, of one of the things that make local folk memory potent and make Glenkeel different from Glenroe, Garron or Donegal Town.'

'It isn't I who decided in favour of a table-top altar,' said the Canon. 'It's a feature of the new liturgy. The general instruction of the Roman Missal, 1970, says that the main altar should be free-standing so that ministers can easily walk round it.'

'The new liturgy is ill-conceived,' said Potter. 'It is the creation of men who are so lacking in a sense of history that they must tinker rather than leave well alone. Your argument that familiarity leads to sleep may well be valid—'

'It is certainly valid in marriage,' laughed Roarty.

'—but there are times when satisfied sleep is preferable to disgruntled wakefulness. What all these liturgical changes are achieving, and what your new church has achieved, is to wake people from the sleep of centuries. They are weakening tradition and the habits that make tradition possible. You want us in the new church to sit up and take notice, but the awareness you mention will foster the spirit of criticism, and not merely self-criticism. Now, that in my view is a fine thing, but I doubt very much if it is the outcome that you as an Irish parish priest most desire.'

'If you weren't English, I'd say you were taught by Jesuits,' said the Canon.

'As a matter of fact I was, though I fail to see its relevance.'

'I'm merely saying, Mr Potter, that your subtlety is lost on me.'

'We've rehearsed these arguments among ourselves a score of times,' said Cor Mogaill, 'and we're all convinced that the old altar must stay. We were serious the night we founded the the Anti-Limestone Society and nothing has changed since then. As Roarty says, the altar is a chunk of local history which only a Glenkeel man can appreciate. But perhaps it is not too much to expect a man of the cloth to realise that the Last Supper and the first Mass was celebrated at a wooden table.'

'We can discuss our differences without showing disrespect for the cloth. There is no need to insult the Canon,' said Rory Rua.

'The Canon can look after himself,' said Loftus severely. 'The observation that the Last Supper was eaten off a wooden table might have come more appropriately from a man who attended Mass and received the Sacraments more regularly than you, Cor Mogaill.'

'HOOA! HOOA! HOOA! said Cor Mogaill with upraised fist.

'I didn't invite you here for an unseemly quarrel,' said the Canon, 'but to put to you what I shall describe as a modest proposal. For some time I have been observing with interest the operations of Mr Potter's firm Pluto Explorations Limited. To explain my meaning I shall recount a piece of local history, which most of you in your enthusiasm for the Anti-Limestone Society may have forgotten. Since the seventeenth century the mineral rights and the surface rights of the south mountain have been held by the Church of Ireland, which for Mr Potter's benefit can be translated as the Tory Party at prayer in Ireland. And Mr Potter is of course sufficiently literate to know that the word "Tory" is Irish in origin.'

Roarty observed a twinkle of enjoyment in the Canon's eye which he construed as nothing less than a twinkle of mischief. He had rested his taurine head against the back of the chair and folded his arms over his capacious stomach, and he was clearly surveying the company with the detachment of a man who knows that the tenor of the conversation is his to manipulate. Roarty leaned forward to catch every word and he noticed that Rory Rua and Gimp Gillespie were doing likewise. The Canon cleared his throat and continued:

'For hundreds of years local farmers paid a rent to the Church of Ireland for grazing rights on the mountain but for a reason I have been unable to divine the rent was discontinued in 1926. I do not know how the first title to the mountain originated but I have it on sound legal authority that you local farmers have acquired at least what may be called "squatters' rights" to the grazing in the fifty years that have elapsed since 1926. The more complex question, and therefore the more costly to determine, is whether you have also acquired other rights in the mountain. Now, Mr Potter's firm has secured a five-year option on the disused mine from the Church of Ireland with the right to take up a 25-year lease on the mountain at £5,000 and a modest royalty if mining of barytes should restart. There is no doubt about the party which has the best deal: it is Mr Potter's firm. And there is no doubt about the party with the worst deal: it is you local farmers whose rights have not been consulted.'

'All this is a fictive confection, the like of which I had not expected to hear even from an Irish shanachie,' said Potter with a laugh of incredulity. But the other members of the Anti-Limestone Society were not listening to him; they were listening to the Canon.

'It may seem far-fetched now, but will it seem so in ten years? Ireland is a major supplier of barytes—the Silvermines deposit in Tipperary exports over £2½ million worth a year. Now, I have been making enquiries in Dublin, and I have learnt that the south mountain deposit could contain as much as 700,000 tons. At £25 a ton for the untreated rock the total deposit could be valued at £17½ million, most of which will line the coffers of Mr Potter's American firm. The Americans will pay a pittance to the Church of Ireland, which is no better at business than theology, and they will ship out the unmilled rock, leaving this country with the minimum economic advantage and the farmers whose rights they have usurped without a brass farthing.'

'This is a figment of your extravagant imagination, Canon,' said Potter. 'I don't know whom you talked to in Dublin but I suspect he was a romancer, possibly a journalist with a story no editor would print. No one denies that there is barytes in the south mountain, but is it workable? In the samples that have so far been analysed the percentage is too small to allow economic mining. The current feeling at head office is that there's nothing in it. I have been told that if the last batch of samples we sent to Dublin are no better than the others the team will be recalled before the end of the year.'

'It is in Pluto's interest to conceal the size of the deposit and stress the operational difficulties. That's how most successful businessmen get their way: by saying one thing and doing another. But Pluto hasn't reckoned with a certain Canon of the Diocese of Raphoe. I propose to organise the local farmers into a vociferous and single-minded group that will first of all find out what their rights are and then demand that they be acknowledged. As it happens, all of you here this evening, except Mr Potter, have grazing rights on the south mountain and there are many others like you in the village and in neighbouring townlands. Quite simply the time has come to disband the Anti-Limestone Society and raise the flag of the Anti-Exploitation Society.'

'We are sufficiently ambidextrous to manage both,' said Cor Mogaill.

'No, because if you want me to preside over the Anti-Exploitation Society, you will have to bury the other. I'm not being immodest when I say that I have friends in high places (I refer to this world, not the next), and friends in the legal profession on whose service we shall have to call. You all know me well enough to know that I'm not a loser, and in this venture he who is not with me is against me. Are you with me, Roarty?'

Roarty studied the challenging thrust of the Canon's chin. He was a blunt man with none of Potter's polish, but he had found the answer to the Anti-Limestone Society. There was gold in the south mountain, and some of it might help to pay the blackmail.

'Well, Roarty?' asked the Canon.

'I'm with you, Canon,' said Roarty, not daring to look at Potter

'Rory Rua.

'You can count on me, Canon.'

'Gillespie?'

'I have my regrets but I'm still witn you.'

'Cor Mogaill?'

'Go to now, ye rich men, weep and howl for your miseries that shall come upon you. Your riches are corrupted, and your garments are motheaten. Your barytes is cankered; and the rust of it shall be a witness against you, and shall eat your flesh as it were fire.'

'A Marxist can misquote Scripture for his purpose. And talking of Scripture, it may interest you to know that James in the same chapter says: "Behold the hire of the labourers who have reaped down your fields, which is of you kept back by fraud, crieth; and the cries of them which have reaped are entered into the ears of the Lord of sabaoth". 'Here, my dear Cor Mogaill, we are on the side of the angels.'

'You surprise me, Canon,' said Cor Mogaill. 'Or should I call you Machiavelli?'

'There is nothing devious in my methods. On the contrary I have been perfectly frank. I have said that if you want my assistance, you must give up the anti-limestone business. And most of you have agreed because you know that I stop at nothing. You will get a share of Pluto's profits, and a tithe of your share will, I hope, find its way into the collection plate on Sunday. In short, this is one of the rare and satisfying occasions when it is possible to serve God and Mammon.'

Cor Mogaill gave a high-pitched squeak of a laugh and delved madly into his rucksack. He pulled out a bundle of tattered newspapers and held one of them up before the company.

'All I will say is this,' he roared, finding his place.

' "Let us always be truly poor," he read. "If we have nothing, no one can take it from us. If we are attached to nothing, nothing can defeat us. If we own nothing, nothing can own us. Only an absolutely poor man is absolutely free." '

'A fine Marxist you are!' the Canon jeered.

'I'm a Marxist with a difference. I don't seek a redistribution of wealth but a redistribution of suffering. And you know who is the distributor of that!'

'A Marxist would surely say that if you redistribute one you redistribute the other,' the Canon laughed.

'I expected you to jeer. Time was when pastors realised that truth was to be found in the cut and thrust of *odium theologicum*, not in the papering of cracks but in bitter antinomies.'

'To be bitter, antinomies must have equal force,' said the Canon. 'But, my dear Potter, you are curiously silent.'

'I am flabbergasted at the speed with which my friends turned Turk. Only the other evening they were quoting the penny catechism and papal bulls in support of their anti-limestone ideals.'

'The vagaries of the human mind and heart are what makes human life so unforgettable. It is the best argument for the immortality of the soul that I know,' said the Canon expansively. 'But now we have business to do, business which may embarrass Mr Potter. As a servant of Pluto you can hardly be expected to participate in a plot to deprive them of their profits. We shall, therefore, understand if you should wish to withdraw.'

'I have no desire to stay,' said Potter with a scornful

glance at the shamefaced ex-officers of the Anti-Limestone Society.

'And neither have I,' said Cor Mogaill, joining him.

Roarty watched the Canon as he showed them both to the door, and he wondered what on earth he would say to Potter the following evening. The Canon came back rubbing his hands.

'Now, we can put our heads together,' he said, pouring another drink, much to the surprise of Roarty.

SIXTEEN

Potter was sitting by the window of the cottage with an oil can and a wad of tow on the chair beside him. He had been shooting that morning and now he was cleaning his shotgun. It was almost three o'clock, about forty-five minutes before sunset, and the November light was quickly fading. The sun was hidden somewhere in the west but it had permeated with brilliant evening colours the feathery clouds that hung like still curtains in the high heavens. Below them were long streaks of blue-black cloud racing wildly into the east in dark contrast with the quiet, heavenly light in the upper reaches of the sky. Were those bright yellowy clouds really becalmed? Imagining a picture by Tiepolo, he closed one eye and looked at them through the branches of the mountain ash. They were moving eastwards very slowly, almost imperceptibly, and he wondered what a meteorologist would make of the different speeds of the wind. Would he say that beyond a doubt there was a change in the weather?

Ever since the beginning of November it had been hard and dry. Now for the first time in three weeks the sky looked like rain. He had enjoyed November because he had never before realised the beauty of the countryside in early winter. As the sunrise was late, he saw it every morning; and one morning in particular he would never forget. The sun climbed slowly over the mountains in the east, a great orange ball which seemed bigger than any sun he could remember, and as it rose into the frost-clear sky it lost its brilliant orange until by eight o'clock it had turned to gold, colouring the barks of the garden trees as if it were a summer evening.

Frosty mornings made him shiver, partly at the ghostly beauty of the countryside and the scores of objects which seemed to take on the quality of rudimentary ornamentation: fallen leaves in the laneway with their veins and serrated edges picked out in grey, twigs that looked as if they had been furred by an unseen hand in the night, the worn gate post with hoar frost like grey fungus on its top, and the bare black trees with thrushes like birds of ill-omen in their branches.

He had got up early that morning to go bird-watching on the Ross Mór. The sun was hidden in cloud and the grey rime was everywhere: on the tiled roofs of houses, on the zinc roofs of byres and barns, on the coping stones of walls, on hard cabbage heads in the gardens, and on the paving stones in the laneway from the house. He noticed, however, that it had not fallen on the black earth beneath the weeping willow. After breakfast he went into the garden. The sun had emerged from cloud and most of the hoar frost had melted. The upper side of the branches of the apple tree where the frost had lain were black and shiny, and clear droplets hung like pearls from the under-sides, dripping luminously as the sun rose higher. It seemed to him for a moment that this melting and dripping would never end. And he realised quickly that his time here was almost over, that he was living out the final weeks of his sojourn. The realisation came to him as a shock, as if he had discovered rather late in life that he was mortal.

He had been lucky on the Ross Mór. He saw a male merlin flying down a meadow pipit, and later a hen harrier which according to his book was rarely seen in Donegal. He took out his diary, opened it at Saturday, 27 November, and made a note:

> Ross Mór 10.0–12.0 am—One male merlin decapitated a meadow pipit. One hen harrier flying uncharacteristically high.

He got up and looked out of the open window. Rory Rua's donkey was rolling in the road, his hind legs reaching heavenwards, his forelegs bent. After he had got to his feet he was joined by another donkey that began to scratch his neck in playful camaraderie which soon took on the guise of unhurried sexuality. He watched them with voyeuristic contentment, two homosexual jackasses unselfconsciously sniffing each other's groins, their two black pintles lengthening like hanging concertinas. Rory Rua's dog came up the road with a bone. Carefully he scooped out a shallow grave in the next field, covered the bone, and examined his footwork with a sniff before putting the donkeys off their stroke with a furious fit of barking. As he watched them, Potter smiled and thought that he might easily have been among the motley press of Soho. All human life, or at least its less sophisticated equivalent, was here.

He was about to turn away when he noticed a movement by the garden wall, a grey rat with an ugly tail vanishing into the darkness of a hole. He took two cartridges from his pocket, loaded the gun, cocked the safety catch, and rested the barrels on the open window. He remembered a bright Saturday morning in October when Rory Rua was threshing, and how he had stood back from the corn stack with his 12-bore and blasted each rat up the arse as it fled. It was an expensive method of extermination but it pleased Rory Rua and provided a morning's sport when he had nothing better to do. The rat sniffed the entrance of the hole with its pointed nose, looked to and fro, and made for a half-eaten potato by an upturned creel. Almost without a movement Potter pulled the trigger and plastered its head against the stone wall. Unnecessarily he held the gun for a moment with the heel of the stock firmly against his shoulder but the rat did not move. He took the tongs from beside the fire, lifted the flabby body, and flung it over the garden wall. Then he returned to the house and sat down to clean his gun once more.

He would not go to Roarty's tonight, he decided. He would stay at home, read a book, and broach the bottle of Glenmorangie which he kept in the dresser for such evenings. He had not been going to Roarty's as regularly as before. Ever since the meeting with Loftus he had felt that neither Roarty nor Gillespie were the upright men he had imagined. He should not have been surprised by the discovery because the Irish, in spite of a handful of anticlerical writers, were by nature priest-servers. In their porter they might make fun of their clergy behind their backs, but confronted by a cassock and cotta they tugged the forelock and said 'Yes, father' with an alacrity which had as much to do with superstition as religion. And that was not merely a survival of attitudes from penal times when the priest was thought to bear the future of the race with the housel in his pyx. As far as he could discover, there were no satirical portraits of randy friars or worldly pardoners in classical Irish literature. There was no fourteenth century Irish Chaucer, no Irish Wycliffe, only the earlier excesses of unworldly monasticism. But the undertow of racial inclination did not excuse Roarty, Gimp Gillespie and Rory Rua. All three were men of unusual intelligence. They knew what they were doing, and they did it not merely to please the Canon but in the vain hope of lining their greasy pockets. In a way he was pleased by what had happened. He had been too sympathetic, over-eager to absorb what he had seen as the genius of the country. Now he was more detached, less ready to applaud because of a picturesque phrase in a pub; and he felt that his new-found ambivalence was an emotional and perhaps an intellectual enrichment.

He put away the cleaning rod, oil and tow, and placed the gun on its rest above the kitchen door. He switched on the light, closed the door against the descending night, and poured himself a long enough drink to keep him sitting for an hour. As soon as the light came on and he had drawn the window blinds, the intimate comforts of the small cottage leaped to the eye. It was a genuine peasant cottage, two hundred years old, with a low thatch roof, flagged floor, limed walls, a curtained kitchen bed in an outshot, a garret above the kitchen and a loft above the lower bedroom, the very antithesis of the modern cottages which were being slapped up for tourists by profit-hungry contractors who put asbestos sheeting under the thatch and introduced such anachronisms as tiled floors, ceilings, central heating and piped water. Potter's cottage had brown scraws and smoke-blackened rafters under the thatch, an open fireplace with a sooty crane, a half-garret of barnacle-eaten beams which spanned the width of the house and supported an old wooden tester and which obviously had been cast ashore, flotsam from a wreck in the days of sail.

What he liked most about the cottage was the open fire. There was a gas cooker at the other end of the kitchen but he never used it except to make a quick cup of tea in the morning. He preferred to cook over the peat fire because of the subtle flavour it gave the food, a tang which he liked best in lamb stew made from mountain 'mutton'.

He took down one of Gimp Gillespie's books from a shelf, an account of Ireland during the Famine by an English philanthropist: *Narrative of a Recent Journey of Six Weeks in Ireland in Connexion with the Subject of Supplying Small Seed to Some of the Remoter Districts: with Current Observations on the Depressed Circumstances of the People, and the Means Presented for the Permanent Improvement of their Social Condition*. He sat down by the fire, stretched his legs and began the first chapter, vaguely wondering if he could interest a London publisher in a similar composition. On the third chapter he looked up, wondering if a mouse had stirred in the wall. He heard the noise again, a soft tap like that of a forefinger on a hand drum followed a second later by a metallic ping. He took out his watch and looked at the second hand to find that the pings were occurring at four-second intervals. It must be rain, he thought, though he could not hear anything between the taps and the pings. He opened the door, surprised to see how heavily it was coming down. The night was full of the sound of falling and running waters dripping from the eaves, whispering in the trees, gurgling in the runnel by the lower gable. Try as he might, he could not identify the source of the tapping, but the ping was coming from the water running off the edge of the stone outshot onto the side of an overturned bucket by the door. He returned to the fire full of an unexpected sense of well-being and the sense of security of a man of forty who is in good health and has long since solved life's economic problem.

Suddenly the door opened and Nora Hession came in out of the night, water from her grey raincoat forming a circle on the floor flags.

'I didn't knock, I was so anxious to get in out of the wet,' she said.

He took her coat and hung it on the back of the door, then led her to a seat in the corner and invited her to take off her wet shoes.

'The Canon went to Donegal Town and he won't be back in the parochial house until after confessions at nine.'

'It's as well he performs a few of his duties. Otherwise I should never see you.'

In a moment she had transformed the small cottage with the mystery and excitement of the night. She sat by the bright fire, her face glowing with the pleasure of small talk, her stockinged feet on the pebbled hearth, and she took the drink he offered her as if it were a queen's ransom. That was one of the things he liked about her, the fact that she was possible to please. She was not a strident, modern woman full of half-baked, pseudo-philosophical ideas about her station, with a unilateral declaration of independence tattooed on her tits and 'All hope abandon, ye who enter here' engraved above her atrophied clitoris. She was intelligent without being an intellectual, sincere in what she said, at least on the day she said it, with the crowning attributes of a voice that was soft and eyes that in their dark depths bore an intimation of the ultimate loneliness of the night.

'I was thinking today that my time here is nearly over.'

'If only you'd found enough barytes,' she laughed.

'In a way I'm glad we didn't because it will teach those two arch-toadies, Roarty and Gillespie, a lesson.'

'I don't share your view of the Canon, I'm afraid.'

'Nora, come away with me. Come to London, to a new and wider life. If you like we'll come back here in the summer and put up at a cottage and have fish and chips in Garron.'

'Why don't you stay here?'

'When this job ends, there is nothing left for me to do.'

'You could get a job with the county council.'

'I can imagine the pittance they'd pay me, nothing like enough to keep you in the style to which you should be accustomed. Think about it, Nora. Come to London.'

'But I've been to London and came back. When I think of London, I think of being lonely in public parks on Sunday afternoons and fainting in the Underground from stale air.'

'It will be different with me. I have lots of friends, a nice house and a big garden. You could grow leeks and tomatoes and, if you like, potatoes.'

'But your friends will laugh at my Donegal accent.'

'Not my friends. They're too well bred,' he laughed.

'But they'll laugh behind my back.'

'Nobody will laugh at you if you are yourself. Oh, we'll have splendid times together. I'll tell you all about the London suburbs and how to size up everyone you meet. In spite of the intricacies of the English class system, there are only two classes in the suburbs, the borrowers and the lenders, and I belong to the latter. I've got two motor mowers, twenty-six planes, eighty-eight chisels, three electric drills and eleven spirit levels, all of which I lend out of a sense of *noblesse oblige*. You were meant to laugh at that!'

'I'm not going to London,' she said humourlessly.

'Then come to bed, you impossible creature.'

He bolted the door, switched off the light, and heaped his clothes on the back of a chair while the leaping fire flames cast grotesque shadows on the walls. He watched her take off her clothes while the firelight caught her white thighs and the low droop of her backside, making him wish that Velázquez had seen her before painting the *Rokeby Venus*. He caught her elbow and spun her into his arms, and they stood locked on the hearth, the heat of the fire pleasurably probing their exposed legs and thighs. He carried her to the outshot bed behind the curtains, and they lay between the warm blankets with the firelight glowing through the light fabric, reddening the wall to contrast with the blackness of the rafters above them.

They lay quietly in each other's arms because any movement, even the simple act of kissing, would have seemed superfluous, so perfect was their pleasure in each other.

'What's happened to your sheets?' she asked after a while.

'They're in the wash, and they're the only ones I've got.'

'It's nicer between blankets. You're more conscious of them on your skin than sheets.'

'To those of us who are not sheiks they are more erotic than silks.'

He kissed her tenderly on the lips, eyelids, neck and breasts, and they lay still again, their legs intertwined and his erect penis pressing against her flat belly. She was as thin and straight as a rake but there was strange comfort in the hardness of her body, more pleasurable than the pneumatic bliss of bosomy blondes. It was as if the very lack of flesh on her bones increased his sense of being closer to the living centre of her. It was the same with her breasts. He had mauled enough bristols in his time, bristols that rose before his mouth like fully inflated balloons, and bristols that without a supporting bra hung like gross tropical fruits to the midriff, but he had difficulty in finding Nora Hession's. They were only the size of pears, so small that he questioned the origin of his desire to kiss them. But kiss them he did, and suddenly and unexpectedly she was ready to receive him. He had to move carefully because of his tight foreskin, and Nora Hession's anatomical peculiarities did not make his task any easier. His foreskin was a problem when he was a bachelor and going out with different women every week, so much so that he had sought the advice of a Harley Street consultant. 'Not quite phimosis,' he said, 'not sufficiently serious to warrant surgery, just a nuisance up with which you will have to put.' Then he met Margaret whose capacious accommodation ended his problem, but Nora Hession alerted him again with this warm ache at the tip of his penis that both protracted and intensified his pleasure. The Harley Street consultant clearly did not understand because a man who could describe this ineffable fusion of pain and pleasure as a nuisance had no poetry in him. A tight foreskin, he was prepared to argue, was the beginning of philosophy for without it how could a man have anything like an adequate idea of the magic and terror of sex? There were many men in history who would have been the better for personal experience of his problem. If Henry VIII, for example, had had a tight foreskin, the history of England would have been different.

'It was a very quiet one,' she said when he had exhausted himself. 'It's curious that it's never the same twice. Is it different for you each time?'

'I don't consider these matters as carefully as you.'

'I do believe that men are too insensitive to appreciate sex to the full,' she laughed.

'Each can enjoy it only to the extent of his capacity.'

'If it's different each time, why do some couples get tired of each other?'

'Perhaps it isn't different for everyone. Maybe we are the chosen.'

'You bring élitism into everything. Is that an English foible?'

'That's a complex question where "yes" or "no" won't do. Ask me again one morning and I'll take the day to answer you.'

She went quiet in his arms like a child who had fallen asleep, and he closed his eyes and shivered in the shadow of Diana Duryea. He had just come down from Cambridge and he had taken a job with a firm which manufactured soil pipes. During his first week they held a press conference to launch a new soil pipe on an unsuspecting world. He had never thought of press conferences before and, if he had, he would have assumed that they were sober occasions for the dissemination of useful information. But he realised the depth of his innocence when he saw the pack of journalists from the technical press which descended on the campari-and-soda and the gin-and-tonic.

'You should do this more often,' an old stager said to him as he dispatched a double whisky and a canapé almost in the same mouthful. 'It's already a success and not a drop of ink has been spilt. There isn't a free-loader I know who isn't here. It can do you nothing but good.'

The shameless audacity of the man took his breath away He looked round for someone younger who might have come out of a love of soil pipes when whom should he meet but Diana Duryea.

'I hope you won't think me ignorant,' she said in a penetrating American accent as she came up to him, 'but could you possibly tell me the why and wherefore of soil pipes?'

She was dressed in the worst of taste, in a crimson suit with crimson lipstick and crimson rouge to match, and he bent over her crimson beret and whispered an answer in her ear.

'Oh, you are a one,' she laughed. And then she told him that her name was Diana Duryea, editorial assistant on the magazine *Lift*.

'Lifts that go up and down?' he asked.

'Yes, elevators, you know.'

'And what might you be doing with soil pipes in a lift?'

'I asked my editor the same question but he told me to keep mum and enjoy the drinks.'

'So you did know about soil pipes.'

'Yes, but I thought my question a good conversational gambit.'

They had several drinks together, and after the press conference they went to a pub in Chelsea and then to his flat in Fulham. By this time she was Brahms and Liszt as she kept saying in imitation of her Cockney flatmate, and she lay on the bed with her long legs apart and her arms shading her eyes from the light. He made her black coffee to put her off guard and, as soon as she had drunk it, made love to her with a French letter protecting his vulnerable foreskin.

She dressed with quick efficiency and combed her hair in front of the mirror while he thought about her blue-veined breasts and how far apart they were, how unsuitable for intermammary aberration.

'That was a clitoral,' she said, letting the hairs from her comb fall on his newly shampooed carpet. The word 'clitoral' came as a shock because he had never heard an American pronounce it before. He had heard the voice before, though. He had heard that strident assurance on a June day on the Acropolis, a middle-class American housewife saying of the Parthenon: 'Those columns are Doric—I can recognise them even here'.

'That was a clitoral,' she said again. 'I thought you might like to know.'

'And what on earth is a clitoral? It certainly isn't English.'

'A clitoral as opposed to a vaginal orgasm. You do surprise me, honey. I thought that a self-confessed member of the technologico-Benthamite society would be capable of such a fundamental distinction.'

'Don't think I'm being offensive but my answer to that is simply: "Get stewed".'

'You're not being offensive, just mildly boring.'

'I'll be even more boring and say that the two-orgasm theory of sex will have as many proponents in a hundred years' time as the four-humour theory of medicine has today.'

'What I like about you is not so much your wit as your small ass. It might interest you to know that in a recent poll thirty-nine per cent of women in Greenwich Village thought a small bottom the most attractive thing in a man whereas only two per cent yearned for a large penis. We women, you see, are not the vultures you make us out to be.'

He led her down the stairs into the night and never saw her again, but he could not forget her combative insensitivity nor the way she had almost devoured within the space of an hour his most sensitive part. The most memorable hurts were always administered by women. If only men were masochists, what a feast life would be.

Nora nudged him and he realised that he had been asleep.

'I must have dropped off,' she said. 'It's nearly nine o'clock. I must get back before the Canon does.'

They dressed in the dark, shivering slightly because the fire had died down while they slept. He switched on the light and kissed her in grateful wonderment at the stroke of luck by which he had found her.

SEVENTEEN

He drove her back in the rain to the parochial house gate
and, in spite of his earlier plans, went straight to Roarty's.
As it was Saturday night, the bar was crowded but he
found a quiet corner with Gimp Gillespie, Crubog and
Cor Mogaill who were trying to decide without benefit of
science whether lugworms are hermaphrodites. Potter
drank and listened but his mind was on Nora Hession
and the way her unexpected visit had taken the edge off
his disaffected thoughts.

He arrived home at twelve and, not wishing to go to
bed just yet, put more peat on the fire, made himself a cup
of coffee on the gas cooker, and opened Gimp Gillespie's
book at chapter three. It was a good book but in his
present mood he would have preferred a thriller if he
could have laid his hands on one. It struck him as appropriate that he should wish for a thriller now. Ever since he
arrived in the glen he had been busy savouring the local
life but now he had withdrawn to take stock and in the
unwonted quiet there was time for light reading. He was
not a habitual reader of thrillers. In London he simply
did not have time, and besides he felt that they lacked the
imponderable ingredient that makes fiction truer than
fact, and that those of them that sported an intrusive

infrastructure of fact lacked the ingredient all the more conspicuously. But in spite of all that, he could enjoy a good thriller just now with the wind and the rain outside and the sea thundering over the rocks below.

He finished the book at two o'clock, covered the dying coals with ashes, and prepared for bed. The house had lost its warmth, and he could feel on his bare ankles the draught coming in under the back door. The bed curtains moved in the draught, and the thought that in a moment he would be behind them under the warm blankets gave him a sense of creature comfort. He pulled the blankets beneath his chin and closed his eyes, surrounded by the sexual odour of Nora Hession. The door strained at the latch, the mountain ash scratched the window pane, the rain beat on the stone threshold, and the wind raced over the roof, bending the sapless rafters. They were all distinct sounds which he tried to count but they merged into a Wagnerian flow that dulled his brain on the verge of sleep.

He woke to what seemed like a dull thud and the splintering of glass, and then he realised that he had also heard a rifle shot at close quarters. In a flash he had rolled out of bed and was lying on the cold flag floor, waiting for either a second shot or the sound of retreating footsteps, but all that came to his ears was the confused noises of the wind and the rain. With his head down he crawled across the floor to the window and came on a triangle of broken glass with his hand. Someone had fired a shot through the window, and whoever it was might well try again. He groped in the dark for his socks and, unable to find them, put his shoes on his bare feet. Still keeping his head below the level of the window sill, he went to the back door, pulled on his overcoat over his pyjamas, took his shotgun from the wall, put two cartridges in the breech and stuffed four more in his pocket. The shot had come from the front of the house, so he gently unbolted the back door and slipped outside without a sound. He stood with his back to the barn wall, trying to peer into the darkness on each side, waiting for a telltale noise or movement. It was still raining, and the water running off the eaves trickled coldly down his neck. He edged his way along the wall, and then stooping under the coping stones of the garden wall made his way stealthily behind the hedge at the front corner of the house. Slowly he raised his head but in the darkness not even the whiteness of the house was visible. The sky seemed only three feet above him, and all he could do was wait for a noise with the safety catch of his shotgun cocked, ready to release both barrelfuls in its direction. He picked up a stone and flung it over the hedge so that it landed with a thud on the flags before the front door but not a sound followed. There was no point in staying outside any longer with the wind whipping his ankles and the rain making runnels down his neck and chest. Carefully and quietly he retraced his steps and entered by the back door. Once inside he rebolted the door and stood in the dark, wondering what to do next. It was only three o'clock; he would have to wait five hours before he could investigate in the relative safety of daylight. He took off his coat, towelled his hair and neck, and poured himself a stiff whisky to steady his nerve. He did not want to put on the light, so he hung over the raked fire in his dressing gown, warming his hands above the embers and his feet on the still warm hearth, his sense of incredulity so strong that he could barely think. What had he said or done to arouse such animosity? And in a place at the world's end where plain living and plain thinking had made the inhabitants so philosophical that they always put off until tomorrow what they need not do today. But whoever did this was no philosopher, and besides he knew something of his habits. It would have been natural to assume that he slept in the bedroom but whoever fired the shot knew better. During the summer he slept in the small bedroom but when the weather turned cold at the end of October he moved to the kitchen bed which was near the hearth fire and therefore warmer. The number of people in the glen who knew this could not be many. He remained by the fire until four, and when he went to bed he lay with his head at the foot as a precaution. He did not expect to sleep but he did. And when he awoke, daylight was already visible through a round hole in the window blind.

He rolled up the blind to find that one of the panes in the lower sash was broken. He looked round the walls to see where the bullet had gone and noticed a hole in the bed curtains. The bullet was buried in the wall of the outshot no more than six inches from where his head had lain on the pillow. He went outside in his dressing gown and found what might be a clue to the identity of the madman who had shot at him. Pinned to the front door was a sheet of notepaper and written on it in red ink was the simple warning: 'Hands off my maid'. His first thought was that this must have been the work of a practical joker, but then he asked himself if a joker would have shot with such uncanny accuracy. No, he must take this seriously. He must go to McGing.

He made himself a pot of coffee and sat at the table, looking out of the broken window at the light breaking through grey mist as in a late Turner. On the other side of the window droplets fell from the slender branches of the mountain ash, not the bright droplets of a summer morning but the grey droplets of winter light. He counted four drops hanging from the underside of one of the branches. A thrush came to rest on the end of the branch and three of them fell, glancing off another branch on the way down. On any other morning he would have delighted in the minuteness of his observations but today they meant nothing to him. It was as if the force which propelled him was spent. He had been wrong, very wrong. He had romanticised Glenkeel and its inhabitants out of all reality, but romanticism was not a crime. In a civilised country not even a desiccated classicist would shoot you for it.

He found McGing eating breakfast in uniform with his cap on the table beside a piled plate of liver, bacon and onions and a mountain of buttered toast.

'And what can I do for you so early on Sunday morning?' he asked.

Potter sat down at the table and took a mug of coffee but declined the offer of toast.

'Someone took a pot shot at me in bed last night, and I want to know who.'

As if in response to Potter's seriousness, McGing put on his cap but he continued eating without looking across the table.

'Go on, I'm listening,' he said after a while.

'He broke my window, missed me by inches, and pinned this note to my door.'

'Hands off my maid,' McGing read through a mouthful of streaky bacon.

'Do you think it could be Loftus?'

'No, whatever may be said of Irish parish priests, they don't go about shooting their parishioners.'

223

'But he has spoken to me before about Nora Hession. He doesn't approve of our relationship.'

'You're right to tell me. We mustn't rule out a man just because of his collar but we mustn't rush into accusations either. It's highly unlikely. He comes from a sporting family, you see. His brother, the doctor, is the best shot in the county. The Canon might shoot you on the run, therefore, but he'd never shoot you as a sitting duck.'

'What do you make of it then?' Potter asked.

McGing slowly munched a piece of gristle in the bacon and spat it out on the side of his plate.

'There are two possibilities. Someone did it for fun or someone did it in earnest. Now, there aren't many people who'd do it in earnest but there are lots who'd do it for fun. You see, in Ireland so many people have a sense of humour.'

'Of grisly humour.'

'If you ask me, it was done in earnest. And in that event I have a shrewd idea of the man who did it.'

'Who?'

McGing poured himself another cup of coffee and began picking a tooth with his finger nail.

'It won't help you to know at this stage.'

'It might help me to guard against another attack.'

'All right then. The prime suspect is Gimp Gillespie.'

'But he's my friend!'

'I say Gimp rather than the Canon for a very good reason. Because it's more dangerous to come between a man and his fantasy than between a man and his maid.'

'You speak in riddles, sergeant.'

'Gimp is mad about Nora Hession, always has been, only she won't as much as look his way. It's the cruelty of life. She herself went through hell and misery because of a good-for-nothing brat, and now she's giving Gillespie the same medicine. Have you ever heard of the Case of the Tumbled Trampcock?'

'Yes, it's a classic of detection in these parts,' said Potter, realising that if he wanted the truth he would have to bear with McGing.

'Well, there's a stranger case that happened the previous year, the Case of the Priest's Maid's Knickers. They were stolen from the clothes line in the priest's garden, three pairs belonging to Nora Hession. I got to hear about it and went down to the parochial house to investigate. But the Canon was adamant. He wasn't going to have a scandal about women's underclothes involving the parochial house. The whole thing was best forgotten, the work of a passing tinker who had now gone out over the hill, more than likely. But the Law is not the Church; it is not so easily appeased. I began keeping an eye on the priest's garden unbeknown to Loftus, and three weeks later, not far off midnight, I caught my bold Gimp jouking under a pear tree, not a hundred miles from a certain clothes line on which were two pairs of Nora Hession's pink drawers. So I marched him out of the garden and knocked up the Canon.'

' "What's all this?" he asked, putting his head out of the bedroom window. "Is it a sick call?" '

' "It's the law," I said. "I've just caught Gimp Gillespie trying to steal two pairs of your maid's underpants."—I couldn't say "knickers" to the priest. When he came down, I told him what had happened, that I'd found Gimp skulking under a pear tree.

' "And what do you think you were doing in my garden at this hour?" the Canon demanded to know.

' "I came to steal a pear," said Gimp.

' "A pair of what?" asked the Canon.

' "I was reading St. Augustine's *Confessions* before turning in and I came to the place where he steals pears. Well, I couldn't resist the temptation of the pear tree in your garden, father."

' "I didn't know Augustine stole pears," said the Canon. "I thought his offence had more to do with unholy loves."

' "He stole pears too, Canon," said Gimp.

' "The *Confessions* are good Catholic reading. You should be ashamed of yourself to find them an occasion of sin. *Tolle lege, tolle lege.*"

' "Shall I book him, Canon?" I asked.

' "Release him," said the Canon. "Tell him to go his way and sin no more." That's the Canon, no stomach for the law. But I know, and everyone else in the glen knows what Gimp Gillespie was doing in the garden. Now, a man who could find such a potent loadstone in a priest's maid's knickers could well take a pot shot at the man he thinks has put his hand up them.'

'I beg your pardon,' said Potter, suddenly very English in phrase and posture.

'Luckily, fetishists are notoriously ineffectual.'

'You wouldn't have called this one ineffectual if you'd heard the whistle of his bullet.'

'You can see the pattern emerging, can't you?'

'Which pattern?'

'Drawers,' said McGing, getting up and going to the window with a mug of coffee, just as detectives do in the movies.

'Drawers?' enquired Potter, convinced that McGing was raving.

'Knickers,' said McGing, eyeing him as if he were a simpleton.

226

'What about them?'

'First Nora Hession's vanishing from the clothes line, then the torn knickers on the tumbled trampcock, now a shot at you in the dark. All three are connected.'

'But didn't you say that it was Gimp Gillespie who stole the first lot and Cor Mogaill who tore the second?'

'It's more subtle than that, the connections too shadowy for the crudeness of language. Even I can see it but darkly. But of this I am sure: something is rotten in the parish of Glenkeel. For years the only offences here were poaching and after-hours drinking and the odd run of poteen at Christmas, all manly crimes, signs of a healthy community. Of course I did my duty as a policeman and tried to stamp them out, but in my heart I had a secret respect for the men I brought to court. Now, in the last six months, if you take the enormity of the offences into account, the crime rate has gone up a thousand per cent. We've had robbery, murder, more robbery and now attempted murder. It cannot be that the population has suddenly turned criminal; it's more likely to be the work of one man, a village Moriarty. But in me he will meet his Holmes, so help me.'

Potter scratched his head and wished for an unimaginative English constable who would make a few notes and draw sensible conclusions.

'If you know the identity of the criminal, what are you waiting for?'

'Evidence. The only evidence I have is a thing of hints and hunches. But time is on my side. I'm gradually amassing the circumstantial details with which to confront the bugger at the psychological moment. My tactics will be to pretend to more knowledge than I have, make him shake in his shoes till he confesses all. Which reminds me that we must hurry to the scene of the crime. Have you got the bullet?'

'No, it's still in the wall.'

'Good. An amateur digging out a bullet with a pen-knife will only scratch it and maybe obliterate the rifling marks which provide the evidence. The bullet will tell us a lot. We'll know, for example, whether it could have come from Dr Loftus's stolen rifle. Have you got the cartridge case?'

'I'm afraid I didn't notice one.'

They both got into Potter's car, and on the way to the cottage McGing delivered a lecture on forensic ballistics of such cogency that for a moment Potter felt that he could not be in better hands. McGing was two men in one. The first, who had a mind like a magpie, was a treasury of forensic knowledge. The second, who drew conclusions, was an inept imbecile

EIGHTEEN

Potter dressed more carefully than usual because he was going shooting. He believed that the success of a shoot depended to some extent on the suitability of the sportsman's gear. And besides, shooting, like going to the opera, was something of an occasion; it behoved one to look and feel the part. So he put on his thornproof plus fours, heavy roll-neck jersey, tweed jacket and balaclava helmet, looked at himself in the mirror, and pronounced the transformation in his appearance a distinct success.

He had brooded a lot over the past week but he took the day off in the hope that a morning's shooting would help to take his mind off his troubles. Ever since the pot shot he was dogged by a feeling of insecurity. Though he did not live in fear he was troubled by the incomprehensibility of what had happened to him, and he took certain precautions such as sleeping in the corner of the bedroom on the same side as the window. His friends, particularly Roarty and Gimp Gillespie, had shown genuine concern for his safety but somewhere in the glen was someone who wished him dead. It was an eerie thought which made him wish that he were back in the London suburbs, commuting to Charing Cross every morning and complaining about the irresponsibility of the trade unions and the lateness of the trains.

He stuffed several handfuls of cartridges into his pockets, hung his sidebag on his shoulder, took his shotgun from the wall, and put a padlock on the door. It was a dry morning but the cold of the north-east wind would skewer an arctic fox. A great red sun sat on the saddle of the hill, and as he drove to the village he found that he could look it in the eye without blinking because of the haze. He entered Roarty's by the back door because it was only half-past eight and the bar was not yet open. Roarty, however, was seated behind the counter with the shutters closed and the lights on and a smell of stale stout and cigarette smoke hanging like a halo over his head.

'You're early,' he remarked.

'You said we'd go before nine.'

'Have a drink on the house to warm you up. I'm having a few quick ones, only enough to take the tremble off my hand.'

'It's cold,' said Potter.

'Did you notice the smell on the wind?'

'No.'

'You only get it here when the wind is north-east. Crubog calls it a *gal fiútair*. He says it's coal from Derry.'

Roarty came out from behind the counter and they both sat by the fire and lit their pipes.

'It's a good morning for a snipe shoot,' Roarty said after a while. 'They'll be sitting close, and they should be in good condition after a week of thaw. They're always plump soon after a frosty spell because the worms come to the surface when it thaws.'

'They were feeding all last night in the full moon.'

'That's what I mean. They'll have full crops this

morning, too sleepy to move till we're within range. We'll make two good bags, wait and see.'

'As Rory Rua says, it isn't the bag that matters but the places you go to fill it. He reckons that the wild places in the hills leave a mark on a man's soul.'

'Rory Rua hasn't a penn'orth of interest in the ways of wildlife. He sees no farther than the ends of his gun barrels and, worse, he eats his game straight from the gun.'

Roarty spat into the heart of the fire and Potter looked at him, surprised by such vehemence so early in the day.

'Have you ever shot with him?' Roarty asked.

'Once or twice.'

'He's got two rotten molars that stink when he laughs, which is why I always walk on the upwind side of him.'

'It's a sportsman's solution,' said Potter, noting the slight tremor in Roarty's hand as he raised his glass and knowing that he swung his gun so quickly that it would not matter.

Ever since the evening with the Canon, he had been aware of a muddy undercurrent in his relationship with Roarty. It was as if Roarty had some grievous secret that he wished to share but could not find words to express. He would begin sentences and leave them unfinished or forget what he was about to say. He would ask him to stay for a drink after closing time or go for a morning's shooting, and all the time he would behave as if he were about to make some searing revelation. But nothing ever emerged except sportsmen's small talk about whether to walk snipe upwind or downwind or use number six or nine shot. Potter listened to him, and though he would have liked to help him in his difficulty he could not. He simply came to the conclusion that Roarty had a guilty conscience because of the way he had deserted the Anti-Limestone

231

Society or that he was lonely and sought the kind of relationship he could not have with a local man.

At nine o'clock they said good-bye to Susan Mooney and climbed the side of the hill above the village with Grouse, Roarty's springer spaniel, following at heel. Roarty was wearing a buff donkey jacket over an Aran sweater to keep out the cold, and he was carrying a rucksack big enough for the most optimistic sportsman. They climbed slowly, pausing every now and then to look back at the houses beneath them and the snake-like village street. When they reached the plateau, they loaded their guns, and at a signal from Roarty the dog went ahead, quartering the ground with eager thoroughness. He was an experienced gun dog, and no matter how fiendishly he worked he seemed to keep his mind on Roarty, ready to obey his every command. Soon he turfed out a jack hare from a mound of rushes. Roarty swung his gun barrels over its ears, and it cartwheeled in the air and went down, shot cleanly in the head. In spite of his morning tremor, there was nothing the matter with Roarty's shot, Potter thought.

They had decided to walk the snipe downwind to make for easier and quicker shooting. The snipe would rise, facing them, against the wind, and as it paused for a moment before turning it would present a more stable target than in a going away shot. The difficulty of walking snipe downwind is that the sportsman's approach is less silent, but they decided that after a bright, calm night the birds would be sitting well in the early morning. Potter's turn came next. With a loud 'scaap' a snipe rose out of a poached track before him, and he snapped it as it hung momentarily in the air before turning on its zigzag retreat. He was not so lucky the second time. With a white and brown flicker another snipe rose close to him, and he decided to let it come out of its jinking flight before trying a going away shot. But he must have misjudged the distance or failed to make enough forward allowance; and Roarty, a hundred yards away, raised his hands in mock horror. As Potter signalled his despair, another snipe rose before Roarty who raised his gun in an effortless swing and snapped the bird in mid-jink as the very best snipe shots do.

By eleven o'clock they had traversed the hill and examined all the favoured sports, the pools and drains and spongy patches which Roarty knew so well. Potter was pleased with the morning's sport. He had bagged a pair of hares and eight snipe, with a kill-to-cartridge ratio of four to five for the snipe. A sharp shower of hailstones coming in from the north-east took their minds off sport for a while. They both made for the shelter of a ruined cow house which had been turned into a sheep pen, Potter running with his sidebag bumping against his hip.

'How did you do?' asked Roarty as they sheltered under the unmortared stone wall.

'A pair of hares and four couple. What about you?'

'A jack hare and seven couple. It was one of my better days; I didn't waste a single shot.'

They lit their pipes and listened to the hopping of the hailstones on the other side of the wall and watched them whitening the greenish-brown mountain before them. Grouse came up with his nose to the ground, and Roarty chucked him under the chin and gave him a digestive biscuit.

'On a morning like this he is worth his weight in gold,' said Potter.

'A pedigree retriever would be wasted here. Though his

affiliation is undecided, Grouse has got a nose and brains and kens how to use them. His great quality is that he can do a bit of everything.'

'I was just thinking,' said Potter, 'that if everyone went about his work with such intelligence, the world would be a more efficient place to live in.'

'Have you heard from McGing?' Roarty asked after a while.

'He told me that he knows the criminal, that all he now needs is the evidence.'

'I hope for your sake that he gets it. Being shot at can't be good for your peace of mind.'

'But it does make you see yourself more clearly. It makes you dare to think beyond the next drink.'

'It's good to be confronted with evil if only because it reminds you of the residue of good within you.'

'Why call it "evil"? Why not "disorder"? Use the word "evil" and you are swamped in theology.'

'If you'd ever sensed the physical presence of evil, you wouldn't call it "disorder". Evil can manifest itself as a bad smell that pervades the house. It lingers in your nostrils in every room, and when you go outside you can smell it on the wind.'

'Whatever it is you're talking about is within you. The mind that apprehends evil does so only because it is a vestigial presence in the mind itself.'

'I've been aware of evil as a continuous presence for the past fortnight. Sometimes it smells like a field of rotting cabbage and sometimes like sweaty feet. I was glad of the smell on the wind this morning because it went some way towards smothering the other.'

'But there was no smell on the wind this morning,' said Potter, drawing on his pipe and watching the wind-driven hailstones bouncing off a rock in front of them. Two months ago he thought he knew Roarty, but now he was not so sure. He had imagined him as a practical man of strong principle who never gave a thought to anything the mind could not dismiss. But now he felt that all he had seen was the picturesque beard, that he had not spotted the mildewed kernel.

Roarty was telling him about the two manifestations of evil: evil which has a physical embodiment and evil which is unrelated to anyone or anything—the most frightening form of all. He listened indulgently without understanding a word, and it seemed to him that Roarty wanted him to give a sign, to say something that would confirm his perceptions and free him for ever from the burden of self-doubt. But Potter smoked his pipe and wondered if Roarty were a latent homosexual who had missed a turning.

'Were you afraid the night you were shot at?' Roarty asked as if it followed quite logically from his discourse on evil.

'I was too angry at being woken up to be afraid.'

'You're rather isolated in that cottage. If you like, you can come and stay with me. You'd be living above the bar, an inestimable boon for a drinking man.'

'It's very kind of you, I'm sure, but I think I'll stay put nevertheless.'

'It was just a thought,' said Roarty, noticing that the hail shower was over.

They walked down the hill without a word, and Potter wondered if Roarty was thinking that he had failed him.

NINETEEN

Sunday, 19 December
A 'large grebe' on the Lough of Silver turned out to
be a goosander, rare in these parts. Took off for the
Lough of Gold with a 'kraah', leaving me alone
with a moorhen flashing white underparts. Failed
to see Roarty's black water bird. A manifestation of
evil visible only to himself?

Potter closed his diary and put more peat on the fire.
Over the past fortnight the weather had turned colder. A
damp, creeping cold that seeped through your clothes and
that only whisky could keep from freezing the marrow
of your bones. The days were noticeably shorter than in
London, though Donegal was only three degrees farther
north, and the mornings were the worst part as he drove
to work with headlights on, the upturned collar of his
overcoat rubbing cold into the back of his head and his
feet stiff in his damp gumboots.

That morning he woke in confusion. At first he thought
that the alarum had gone off too early because of the
darkness outside the window, but when he pulled the
curtains he saw that it was not night but a foggy morning.
The sky seemed to have swallowed the hills, and the

cottages by the sea down below loomed vaguely through a heavy shroud of grey. He went to early Mass and spoke to Nora Hession who told him that she would be coming to see him that evening, and then he went home without stopping for a drink in Roarty's and spent the short day by the loughs watching water fowl through his field-glasses.

He was glad to be going away but Nora Hession tempted him to look back. She would not come with him, and that he could understand. Perhaps she was wiser than he. Perhaps this was her proper, her only, home. Here she could float gently into the loneliness of spinsterhood and still be herself, knitting or reading by the parochial house fire in the long nights and aware of Gimp Gillespie's hungry eyes on her face on Sundays. She would be lost in suburban London because she was too serious about human relationships to suffer the exiguity of the shards from which suburban man fabricates a life. He would leave her, regretfully perhaps but also in sympathetic understanding. He realised that if he took her away she would only pine, and in pining lose her sweetness. Life, he felt, was fraught with possibilities that did not beckon, bridges that loomed before you cared to cross them. He poured himself a drink and turned the newly washed sheets that he was airing on the backs of two chairs by the fire.

It had been a week of irritations which began with Gimp Gillespie's sensational article in one of the Dublin Sunday papers. Under the cumbersome heading 'Exploitation, Reformation and Attempted Murder in Donegal', Gimp told of an English engineer who was nearly murdered in his bed as the representative of a foreign firm that was trying to get the most valuable deposit of barytes in the country on the cheap. The engineer seemed to be a well-meaning simpleton on arrival. He had seemingly come to Donegal with the idea of converting the people to Lollardism which, for the benefit of his readers, Gimp described as pre-Lutheran Protestantism. In the pursuit of Lollardism he founded an Anti-Limestone Society and converted many of the innocent locals to his beliefs, only to be exposed by the vigilant parish priest who saw the Anti-Limestone Society and the Lollardism as a cover-up for surreptitious exploitation. Potter could hardly believe that he was reading about himself. He had thought of Gimp Gillespie as a friend or, if not that, as a provincial journalist who found literary fulfilment in innocuous notes on bumper potato crops, marauding foxes and shoals of mackerel in season. He could not believe that he would be capable of such a monstrous betrayal after drinking his Scotch and eating his roast snipe carefully skewered by their own beaks.

A telegram from Dublin summoning him to head office took his mind off Gimp Gillespie for the moment. But when he saw his American boss, Ben Shockley, he knew that Gillespie had done more damage than he had imagined.

'I can explain everything,' he said to Shockley. 'It's all in the imagination of a provincial journalist, the ugliest man you ever laid eyes on.'

'Did you or did you not found an Anti-Limestone Society?' asked Shockley with American shrillness.

'Yes, but—'

'And did you say that you were bringing Lollardism to Ireland?'

'That was a joke.'

'You're out of your mind, Potter, and I'm not joking. I'm surprised they didn't shoot you and have done with it.'

'The whole thing has been exaggerated out of all——'

'Do you know that you have set the business of this company in Ireland back ten years. You have dragged the image of Pluto in the dirt. We're in a politically sensitive field, where charges of exploitation come easily, where tub-thumping politicians are only too willing to get up on their high horses. What we want is to keep a low profile and maximise profits in peace. We don't want trouble. We don't want publicity. And what do you do? You go up to Donegal with your 12-bore and plus fours and begin preaching Lollardism to the natives. You are a dangerous simpleton, Potter, and I'm recalling you to head office and a desk job. You're not fit for the field, that's your trouble.'

'Get stuffed,' said Potter.

'Take that back,' said Shockley.

'You can stick your job and your low profiles and your maximisation of profits. I'm leaving. I'm going back to Donegal to pick up my things.'

'The sooner the better,' said Shockley. 'Please don't consider yourself under any obligation to give a month's notice.'

'Thank you,' said Potter, marching out of the room.

He discovered from someone in the corridor that operations in Donegal were being suspended and that the other engineers were being recalled. He did not care. He had decided to go back to London and leave Margaret to follow or not as she pleased. He had two more days left in the glen. He was leaving on Wednesday morning.

Nora Hession came at six and cooked him jugged hare over the peat fire. They drank Scotch and water while it simmered, and then at the last moment he opened a bottle of claret as an afterthought and saw her eyes light up with pleasure. Over dinner they talked quietly of the people of the glen, of almost everyone except themselves, and when they had finished he took her hand and she looked at him shyly and said in a whisper:

'I've been meaning to tell you, Kenneth. I'm pregnant.'

'How long have you known it?'

'This is the second month.'

'That's the best news I've had since I've been here.'

He really meant it. He and Margaret had tried for a baby more times than he cared to remember but they were always disappointed. The doctor told Margaret that she was capable of conceiving and recommended that her husband have a test. The test confirmed the doctor's suspicions: Potter's sperm count was low. This news was a shot in the thigh, however. Obviously what his seed had needed all those years was a sufficiently fertile tilth. And you would not think of fertility to look at her, this sliver of a girl with her small breasts, thin jaws and straight haunches.

'Is it good news?' she asked.

'You'll have to come away with me now,' he said, getting up to open another bottle of claret.

'You will come with me,' he said, refilling her glass.

'If you want me to.'

'I do, Nora. Oh, we'll have lovely times. I'll have to get a job first but that should not be difficult. With a bit of luck my old firm will have me back.'

'Where will we love—I mean live?' she laughed.

'I've got a house in the outer London suburbs and a snug little cottage in Herefordshire. We could go there at week-ends to do a bit of gardening and walking and maybe fishing and shooting. Do you like fishing?'

'I could dig for the worms.'

'No, this is fly-fishing. I shall teach you how to do it. There's nothing to it, and there are women who are very good at it.'

'I'll do all the things you do except shooting. I don't think I could learn to like shooting. When are you going away?'

'I was thinking of leaving on Wednesday but now I'll wait for a few more days to give you time to get your things together.'

'I'll need a week. The Canon must have time to find a new housekeeper. What shall I tell him?'

'Tell him we are going to be married.'

'Are we?'

'If you say yes.'

She squeezed his hand, quite tipsy from the wine.

'There's one little problem,' he continued. 'I'm already married. But it isn't an insuperable problem. My wife and I will simply get a divorce, and then we shall be free to marry. A divorce may take time, however. It is possible that our child may be born first.'

As he looked at her, she burst into a fit of laughter, high-pitched, painful laughter, involuntary as the hiccups. He had expected her to cry. He had not expected her to laugh.

He reached over and shook her by the shoulders until she stopped.

'Why are you laughing?'

'I just realised for the first time that you were a stranger.'

'I hope you're not disappointed in me.'

'Does it matter?'

'Yes, it matters to me.'

'I'm not disappointed in you. I'm disappointed in myself.'

'Why is that?'

'When I began going out with you, the Canon said to me: *Pós ar an charn aoiligh.*'

'And what does that piece of mother wit mean?'

'Marry on the midden: marry someone you know. I laughed at him then but now he could laugh at me if it were a laughing matter.'

'You take all this far too seriously. My wife and I have long since gone our separate ways; it will be a divorce without regrets, without a legacy of mutual hurts. She is quite happily looking after her arthritic mother, and I'm quite convinced that if she did not have an arthritic mother to occupy her she would have left me long ago.'

'If you're both Catholics, how can you get divorced?'

'Don't bring religion into this. Religion is a bauble that every age repaints to its liking. Compare the Church ten years ago with the Church today. The form of the Sacraments has changed. The liturgy of the Mass is unrecognisable. Roman Catholics are receiving holy communion in Anglican churches and Anglicans are singing Roman Catholic hymns. The martyrs of the Reformation have died in vain. And the Church, while professing an immutable doctrine, is tacking for all it is worth against the dirty weather of secular indifference. But you can't tack without changing course. Mark my words, in twenty years' time divorced Catholics will be able to remarry in the Church—provided they say a special prayer and pay a hefty fine. But why wait twenty years? We'll both be past it by then.'

'If I can't get married in the Church, I won't get married at all.'

'We don't have to get married. We can live together until such time as we are free to marry as you wish.'

'No.'

'Why?'

'I wouldn't be happy.'

'And what will you do with the child?'

'Bring it up.'

'You needn't have it, you know. If you come to London with me, I shall make all the arrangements.'

'For what?'

'An abortion, of course.'

'You can't be serious.'

'You mean you won't have an abortion?'

'I've gone this far, and now I'll go the rest of the way.'

'I shall send you enough money to support the child, but what about yourself? As an unmarried mother, you will not be able to stay with the Canon, and you won't get a job as a teacher either. Come to England with me where no one takes any notice.'

'I'll be all right.'

'You have a touching faith in the future.'

'I'm only doing what's right for me.'

'Think it over.'

'I don't need to ,' she said, getting up to go.

'Shall I see you before I go?'

'You know where I am if you wish to see me.'

He offered to drive her back but she said that she would walk, that there were things she could think about better in the dark. He pressed her hand at the end of the lane, and she vanished into the night without a word, leaving him with a disconcerting sense of life's, and possibly his own, inadequacy.

When he had heard that she was pregnant, he was overjoyed. A son—it could conceivably be a boy—was something he had wished for at odd moments on empty

Sunday afternoons in the suburbs, and a son from Nora Hession would surely have a streak of originality. When she refused to come away with him, he saw his son growing up in a narrow glen without the advantage of a father and the start in life which only a prosperous father can ensure. Such a son would not be his, he thought, and the thought made him suggest abortion. Now he was somewhat ashamed of himself, but he could not help blaming Nora Hession for the tangled, torn state of his feelings.

When he got back to the cottage, he found two empty claret bottles on the form inside the door, and he felt as sober as if Nora Hession had drunk them both. The cheerlessness of the bedroom was unbearable, and he put on his coat and drove straight to Roarty's, desperate for the harmless deceptions of male companionship.

TWENTY

Roarty held a glass beaker of his urine against the bathroom light, turning it slowly in his hand like a landlord testing the first glass from a fresh barrel. It did not look like his urine. It rather resembled a malt whisky, and with justice, he thought with a smile. He sniffed the contents of the beaker and, noting the heavy sediment in the bottom, wished that it were something as innocuous as hops or smegma. He emptied the beaker into the lavatory bowl except for the half-inch at the bottom which he decided to preserve in an empty pill bottle for the sexually dextrous McGarrigle.

Quietly, he returned to his bedroom after making sure that Susan Mooney had switched off her light. He locked his door without a click and took Dr Loftus's rifle from the bottom of his wardrobe. He had retrieved it from the culvert the previous night, and now he balanced it on his hands and rubbed his forefinger along the slightly worn fore-end piece. It had obviously had a fair amount of use but it had got good care and was in beautiful condition. It was one o'clock. He still had an hour to kill, long enough to take in Schumann's first and fourth symphonies. He put the first symphony on the gramophone and lay on the bed, looking through the article on 'Bridges', one of his favourite pieces in *Britannica*.

After memorising a few of the formulae he laid the volume beside him on the coverlet and closed his eyes. For the past few days he had been more than usually aware of the transience of human perceptions. Our insights come, give a moment of pleasure or displeasure, and are gone. Even in a man with a good memory the experience of one day never survives the next, for those experiences that return to torture or delight undergo a sea change each time we recall them. Life, he thought, is a palimpsest of expunged experiences. His memories of school, for example, were vivid, but did they represent the reality of school or were they fictional accretions of his own fabrication, suffering a renewed transmutation with each recalling?

Now as he looked back he saw his schooldays overcast by a blighting sense of unreality. While the other boys dreamed of becoming doctors, lawyers or engineers, he sat in the classroom wondering where all those words might lead, curious only to discover if they related to anything except one another. History, which should have enlivened his boyish imagination, died as it fell on his ear. The master maundered confusingly about the campaigns of Wallenstein and the complexities of the Thirty Years' War so that Wallenstein remained for him a name, not a man, and the duchies of Friedland, Sagan and Mecklenburg were places that conjured up nothing but the sickly fear with which he beheld pink examination papers. And when the master told them that Wallenstein was murdered after a banquet by Scottish Protestants and Irish Catholics from his own army, Roarty was neither surprised nor saddened but rather overcome by the futility of a further nugget of information which would keep rising like flotsam to the surface of his mind for the rest of his life.

In his last year at school, when other boys were preparing for university, he could not imagine what he wanted to do because the days seemed two removes away and there was nothing in the world that he truly desired. Tentatively, he concluded that the battle was to be fought not in the world but within himself, an opinion which was confirmed for him by a conversation he had overheard between a Christian Brother and a lay teacher.

'And how are you finding the great world?' the brother asked.

'Do you want to know if you did right in forsaking it?' the lay teacher laughed.

'I know it well,' said the brother. 'It's a thin world. You could travel it from end to end and return empty-handed.'

This brief exchange left an impression on Roarty, and when a Holy Ghost Father came to the school to proselytise, he promised to join the order almost as a matter of course. He joined not out of love for humanity but from an absence of love and a romantic attachment to an asceticism of which he found little evidence in the seminary.

The burden of experience weighed on him like a lifetime of years. His schooldays had been unhappy but he had survived them. It was only now in remembering them that they had begun to eat his innards. He felt that if he could re-experience his life as it had happened he would be healed, but in recalling over the years he had pruned and refined, eaten away the fruit until he was left with the poisonous core. His memories did not encompass experience; they were toxic distillations of experience that had become lethal in their potency. If only he could

247

exchange his memories for those of, say, Potter, he could live in peace without having to struggle daily against the venomous toad in his heart. But if he bartered his memories, would he not be surrendering the personality he was at such pains to preserve?

His memories of the seminary were more destructive than those of school because in the seminary he had been tortured by the knowledge of how his mad uncle had met his end. In his final year the president of the college called him to his study and handed him an anonymous letter which said that he had an uncle who died in the asylum because of his habit of putting schoolgirls astride his erect penis. And the letter writer asked the simple question: 'Has the nephew of such a man the purity of heart necessary to become a priest?'

'Is this true?' asked the kindly president.

'In essence, yes,' said Roarty.

'We are all subject to temptation, some sadly more than others, and we all must combat it with what weapons the Lord in His love and wisdom has given us. Look into your heart, my son, and see what you find there. Should you ever wish to talk to me, I shall be here at your disposal.'

Roarty did look into his heart only to find the stench of pent-up concupiscence. He remembered how on holiday he had watched young girls in white first communion dresses returning from the altar rails and how in his heart he had desired them. He did not get up from his pew as Lanty Duggan might have done because he had not yet strayed sufficiently from reality. But what if he should in years to come? Lanty Duggan lived within him, an evil-smelling old man, a corrupter of innocence. He left the seminary to escape from that old Adam whom he knew would haunt him unrelentingly in a life of celibacy. Now in his middle age the battle had begun to go in the old man's favour. As it happened, he was impotent but his impotence made his desires all the more fantastical. Already he could sense them driving him off the highroad into hedges and ditches like a wild tramp of the hills. Lanty Duggan still lived. He was a maggot within his brain that threatened to consume his reason.

He picked up the rifle, opened the bolt, and pressed five rounds down into the magazine.

'Victorian man feared the workhouse,' he said to himself. 'But modern man fears the madhouse.'

He stole down the stairs backwards so that the loose tread would not creak. Outside, the sky was low and starless. It was pitch dark between the houses, and cold enough for snow. He pulled his woollen scarf up under his chin and took the fenceless road that climbed the hill in the direction of Rory Rua's cottage.

Crubog had come into the bar that morning crowing like a cock about the great bargain he had driven. He had sold his farm to Rory Rua for £3,500 and a hot dinner every day for as long as he lived.

'I didn't sell it for the money,' he explained apologetically, 'but for the hot dinners. At my age a man doesn't want to spend what little time he has left in the kitchen.'

'You could have chosen a better cook,' Roarty laughed. 'You could have sold it to a man with a wife. All the cooking Rory Rua ever does is to boil eggs and potatoes. You may find yourself on cold collations in your old age.'

'I've taken care of that. He is to cook me something different every day, meat five days a week and fish on Wednesdays and Fridays. Leave it to Old Crubog. He's as good as any lawyer.'

249

'So it's all signed, sealed and delivered,' said Roarty as if he could not care less.

'No, we're going to see the solicitors next fair day.'

That gave Roarty an idea. He was not uninterested in the sale; he was incensed by it. He had had his eye on Crubog's mountain acreage for the last ten years, and if he had failed to buy it, it was not for want of bidding. He felt that the number of free whiskies he had poured down Crubog's wattled neck gave him a personal stake in the land and that Rory Rua had wrested it from him by foul means, not fair. If he had known that Crubog wanted a hot meal every day of his life, he could have provided it. Susan was a passable cook, and Crubog could have had his meals as well as his drinks in the pub. But all was not lost. The conveyancing was not complete; there was still time to frighten Rory Rua into backing out. He was not sure about how he would frighten him but he suspected that the fizz of a bullet at his ear as he slept would make him think twice before completing the deal. To clarify matters he had prepared a little note which he would pin on Rory Rua's door, but in different handwriting from the one he had left for Potter.

As he approached Rory Rua's, he moved onto the green verge of the road to muffle his tread. Strangely enough, the farmyard gate was open, and he stood by one of the piers and cocked the safety catch of the rifle. A tom cat squealed somewhere among the trees on his left, and he squatted on his hunkers to see if he could detect the outline of the house and farm buildings against the sky. A muffled noise like the coughing of a cow followed by the jingle of a chain came from behind the house. He edged his way forward, keeping his back to the high hedge, and sidled across the yard with one arm outstretched until he

250

felt the pebbledash of the gable with his fingertips. He moved along the gable wall, placing one foot carefully before the other in case he should overturn an empty pail or bottle, and peered round the corner. The byre door was open and a dim light shone from inside. Rory Rua had evidently sat up to look after a sick cow. It was too risky to advance any farther. He would go home and wait for a more auspicious night.

As he turned, two powerful arms gripped him from behind, pinning his elbows firmly to his sides. Roarty swung round with all the strength of his huge body, and the other man, trying to topple him, lost his grip and grasped the barrel of the rifle in an effort to keep his balance. There was a loud report and the rifle recoiled in Roarty's hands. The other man sank to his knees with a groan, clutching the legs of Roarty's trousers. Roarty freed himself with a kick and was about to hurry off when a single word stopped him. 'Bogmail.' He recognised the gruff voice of Rory Rua and sensed somehow that the word might be his last. He bent over the dark heap and ejaculated with throbbing fear in his trousers. He caught the other man's wrist but there was no pulse that he could feel. His hands were shaking badly and a cold sweat had broken out on his chest and forehead. His initial impulse was to hoof it back home as quickly as he could but first, he thought, he must make sure that Rory Rua was dead. He dragged the deadweight into the house and switched on the light in the kitchen. Rory Rua had been shot in the chest; he had tickled his last trout, baited his last lobster pot, eaten his last hare straight from the gun. He stretched the body on the outshot bed, drew the curtains closed, and examined his own clothes for blood stains. He had been lucky. There was only one smallish splash on his donkey jacket and he would see to that when he got home.

He locked the door of the house, extinguished the storm lantern in the byre, closed the farmyard gate behind him, and trudged down the lane, his fingers clutching the rifle in involuntary spasms. He tried to think but uncomprehending fear filled his mind, and he was surprised when he reached the culvert by the Minister's Bridge because he had not been conscious of wishing to go there.

TWENTY-ONE

It snowed in the night, and at nine o'clock the following morning the floating, whirling flakes were still muffling the air in their descent on the whitened glen. From an upstairs window Roarty watched them blowing against the rough boles of the garden trees, forming white, silent bells on the knots and loading the branches until the black undersides looked like impossible shadows. The snow lay in great white daubs along the eastern side of the dead conifer, white blooms like June roses, as if the sapless wood had suddenly burst into flower. In the distance the whitened south mountain was scored in black where rivers ran down its side, and the fenceless road that came down from Rory Rua's cottage had vanished in the general whiteness of field and hill. The whole glen looked as if it had become overgrown in the night by a beautiful but deadly fungus. Roarty sighed wearily. Though he could feel the warmth of the first drink of the day within him, he sensed that he too was being choked by a fungus against which there was no earthly protection.

He would never have guessed that the blackmailer was Rory Rua; he had been so certain that it was Potter. If Rory Rua had told the truth in his last letter, the story of the murder and the whereabouts of Eales's body would soon be known to the police. More investigation and more tom-fool questions. He would have to sit tight, keep his nerve, and, as Asquith said, 'wait and see'. Circumstantial evidence alone, even two trout in the milk, would not convict him. But what of the murder of Rory Rua? That was the next problem. Assuming that there was no evidence of blackmail, however, even the most astute policeman could not guess why he should murder him. After all he had been one of his best customers, a man with whom he had never exchanged an unfriendly word. The thought came like a flow of oil, smoothing the ruffled surface of his mind.

He went downstairs and breakfasted cheerlessly off a kipper before throwing the backbone to the cat. He lingered at the table over a second cup of coffee, glad that Susan was polishing glasses in the bar. He had come within an ace of committing the perfect murder. In fact he might now have committed two. But though he had so far escaped the retribution of the law, his life was changed for ever. To be a successful murderer you needed the temperament and constitution of an ox. He himself had always been strong of limb but that was not enough. His Achilles heel lay elsewhere; not in an overtender conscience that brooded on a rooted sorrow but in the obsessive cast of his mind which had not given him a moment's peace from either the blackmailer or McGing. His suffering was not a visitation from above but a constitutional flaw; the seeds of suffering sprouted within his skull. He wondered where it would all end. He was going to Sligo Hospital for a check-up tomorrow. Was that where it would end? Having asked himself the question, he had to answer truthfully that he did not really care. His joy in life had gone, and even each drink had become a wearisome turnstile through which he had to pass to reach the next. Cecily, once an angel, had left him, and he had nearly murdered the man whom he would have liked to call his friend. He felt that he had unwittingly become a stranger to himself, that the man he prized most, the reclusive would-be scholar who memorised *Britannica* and listened to Schumann in the small hours, had been devoured by his opposite.

He went to the bar, poured himself a drink, and sat by the turf fire waiting for opening time and trying to imagine how customers saw him behind the counter. The morning went by slowly. Crubog in wellingtons and two over-coats came in at half-past eleven, over an hour late, and Cor Mogaill arrived with snow on his knapsack which left a pool of water on the tiled floor as it melted. At mid-day the postman came with a letter from Cecily. She was coming home for Christmas and she was bringing her English boyfriend who, to judge by the accompanying photograph, was an insubstantial young man you'd blow off your fist and wonder where he'd gone. But he must not prejudge him. He must wait and see; see, for example, if the deletion of Eales had been in vain. What if he did not think him worthy of Cecily? Would he expunge him as well? Life, he smiled to himself, was so full of ironic possibility.

Potter arrived before lunchtime and placed a pair of yellow woollen gloves on the counter before ordering.

'You're for the road today,' said Roarty amiably.

'If I can get out over the hill.'

'The bus made it this morning. You won't have any trouble in your car. That's on the house, by the way.'

'A *deoch a' dorais* as you say. Cheers!'

'I hope you enjoyed yourself here.'

255

'It had its moments, I must confess, and I'm leaving as sound of limb as when I came.'

'It's a pity you didn't discover enough barytes.'

'No, it would have been the ruination of all of you.'

'That's a tourist's view,' said Roarty. 'The animals that live in the zoo might think differently.'

'I think I qualify as being a little higher than a tourist.'

'Well, of course. It's a pity too that we dropped the Anti-Limestone Society. It could have led to great things.'

'It has now become one of the ifs of ecclesiastical history,' said Cor Mogaill from behind his newspaper in the corner.

'You all realise that the only man with cause for satisfaction is the Canon,' said Potter.

'Once we had a Protestant ascendancy,' said Cor Mogaill. 'It's now the clerical ascendancy. And they both rule with the same mixture of self-interest and cynicism. The Canon knew that there would be no barytes but he also knew the power of avarice. He doesn't make his living by the seven deadly sins for nothing.'

'Are you taking the car ferry this evening?' Roarty asked in a voice that betrayed a landlord's easy solicitude.

'Yes,' said Potter with an Englishman's economy of phrase which sounded almost rude in Ireland.

Cor Mogaill banged his fist on the wall and alarmed Roarty with a shriek-like laugh.

'Gimp Gillespie has done it again,' he said, shaking a copy of the *Donegal Dispatch*. 'Listen to this.'

Householders in Glenkeel are mounting watchful vigils on their flocks of hens, geese and turkeys from now until Christmas. They know that their fattening fowls are in dire danger from turkey rustlers who raid the pens in search of prize birds for the lucrative yuletide trade.

He's put in that paragraph every year since someone stole Crubog's pet turkey for a joke nearly a decade ago. But listen to this as well.'

During the past week the gardai under the energetic leadership of Sergeant McGing have been raiding the homes of poteen-makers, many of whom are busier than farmers should be in winter. The raids were described by one seasoned poteen-maker as the most intensive in the long history of the still. It is reported reliably that as much as a hundred gallons of wash and as many pounds worth of equipment have been impounded.

'The man is nuts,' said Cor Mogaill.

'I wish he had stuck to reporting for the *Dispatch*,' said Potter. 'It's what he is best at.'

'Talk of the devil,' said Roarty as McGing's over-coated form filled the doorway. 'A black-and-tan?'

'No less,' said McGing.

'It's a cool one,' said Roarty, handing him his pint.

'It may be cool but it's a good enough day to arrest a murderer.'

'Have you got him at last?' Potter enquired.

'At last,' said McGing.

Roarty went to the till, not trusting his voice sufficiently to speak.

'And who is it, may I ask?' said Potter.

'Rory Rua. I'm on my way to arrest him for the murder of Eamonn Eales, itinerant barman, and for the attempted murder of Kenneth Potter, English gentleman.'

'I can't believe it,' said Potter. 'Rory Rua is one of nature's gentlemen. Ever since I've had his cottage he has given me more turnips, parsnips and carrots than I could eat, all for nothing.'

'He was fattening you only to kill you,' said Cor Mogaill.

'He wasn't at home this morning when I called with the key. The door was locked and curiously enough there were no footprints in the snow.'

'Have you got enough evidence?' Roarty asked as he recovered from the shock.

'More than I need. I've brooded over this in the silent watches of the night, and I've put off the arrest until I could bear the certainty of his guilt no longer. You see, I must tread more carefully here than an inspector of the Yard. In the vastness of London a policeman can forget his mistakes, but not in the country where the relationship between the criminal and the policeman is keenest.'

'I'm astounded,' said Potter.

'What is the evidence against him?' asked Cor Mogaill.

'Mainly circumstantial,' said McGing. 'But then most criminals are trapped by what a famous barrister once called "the probative force of circumstantial evidence". The thing to remember if you are a criminal is that most criminals confess when they need not.'

McGing emptied his glass and left with a show of officious self-importance.

'Highly irregular,' said Potter when he had gone.

'What is?' asked Cor Mogaill.

'McGing coming in here to tell us he's going to make an arrest.'

'He's been obsessed with this murder for the last four months. He couldn't wait for the glory of solving the crime. He had to be the first to tell us,' said Roarty.

'I m sure he's wrong,' said Potter.

'Right or wrong, he's given us a grand topic of conversation for the winter nights,' said Cor Mogaill.

'I'm afraid I shan't be able to join you,' said Potter. 'I must make tracks before I'm served with a subpoena.'

Roarty accompanied him outside, genuinely sorry to see him go. He was a good shot, a good angler, and he had the rare gift of amusing conversation.

They crossed the street to Potter's car. It had stopped snowing and a sharp sun was shining brilliantly on the north side of the glen. The cold came down with the sunlight out of a windless sky, nipping their ears and ankles and stiffening the roots of their beards. It was a day for sitting by the fire with a drink, and Roarty did not envy the gang of workmen who were unloading the new limestone altar outside the church.

Potter started the car and put his hand out through the open window. Roarty grasped it, remembering for some reason how he would wake in the small hours frightened of he knew not what.

'What will you say when you get to London?' he asked.

'I shall say that I went to Donegal for the winter and came back again, and that it was very cold weather.'

'I'm always sorry to lose a good customer, and doubly sorry if he's a friend. If you're ever within striking distance of these parts, do drop in. The Glenmorangie and a hundred thousand welcomes will be waiting.'

'I might take you up on that,' said Potter.

For a complete list of books available from Penguin in the United States, write to Dept. DG, Penguin Books, 299 Murray Hill Parkway, East Rutherford, New Jersey 07073.